Praise for

LOVE

"Morgan is a wonder... and witty... The aut... daytime TV and conve... with assurance. The mystery takes several interesting twists and will keep readers guessing."

—*The Romance Reader's Connection*

"The heroine can be summed up in one word: spunky... rich in characterizations and action... Linda Palmer proves with this fine cozy that she has what it takes to reach the top of her profession."   —*The Best Reviews*

"This is a great book for fans of soap operas and good books alike."   —*Fresh Fiction*

"Full of sharp details, quirky characters, and juicy gossip, Palmer's latest not only promises the goods, it delivers them in high style."   —*Romantic Times* (4 ½ stars)

LOVE IS MURDER

"Divine... the juicy behind-the-scenes soap opera details are to die for!" —Jerrilyn Farmer, award-winning author of the Madeline Bean Catering Mysteries

"I couldn't put it down! [A] vivid backstage portrait of the world of daytime drama... A wonderful read and a fun mystery... Spot-on."   —Barbara Rush, formerly of *All My Children* and *Flamingo Road*

"One terrific read... A delicious mystery... clever and smart."   —Linda Dano, formerly of *Another World*

continued . . .

Daytime Mysteries by Linda Palmer

LOVE IS MURDER
LOVE HER TO DEATH
LOVE YOU MADLY

love you madly

linda Palmer

BERKLEY PRIME CRIME, NEW YORK

THE BERKLEY PUBLISHING GROUP
Published by the Penguin Group
Penguin Group (USA) Inc.
375 Hudson Street, New York, New York 10014, USA

Penguin Group (Canada), 90 Eglinton Avenue East, Suite 700, Toronto, Ontario M4P 2Y3, Canada
(a division of Pearson Penguin Canada Inc.)
Penguin Books Ltd., 80 Strand, London WC2R 0RL, England
Penguin Group Ireland, 25 St. Stephen's Green, Dublin 2, Ireland (a division of Penguin Books Ltd.)
Penguin Group (Australia), 250 Camberwell Road, Camberwell, Victoria 3124, Australia
(a division of Pearson Australia Group Pty. Ltd.)
Penguin Books India Pvt. Ltd., 11 Community Centre, Panchsheel Park, New Delhi—110 017, India
Penguin Group (NZ), Cnr. Airborne and Rosedale Roads, Albany, Auckland 1310, New Zealand
(a division of Pearson New Zealand Ltd.)
Penguin Books (South Africa) (Pty.) Ltd., 24 Sturdee Avenue, Rosebank, Johannesburg 2196,
South Africa

Penguin Books Ltd., Registered Offices: 80 Strand, London WC2R 0RL, England

This is a work of fiction. Names, characters, places, and incidents either are the product of the author's imagination or are used fictitiously, and any resemblance to actual persons, living or dead, business establishments, events, or locales is entirely coincidental. The publisher does not have any control over and does not assume any responsibility for author or third-party websites or their content.

LOVE YOU MADLY

A Berkley Prime Crime Book / published by arrangement with the author

PRINTING HISTORY
Berkley Prime Crime mass-market edition / May 2006

Copyright © 2006 by Linda Palmer.
Cover illustration by Haydn Cornner.
Cover design by Joni Friedman.

ISBN: 0-425-20968-7

BERKLEY® PRIME CRIME
Berkley Prime Crime Books are published by The Berkley Publishing Group,
a division of Penguin Group (USA) Inc.,
375 Hudson Street, New York, New York 10014.
The name BERKLEY PRIME CRIME and the BERKLEY PRIME CRIME design are trademarks belonging to Penguin Group (USA) Inc.

PRINTED IN THE UNITED STATES OF AMERICA

10 9 8 7 6 5 4 3 2 1

To D. Constantine Conte

I AM GRATEFUL . . .

To Claire Carmichael (aka mystery novelist Claire Mc-Nab) for teaching me the art and craft of mystery writing. Thank you for being both so tough and so kind.

To Norman Knight, one of the world's great unsung heroes. You save lives, and mine is one of them.

To Allison McCabe—what an artist you are as an editor. I'm a very lucky author! Thank you for all you do.

To Rebecca Gradinger and Morton Janklow, brilliant agents and treasured friends.

To the sharpest "test readers" with whom any writer could be blessed. You see the manuscript so early and have such great comments that you make me look smart: Carole Christie Moore Adams, Dr. Rachel Oriel Berg, Christie Burton, Rosanne Kalil Bush, Carol Anne Crow, Jane Wylie Daley, Hannah Dennison, Ira Fistell, Richard Fredricks, Judy Tathwell Hahn, Nancy Koppang, Kay Partney Lautman, Susan Magnuson, Mari Marks, Dr. Jeffrey Marks, Nellie Manda Monsrud, Dr. Cecil B. Nichols, Jaclyn Carmichael Palmer, Dean Parker, Caroline Pfouts, Dr. Kathy J. Segal, Corinne Tatoul, and Kim LaDelpha Tocco. "Morgan" and I thank you.

To Betty Pfouts, for "Penny's" bouquet of chocolate rosebuds, and to Nancy Koppang for "Penny's" red rose cake. Thanks to my male friends who want to marry "Penny."

To Linda Dano and Vivien Stern for sharing stories about a colorful "Super Soap Weekend."

To Shelly Berger, Christie Burton, and Claire Carmichael for your knowledge of Las Vegas.

To Bruce Thompson, the "Superman" of computers.

To the remarkable Wayne Thompson of Colonial Heights, VA. Thank you for inspiring "Chet."

Once again, and always, I am grateful to Berry Gordy.

Chapter 1

"DON'T WORRY, JULIE—he'll be wearing a Speedo under the sheet."

Fervently, I *hoped* Link Ramsey would wear it, and not pull one of his pranks by surprising his new acting partner in midscene with total nakedness. *Love of My Life*, the show for which I was both head writer and co-executive producer, was Julie Lawson's first daytime drama, and she was about to do her first bed scene.

Costume supervisor Flo Ryan stood beside me, making notes. "We need some tape to put across Julie's nipples," I told her.

Julie clutched the front of her terry cloth robe, her green eyes wide with curiosity. "But they're only going to shoot my back down to the waist, and from the side when I throw myself on top of Link. The audience isn't going to see my nipples. Why do I need tape?"

"They can do practically anything on cable," I said, "and

they go pretty far with nudity after ten P.M. on the networks, but this is daytime TV. We do *fake* reality. Our network has drawn a line we don't cross—meaning that Link's skin can't touch the"—I struggled for the perfect word—"*relevant* parts of your body."

Flo sucked her lower lip as she assessed Julie's ample breasts. "I'll get the widest roll," she said, and hurried off to raid the supply shelves at the rear of our show's three-thousand-square-foot wardrobe department.

We'd hired Julie two months ago for the role of "Amber," an impetuous medical school dropout who is pursuing "Cody," the part played by daytime's favorite romantic bad boy, Link Ramsey. Because Cody is grieving for his recently lost love, he isn't interested in a new woman. He's been ignoring Amber's advances. For her own devious reasons—which won't be revealed for a few more weeks—Amber has become increasingly bold toward Cody. In the scene we were going to shoot this morning, Amber surprises Cody by jolting him awake in bed.

"Morgan, will this scene air by the time we go to Las Vegas for that weekend soap . . . thing?"

"The Super Soap Fan Weekend," I said. "Yes—it'll air in two weeks, just before we go to Las Vegas. By then our viewers will be very eager to see you and Link live."

Julie clenched her teeth and stretched her mouth into a wide grimace. It wasn't a very attractive expression. "What's the matter?" I asked.

"I read Link's bio—he's been in *plays*, he's done Shakespeare, but I've just been in *Playboy*. I mean, I'm taking acting lessons, but I've never been on a stage, in front of real people. I'm scared."

"It's an audience of *fans*," I said reassuringly. "Tell you what—I'll write some answers to questions the fans might ask, then you won't have to worry about what to say." I started toward the door, but she reached out to stop me.

"Morgan—what if nobody asks those questions?"

"Here's the way it will work: I'll be up on that stage, too.

I'll introduce you and the others, and call for questions. Then I'll take my microphone and go out into the audience. I'll pretty much steer the discussion in the direction I want it to go." I lowered my voice to a conspiratorial whisper. "Joel Davies—you've seen him, he's our production manager—will be out in the audience with a microphone, too. Don't tell anybody, but the makeup ladies and the hairdresser will be sitting among the fans. If nobody else asks the questions you're prepared for, I'll have them rehearsed to do it."

Julie flashed a smile of appreciation.

"Don't fret about the Super Soap Weekend," I said. "The people will love you. You're terrific as Amber—you're striking just the right notes playing her outrageous personality. Now have fun this morning when she's trying to seduce Cody."

"If I can just remember my lines!"

"The *intention* of the scene is more important than the exact words in the script," I said. "If you go up in your lines, don't panic. Link is great at covering."

She relaxed, and I saw a little twinkle in her eyes. "He's cute, too. Is he straight?"

"Definitely," I said. I couldn't suppress a smile. According to industry gossip, Link got high marks in the romance department.

Julie might have misinterpreted my smile because a sudden look of anxiety swept across her face. "You're not going out with him, are you? I mean, even though you're thirty, you're good-looking enough to catch a star."

Catch a star? Yuck! I decided not to make a fishing joke and instead answered simply, "No, Julie. Link and I just work together. That's all it's ever been."

"Maybe Las Vegas *will* be fun," she said.

THERE WAS NO one at Betty Kraft's secretarial desk outside my office at the opposite side of our studios in the Global Broadcasting building, but I saw that Link Ramsey was inside waiting for me. He was standing in front of the window behind my half of the massive antique English partners' desk, staring down at Central Park West.

"What's up?" Indicating the makeup robe he was wearing, I added with mock severity, "You better have something on under that. This isn't HBO."

He didn't laugh, or give the playful comeback I'd expected. The expression on his face was solemn. That was unusual. At thirty-two, Link had the dark-haired, dark-eyed brooding good looks of a modern Heathcliff, the classic tormented antihero, but one of his most appealing qualities, on screen and off, was his sense of humor. Even during technical catastrophes— inevitable when you tape 260 hour-long episodes a year—I could count on Link to lighten everyone's mood with a quip or a practical joke. But this time I sensed he wasn't about to pull one of his gags. He beckoned to me. "Come over here and take a look."

I joined him at the window. "What do you want me to see?"

"Down on the sidewalk—the woman in the blue coat."

All I could make out was a tiny dab of blue. "We're twenty-six floors up. How can you tell it's a woman?"

"For the last couple of weeks, everywhere I go, when I turn around, there she is. She's always wearing that same coat."

"Has she said anything to you?"

"Yesterday, for the first time. It was irritating, seeing her everywhere, so I went over to where she was standing. I was nice about it, but I asked why she was following me. She said she just wants to be near me, that I don't even have to talk to her. Morgan, I'm beginning to think the lady may be a little nuts."

Obsessed fans could be a serious problem. The network employed experienced security staff on each of the floors where Global Broadcasting shows were taped, but outside the studio actors were vulnerable.

"I'll assign one of the guards to leave with you tonight, and I'll have him chat with her."

"No," he said sharply. "I don't trust those apes. They might get nasty. I'm sure she's harmless." Still looking down at the speck of blue on the sidewalk, he added, "She's only pathetic. I'm not afraid of her—I'd just like my privacy back."

"If you don't want a guard, what can I do?"

"When I finish for the day, come out of the building with me. We'll be holding hands, like you're my girlfriend. Maybe she'll leave me alone if you talk to her—woman to woman."

I was dubious.

"*Come on*," Link urged. "She's shy, and—to put it kindly—she's not attractive. I'll bet the sight of a pretty woman with me will discourage her."

Reluctantly, I agreed to give it a try. "But I have a condition," I said.

Link lifted one wild black eyebrow and joked, "Want to go to bed with me, boss lady?" He raised his hands, palms out, in a gesture of surrender. "Like I said: any place, any time."

"We settled that a long time ago, so forget it," I said. "Here's my price: Behave yourself in the scene with Julie today. None of your naughty tricks."

"Killjoy," he growled. But he promised.

"One small detail," I said. "We start holding hands just as we're about to exit the building. I don't want anybody on the show to jump to the wrong conclusion about us."

The phone on my desk rang. I could see from the flashing button that it was my private number. "Go somewhere and run your lines," I said, making a shooing motion with my hands.

Giving me one of the sexy winks that made him such a favorite with the audience, he left, closing the door behind him.

I picked up the receiver. "Morgan Tyler."

"Morgan, thank God you're there!" It was Nancy Cummings, my best friend. "I *need* you." In the dozen years I've known her, since we met as freshman at Columbia, this was the first plea I'd ever heard from her. "If you've got a date tonight, *please* cancel."

"The men in my life are out of town," I said. Homicide Detective Matt Phoenix and his partner were in Washington, D.C., at an FBI seminar, and true crime author Chet Thompson was in San Diego, interviewing a survivor of genocide for the new book he was writing. I had no idea where Philippe Abacasas, the mystery man I thought of as the wild card in my life, might be, or if I'd ever see him again. "I'm free," I said. "What's up?"

"Tonight's when I'm *finally* going to meet Arnold's daughter, Didi, remember?"

"How could I forget? You've been trying to decide what to wear for a week."

"Well, there's a slight change of plans. Arnold wants you to join us."

"I'd like to meet your future stepdaughter," I said, "but I really don't think I should be with you the first time—"

"Oh, but Arnold *insisted.* He said if the two of us join them for dinner, it won't seem as though he's shoving me at Didi."

"I thought Didi knew what a serious relationship you and Arnold have?"

On the other end of the line, I heard her inhale and expel a breath. "So did I—I'm embarrassed to admit that I just assumed he had told her. Even though I should know better than to assume. It turns out he's mentioned me—but so far only as a colleague at Donovan. He said he wanted her to get to know me first, before he tells her about us."

Arnold Rose, one of the smartest and most successful criminal lawyers in the country, headed a division of Donovan, Newton, Lipton and Klein, the firm where Nancy practiced corporate law. From what Nancy had told me, he adored his only child.

I remember being a twelve-year-old girl. We were usually a lot smarter than the adult authority figures thought we were. For Nancy's sake, I hoped that Arnold's little ruse wasn't going to backfire.

Chapter 2

LINK KEPT HIS word, wore his Speedo under the sheet, and behaved like a gentleman.

I watched the scene from up in the control booth, more and more delighted at the on-screen chemistry I saw between the actors. They looked good together, too. Golden blond Julie was an effective visual contrast to Link's darkness. Their short, tangled "Statue of David" hairstyles were similar, but on Julie the cut was feminine and on Link it was unmistakably masculine.

"This pairing's going to work," I told that day's episode director, Will Givens.

Will gnawed a piece of hard candy—his latest device to kick cigarettes. "They make me hot just looking at 'em," he said.

I allowed myself a deep sigh of relief. While our February Sweeps numbers had been high, we'd lost a Super Couple. I'd created the Amber character quickly, hoping to fill the void.

The casting team had put in seven-day weeks to find the right actress; Julie wasn't an experienced performer, but she had an appealing quality on-screen—an intangible something that made the audience like her. It seemed as though our hard work was paying off, and that *Love* was going to have a new Super Couple. I made a mental note to start scheduling fan magazine photo shoots of Link and Julie as Cody and Amber. Considering all the offscreen dramatics that had surrounded *Love* in recent months, we might even break into the mainstream media.

The control room phone buzzed. Will snatched up the receiver with a gruff "Yeah?" then grunted and thrust it toward me. "Your secretary," he said.

I nodded thanks and took the instrument. "Betty?"

"When are you coming down to the office?" she asked. "There's something here you've got to see."

"What is it?"

I heard amusement in her voice. "A description won't do it justice."

I MADE MY way carefully over fat cabies that snaked across the floor, and past the sets we were using for the day's shoot. As I neared my office I saw Betty Kraft, the assistant I share with co-executive producer Tommy Zenos, nibbling a large cookie at her desk. She swallowed and greeted me with an uncharacteristic smile.

"You're looking cheerful," I said. "On a carbohydrate high?"

With what was left of the cookie, she gestured at the large white box on her desk.

I glanced into the box and was surprised to see that it was *full* of cookies—and they replicated the world-famous logo of the Global Broadcasting Network: a globe with a sunburst in the middle. Half of the sunbursts were made of yellow frosting; the other half were in orange.

"The yellows have sugar, the orange ones are sugar-free," Betty said.

I reached for one of the yellows and bit into it. The cookie was so light it practically dissolved on my tongue. I knew only one person who could have created these: Penny Cavanaugh. "Where is she?"

"Over at the Craft Services table. She brought another eight boxes, for everybody in the cast and—"

"Here I am, Morgan." I heard a familiar, slightly breathy voice behind me and turned to see Penny Cavanaugh. As always, she was dressed in casual elegance; today it was a butterscotch cashmere sweater dress topped by a brown wool car coat. A double strand of amber beads and dark brown leather calf-high boots completed the outfit. Looking at her, I felt like an urchin out of Dickens because my ensemble was a New York Knicks sweatshirt over black jeans, and comfortable old black ankle boots.

"These are fantastic," I said. "When did you have time to make dozens of designer cookies?"

"I'm out of work." There was a cheerful lilt in her voice, but I could tell she wasn't as carefree as she tried to pretend.

I hadn't known Penny as long as I'd known Nancy Cummings, but she had become my other closest woman friend. At just over forty, she's ten years older than I am, but with her curvy figure, glowing pink skin, and hair the color of Vermont maple syrup Penny is girlishly pretty. Most people guess her age at early thirties.

I reached out to touch her hand and discovered it was surprisingly cold. I made a quick decision and told Betty, "Penny and I are going to lunch."

Penny's cheeks flushed. "Oh no. I don't want to interrupt your work."

"You're *rescuing* me. I need to get out of this place for an hour."

Penny preceded me as we exited the Global building. Apprehensive, I scanned Central Park West in both directions, and was relieved that I didn't see a blue coat. I hoped that meant Link's infatuated fan had given up.

"Where would you like to have lunch?" I asked. "Anywhere they'll let me in looking like this."

"Let's eat in the park. There's a wonderful hot sausage stand near the Sixty-Sixth Street entrance."

"Sounds good to me."

We turned north and walked a block to Sixty-Sixth. When the light turned green, we crossed and stopped in front of a stainless steel steam cart shaded by a big green and yellow striped umbrella.

The cart's proprietor was a short, stocky man with a dark complexion and wisps of silver hair sticking out from beneath a knit cap the same green as the alternating bands on his umbrella. "What'll you young ladies have?"

"A hot Italian sausage with mustard," Penny said.

I seconded that, and added, "Two diet sodas—and extra napkins, please."

Penny tried to pay, but I was faster. "My treat. You brought us all those great cookies."

About fifty yards into the park, we found an empty bench under a tree, and settled ourselves to eat the delicious hot sausage rolls. It was a lovely day for March: mild, with an outline of the sun visible behind a scrim of pale gray sky. Above our heads a canopy of bare branches were showing their first tiny green buds.

As though she read my mind, Penny said with a sigh, "It'll be spring next week."

I hadn't taken Penny away from the office to talk about the seasons. "What did you mean—about being out of work?"

Penny touched a napkin to her lips, removing a dot of mustard. "Natasha closed her blue and gold doors permanently last Saturday afternoon."

Natasha's-On-Madison was one of the premiere day spas in Manhattan, and for several years Penny had been its star cosmetologist. I never knew how relaxing a facial could be until I'd had one of Penny's. Even Nancy Cummings (an expert on the subject of beauty upkeep) declared Penny gave the best facials she'd ever experienced.

"What happened?"

"Natasha's lease was up, and she decided not to renew. She's going to retire to her house in Palm Beach. No one knew what she was planning until Saturday afternoon, when she handed out envelopes. She left before we opened them. Inside we found checks for three months' salary and a good-bye note."

"That's a terrible thing to do!" I broke off a piece of my bun and tossed to it a nearby squirrel. To judge by his chubby little body and his shining coat it didn't look as though he'd had a tough winter.

Penny shrugged. "I'm not unhappy about losing the job. I'd already decided to quit." Two other squirrels, sensing that there was food to be had, joined the first one. Penny saw them and contributed bits of her bun.

"Didn't you like the work?" I asked as we watched the squirrels.

"Oh, I enjoyed rescuing skin that the clients had treated badly, restoring its healthy tone and color. But people were always confiding their problems and their secrets to me while I worked on them. It got to be so sad. I just didn't want to hear about one more cheating husband, or child who was on drugs."

We'd finished our sausages and drinks and broke the rest of our buns into little pieces for the squirrels—more of them had joined the party—and for the pigeons who'd come upon the scene. We wiped our fingers on the last clean napkins and I wadded them into a ball and dropped it and the empty soda cans into a nearby trash basket.

"What are you going to do now?" I asked as I rejoined Penny on the bench.

"I started thinking about that several weeks ago, before I knew about Natasha. In fact, I tried something." Penny reached into her leather satchel handbag, which she'd put on the bench between us, pulled out a green letter-size file folder, and extracted a sheet of paper with typing on it.

She held onto the page, studying it with a speculative expression.

"I thought, maybe . . . I could write. Would you read this, and tell me what you think? I want your brutally honest opinion."

Hearing those words sent a shot of dread into my heart. Although I tried hard to avoid it, people did manage to press their creative efforts on me—or try to tell me about them. I was good at dodging these attempts, but Penny had just blindsided me.

She looked so nervous and vulnerable that I pushed any negative thoughts away. Maybe Penny could write, and if so, I might be able to help her.

"Let me see it."

Penny handled the sheet of paper gingerly, simultaneously eager and reluctant. Because she was holding onto it, I had to take it out of her hand.

"Don't worry," I said. "I'm on your side."

The title at the top startled me: *The .44-Caliber Kiss*. A second surprise came when I read the name of the author. "Who's 'Stone McConnell?' "

"He's my *nom de* whatever. I couldn't imagine this kind of story written by someone named *Penny*. I thought the author picture on the back could be mysterious—just eyes peeking through thick leaves, like the kind of thing Ed McBain did on the back of his early 87th Precinct novels, when he was trying to keep his real name a secret."

I started to read:

"I was in the middle of a hot dream involving busty blond twins (natural blonds), a can of chocolate Reddi Whip, and a feather boa . . ."

Chapter 3

GLANCING UP AT Penny, I said, "Your first sentence certainly is a grabber." I went back to reading the page in my hand:

"A meaty hand grabbed me by the neck, yanking me back to cold reality. Something hard and heavy smashed against the side of my head. Just before I passed out, a size fourteen foot in a steel-tipped boot kicked a field goal with my left kidney. I recognized that boot; it was the fashion statement of one of Tony 'Bananas' Bonfiglio's gorillas.

"When I woke up—a hundred years of hard time later—I was lying facedown in a shallow pool of wet and sticky. Exploring the substance with my index finger, which was the only part of my body that didn't hurt, I had my first coherent thought: 'Blood really *is* thicker than water.'

"As I struggled to stand up, I remembered something

that a wise old con told me before I took this case: 'Never go up against a guy whose middle name is a fruit.'

"Too late now," I thought.

That was the end of the page.

"Let me read the rest. This is very funny." The smile on my face was genuine.

"I wasn't trying to be funny," she said. "And there isn't any *rest*." Penny took the page back and returned it and the green folder to her handbag. "I couldn't think of anything more."

"That happens to a lot of writers," I said.

"Does it happen to you?"

"Yes, sometimes." We got up and began strolling east along the path. "When I realize I'm on the wrong track in creating a long-term story document," I said, "or when I've written part of a scene in a script and hit a wall because suddenly I don't know what else the characters would say."

"What do you do?"

"Admit to myself that the story line, or the scene, isn't working," I said. "Maybe it's happening between the wrong characters, or at the wrong place in the script. Maybe I don't really need it—maybe I could better accomplish the *purpose* of the scene some other way. What I do then is go back to the last place in the script where I knew I was doing it right."

"I did go back to the last place where I knew I'd done something right, and I was in my kitchen," she said wryly.

"Look, Penny, why don't you take some fiction courses at Columbia, or NYU?"

She shook her head. "For years I've been listening to Matt and his homicide friends telling their stories, so I thought I had all this exciting material—but it took me more than a week to come up with just that one page." She smiled wistfully. "My heart isn't in writing. I need to do something new with my life, but I don't know what."

"I understand," I said. "After I came back from Africa, I had no idea what I was going to do with the rest of my life."

"You found your answer. That gives me hope."

As we walked deeper into the park, I saw signs of the nearness of spring everywhere I looked. On either side of the path, delicate little blades of new grass were shooting up. Here and there hardy little wildflowers sprouted, adding dots of color to the lovely mosaic that was Central Park. Looking at the flowers, I remembered Penny's fabulous Thanksgiving dinner party. In addition to the juiciest turkey I'd ever tasted, she'd created a delicious jelly out of flowers.

"Did you ever think of becoming a caterer?" I asked.

She shook her head emphatically. "I wouldn't like the business part of having a business. Even if I hired someone to do that, I'd still have to decide what to charge and where to get facilities and how to transport food and all that. No—I'm not cut out for commerce. I like to cook and decorate and make a comfortable nest."

We'd reached the carousel in the middle of the park, near East Sixty-Sixth Street, just as a new ride began to the recorded strains of "And the Band Played On."

A dozen or so women stood near the round brick building that sheltered the carousel. They smiled and waved at children who were riding the exquisite, hand-carved horses. Some of the horses had serious expressions; their heads were down and their eyes faced front—all business. Others were in a more joyful posture, with heads thrown back and wavy manes streaming in imagined wind.

A few children were too small to ride the horses. The women with them cuddled their toddlers in the brightly painted sleighs that went 'round and 'round with the majestic horses.

"This is one of my favorite places." Penny's voice was soft, the tone dreamy. "Patrick took me here on our first date. The carousel closes at six, but he paid someone to open it up just for us."

Uh, oh. Patrick—Penny's deceased husband—was a delicate subject because Penny was convinced that he wasn't really dead. I blamed my fellow daytime drama writers for her obsession. They'd written so many back-from-the-dead plots that they'd given Penny, a lifetime devotee of daytime drama, irrational hope.

"Everybody thinks Patrick was killed, but I don't believe it," she said. "I don't care how many days they said they searched the ocean for survivors, or how few pieces of the plane they said they found. I spent a year questioning everybody on the National Transportation Safety Board. They gave me nothing except pitying looks. I was afraid I'd go crazy. That's when I went to cosmetology school—so I'd have something to do until Patrick came back."

She had told me about this before, but I could see that she needed to talk, so I just listened. I couldn't bring myself to remind Penny that the TV stories she followed so closely were *fiction.*

Like Penny, I was a widow. I'd married my husband, Ian, when I was nineteen. He was my first lover, the center of my world, and I'd adored him. It wasn't easy, but after his death I made a new life for myself. *Un*like Penny, I didn't want to return to the past. I'd never written a back-from-the-dead plot for *Love of My Life,* and I'd sworn to myself that I never would.

The ringing of my cell phone interrupted my thoughts. "Sorry," I said to Penny as I unclipped it from my waistband.

It was Nancy Cummings. "Hi, Morgan. Where are you?"

"In Central Park."

"Not with that *Greek,* I hope!"

"I'm with Penny," I said, ignoring her reference to Philippe Abacasas, the one man she didn't want me to be anywhere near.

"Perfect! Penny's the one I'm looking for. I couldn't reach her at home, so I called Brandi Flynn. She said Penny'd been up half the night baking cookies for your show, so . . ."

"It's Nancy," I said. "She wants to talk to you." I handed Penny the phone.

"Nancy, hi." Penny listened with a puzzled frown on her face. "Yes, I'm free on Saturday. . . . What's the . . . oh, you did. Okay. I'll see you there at eleven o'clock. Bye." Penny disconnected and handed the phone back to me.

"What did she want?"

"For me to be at her office Saturday morning at eleven," Penny said. "She left the address on my voice mail."

"Her office? That's strange. Did she tell you why?"

"Didn't even give me a clue." Penny looked at her watch. "We've been gone more than an hour. You have to get back to the studio, and I've got some errands to run before I go home."

We exchanged good-byes and a hug before Penny began walking east to Fifth Avenue.

I started west, then veered north toward West Seventy-Second Street. Before I went back to the Global Broadcasting building I would go home to the Dakota, to change into respectable clothes in order to join Nancy and Arnold and his daughter for dinner.

As I walked, I wondered about Nancy's peculiar call. I wasn't surprised she had said so little on the phone; Nancy was always circumspect about business. But what business could she possibly have with Penny?

Chapter 4

SHORTLY BEFORE NANCY was due to pick me up to go to dinner, Link and I left the Global building, hand in hand, as he'd requested. It was six o'clock, getting dark, and much colder than it had been in the afternoon. Even though earlier the signs of spring were everywhere, now the air was heavy with the possibility of snow.

It was going-home time in Manhattan. People leaving office buildings, including our own, hurried to get to their after-hours lives. Some pulled up their collars and lowered their heads against the March chill to walk a few blocks uptown or down, or to the nearest subway stop. Others scanned the vehicle-crammed street for empty cabs or approaching buses. From the day I arrived in New York City, I've thought "the music of the night" was a symphony of honking horns and squealing brakes.

At first I didn't see the woman in the blue wool coat, but then she stepped out of the shadows on the downtown side of the Global Broadcasting building and into the strong illumination from the street lamps.

She was perhaps two inches taller than my five feet six, with broad shoulders and thick legs. Her face was round, with slightly bulging pale blue eyes set close together. She wore no makeup, and her shoulder-length light brown hair hung limp and lifeless beneath a blue beret with a fuzzy pom-pom on top. Her large hands were encased in blue wool gloves, a shade darker than her coat. Her best feature was her clear skin—naturally pink and virtually without lines. I guessed her age to be midtwenties. She rushed toward Link with a blissful smile on her thin lips.

Then she saw my hand in his.

As though a switch had been flipped, her internal lights went out. She gaped at me. The expression on her face morphed from joyous to bleak.

Link's fingers tightened on mine as she came closer to us.

"Hello again," Link said. His tone was pleasant but deliberately impersonal.

She pointed a chubby blue wool finger at me but kept her gaze fixed on Link. Her voice was strident as she demanded, "Who is *this*?"

Link didn't answer, but pulled me to the curb as he scanned Central Park West for an available taxi going downtown. She followed us to the edge of the sidewalk.

I forced a warm smile and said, "Hello."

"What are you to Link?"

"I'm—a friend of his." I extracted my hand from Link's and offered it to the woman, but she ignored it.

Link hooked his left arm through my right and said, "Morgan's a *very good* friend."

I could have kicked him for referring to me by name, but I tried to keep the party polite by showing an interest in her. "What's *your* name?" I asked.

In an imperious tone that implied I should know the answer, she said, "I'm Lena Ramsey. His *wife*!"

Link was open-mouth stunned. "What!?"

Petulant and childlike, Lena whined, "You said we could tell people now. I want everybody to know I'm your wife!"

Link turned to me. "She's crazy."

"*She's* making you say that, isn't she?"

"You and I are *not* married," Link told her firmly. "I didn't even know your name until just now."

Tears filled Lena's eyes. "Why are you lying? Are you ashamed of me?" She clapped her meaty hands on Link's arm and wrenched us apart, screaming, "Get away from him, you bitch!" Shockingly, the petulant child had turned into a virago.

At that moment, an occupied taxi veered to a stop at the curb beside us, and Nancy's face appeared in the rolled-down back window. Before she could say more than, "Here I am," Link jerked his arm free of the woman, yanked the cab's back door open, and shoved me inside. I fell halfway across Nancy. As we tried to right ourselves, Link jumped into the front seat beside the surprised driver and yelled to him, "Move!"

With heavy weeknight traffic clogging Central Park West, the driver had to watch for an opportunity to wedge his way into the downtown stream.

Lena—if that was her real name—tried to open Link's door, but luckily the driver had locked them all, securing us inside. Frustrated, weeping, she began to bang on the windows with her fists. As the cab managed to pull away from the curb, she followed, pounding on the lid of the trunk until the driver was able to put distance between us and Link's anguished fan. Vehicles behind us furiously honked their horns at Lena, forcing her back up onto the safety of the sidewalk.

Nancy, who had been watching out the back window, turned to me. "What was *that* about?"

Link dismissed the scene with a shrug. "One of my fans. She just got a little emotional."

Even though I was sympathetic to his uncomfortable situation, I was very annoyed. "Why in the world did you tell her my name?"

"Just your first name."

"She saw me coming out of the building with you. If she

thinks to check the show's credits she'll see my name—there isn't any other Morgan at GBN."

"She couldn't be that smart," Link said. "Look, she never did anything before except follow me around. She just got overheated. I blame myself for having us come out holding hands. Forget her." To the driver, he gestured toward the next corner. "Turn there and let me out."

"I think you should report her to the police as a stalker."

"No!" Link was vehement. "No cops. She's harmless."

"And you got your degree in psychology where?" I asked in a tone that was unmistakably sarcastic.

Link had the grace to look sheepish. "Look, I'm pretty experienced with emotional women. She's harmless. She'll get over me."

"I hope you're right," I said.

The cab turned the corner. Link leaned over the back of the front seat, pressed some bills into my hand, and said, "This should take you girls where you're going." He was out of the cab before it had come to a complete stop. In a moment, he had disappeared into the crowd on the street.

Nancy pushed strands of glossy pale blond hair out of her eyes. "Do you want to tell me what happened back there?"

"Not now."

The driver made eye contact with me in the rearview mirror. "Where to?"

Nancy leaned forward. "Jean-Luc's. One hundred and ten West Fifty-Third Street."

"You got it," he said.

Nancy settled back against the seat. "How do I look?"

This wasn't the Nancy I was used to. My tall, supermodel-gorgeous best friend was usually the most confident of women.

"You're perfect," I said truthfully.

She shook her head and waved one freshly manicured hand at me. I noticed that she'd abandoned colored nail polish tonight for clear. "No," she said. "I mean, do I look *okay* to meet Didi?"

She fingered the skirt of her conservative dove gray suit. At her throat was her favorite adornment, a single strand of seven-millimeter natural pearls that glowed softly against the smooth skin of her throat. She'd completed the outfit with a simple black wool cape with a standup collar that reached her ears. Arnold Rose (the first man with whom she had ever fallen completely in love) was five feet seven inches tall and she was five nine; in deference to their height disparity, she wore low-heeled black suede boots.

"Didi should love you," I said. "You'll be the farthest thing in the world from a wicked stepmother, you're crazy about her father—and you didn't break up her parents' marriage."

"No," she agreed with a relieved sigh. "They were divorced for a year before I even met Arnold."

"So you two have a clear conscience. And you actually like children."

Nancy regarded me quizzically. "You mean you don't?"

"All I get to meet are child actors." I said. "I'm sure I'll like real children."

Nancy smiled at that. "From what Arnold's told me about Didi, she's a darling." With a note of determination in her voice, she added, "I'm really looking forward to this dinner tonight."

Mentally, I was crossing my fingers.

Chapter 5

JEAN-LUC'S, LOCATED IN an early twentieth-century town house, was one of the most renowned French restaurants in Manhattan. I paid the driver with the money Link thrust at me. It was more than enough for the fare, so I added the rest as a generous tip.

Nancy and I entered the restaurant through a mahogany-framed stained glass revolving door that swiveled us into a handsome dining room with dark wooden crossbeams and gleaming hardwood floors. When my eyes adjusted to the soft lighting, I saw that Jean-Luc's was furnished with deep banquettes upholstered in shades of ginger and rust. Long cloths in a subtle floral pattern covered the tables. Serene woodland murals lined the walls above the mahogany wainscoting. Diners speaking in quiet tones created a gentle blanket of sound, and delicate scents wafting from the direction of the kitchen combined for a pleasing ambiance.

According to my colleague, Tommy Zenos, *Love*'s other

co-executive producer and also a walking *Zagat Restaurant Guide*, owner Jean-Luc Fortier's devoted regulars were a mixture of the brainy and the beautiful: men and women of genuine accomplishment, and so-called celebrities whose publicists made them famous. Deals and liaisons forged at Jean-Luc's were predicted or confirmed in the *New York Post's Page Six*, or in the columns of Liz Smith and Cindy Adams. Nothing that happened at Jean-Luc's was a secret for very long, but the patrons didn't seem to want it any other way.

While the maitre d' greeted Nancy with warm familiarity, I made a quick survey of the room and spotted Arnold Rose on the center banquette against the wall that faced the entrance. Sitting beside Arnold was a very pretty preteen with long hair that cascaded down her back like a dark chocolate waterfall. She was speaking to him in a spirited rush.

Just as Nancy told the maitre d', "We're meeting Mr. Rose," Arnold saw us and waved. Didi turned to discover who had captured her father's attention. Her animated face went still. Blank.

Arnold got up from the banquette and came around the table to greet us. He took Nancy's hand—briefly—and then mine.

"Hello, ladies. How nice to see you. Are you alone? Or meeting someone?"

Uh, oh. That meant Arnold hadn't told his daughter they were going to have company. I felt a pang of concern, but Nancy picked up Arnold's cue without a pause.

"We're alone," she said.

"Good, then you must join us." He turned to Didi and said, "Honey, I'd like you to meet two friends of mine. This is Nancy Cummings, a lawyer at the firm, and this is Morgan Tyler, who writes for television. Nancy and Morgan—this is my daughter, Didi."

"Hi," I said to Didi.

Nancy gave her a warm, "Hello."

There was a flash of comprehension in Didi's bright hazel eyes as she appraised Nancy. I was certain the girl realized this evening was a setup, and I was equally sure that she didn't like it.

Didi acknowledged the introductions with a carefully expressionless face.

Accustomed to commanding a courtroom, a meeting, or a table, Arnold directed me to sit on one side of the banquette and Nancy on the other, which put Didi in between us. He took the facing chair, saying that he wanted to sit opposite "these three beautiful women." Didi grimaced, but her father was turned away, asking for menus, and didn't see the look on her face.

"Why don't we order," he said, "then we can all relax and get acquainted." His tone was affable but his smile was too broad, like a salesman who was trying too hard.

"You can order for me, Daddy," she said sweetly, reaching across the table to give his hand an affectionate squeeze. In a syrupy voice, she added, "You always know the best things."

Arnold glowed, and I marveled at what an operator his little girl was. I had a suspicion that Nancy was going to have her hands full.

"I haven't been here before," I said, "so why don't you order for me, too, Arnold?" Nancy nodded agreement.

While her father was selecting our meal, Didi turned in her seat to face me, which put most of her back to Nancy. "Daddy said you write for TV. What show?"

"*Love of My Life.*"

"That's my favorite!"

"That's nice to hear," I said.

"It's the absolute best! I cried so much when Cody lost his girlfriend, even though I didn't like her."

"Why not?" I asked.

"She was a *phony.*"

"That's very perceptive of you."

She beamed at the compliment. "Do you want to know what I think about the other characters?" she asked eagerly.

Arnold leaned forward and touched Didi's hand to distract her. "Morgan works hard all day; I don't think she wants to talk business at night." With a quick smile at me, he steered the conversation in another direction. "Nancy's become quite the star in our office. She just arranged the purchase of the Better Living Channel for one of our important corporate clients. Do you ever watch Better Living, honey?"

Didi twisted her mouth in distaste. "It's crap," she said.

Arnold frowned at his daughter. "Didi, that's not nice."

"It's all right, Arnold," Nancy said graciously. "I agree with Didi. The current programming isn't very good. That's why we were able to make such a favorable deal for the client."

Didi flashed her father a radiant *I-told-you-so* smile, then she turned her attention back to me and scanned the moss green suede pants suit I was wearing. "Nice outfit," she said. "Where'd you get it, Bergdorf's, or Bloomie's?"

"Home Shopping Network." I said.

"Oh . . . Well, I like it anyway." Didi changed the subject with the speed of a slight of hand artist. "Is Cody going to get a new girlfriend?" she asked.

"Maybe . . . but I can't reveal any secrets."

"Could I call you sometime, to tell you what I like on the show?"

"Sure," I said, surprised. I wanted to catch Nancy's eye, to see how she was taking this, but Didi was blocking my view of her. I was positive the girl knew her father was interested in Nancy, and that was why she was concentrating her focus on me. To turn Didi's attention away from me and the show, I asked, "Where do you go to school?"

"I don't. Daddy lets me have private tutors."

I tried again. "When you're not studying, what do you like to do?"

"Ride horses. I ride competitively."

Nancy tried to attract Didi's attention. "You're a junior champion jumper, aren't you?" she said. "Your father has a picture of you on his desk—winning a ribbon."

Didi shot Nancy a piercing glance. "Why were you in Daddy's office?"

"Because . . . we had a meeting—"

"I frequently have meetings in my office, with other lawyers," Arnold said quickly. I knew he was telling the truth, but the uncomfortable expression on his face made it seem like a lie.

Didi aimed a parting shot at Nancy. "Just so you know—the *horse* is the jumper. I'm the *rider*." Fast as a bolt of lightning, Didi bestowed a bewitching glance on her father, then turned back to me. "I'm in four big competitions this year, that's why I can't go to regular school. The Del Mar National, that's in California, in April. Palm Beach in June, then the Hampton Classic in Bridgehampton—that's in August—and the Metropolitan National here in the city at the end of October. Will you come see me compete, Morgan?"

"Well . . ." I said hesitantly, "it's hard to know what my schedule—"

"We'll *all* go," Arnold announced.

Didi ignored that and continued talking to me. "My trainer says if I keep working hard, I'll make the U.S. Olympic Team one day. After that it's big money endorsements. I could be on a cereal box. Or even have my own cereal! Anything's possible, isn't that right, Daddy?" she cooed.

Didi went on to tell me that she'd started riding seriously when she was six years old, and that tomorrow she'd be guiding her favorite jumper, Lancelot, over a practice course, then through the "flat" phase where she'd take him through walking, trotting, and cantering around the ring. "During competitions," she said, "judges award points for each part of the performance."

Before I could do more than nod and utter an interested "Hmmmm," Didi asked, "Morgan, are you married?" Her face was the picture of young innocence.

"Uh, no. My husband died."

"Daddy's divorced," she said. *Pointedly*. "You two should go out sometime."

Chapter 6

THE EVENING WAS a total nightmare.

Didi declared that she couldn't have dessert because she had to watch her weight.

I wanted dessert, because I hadn't enjoyed the terrine-de-*something* that Arnold had ordered for me, but when Nancy and Arnold quickly passed on Jean-Luc's famous *mousse au chocolat*, I reluctantly passed, too.

At twenty minutes to eight, the evening was over. Outside Jean-Luc's, Arnold hailed a cab and helped Nancy and me inside. He mouthed "I'm sorry," to her, then closed the taxi's door and returned to Didi, who was watching us from the entrance.

The driver wanted to know, "Where to?"

"I need a drink." Nancy said.

I gave the driver my address. "One West Seventy-Second Street."

Nancy didn't object. She leaned back against the seat and stared straight ahead.

For the next few blocks, we were silent. Usually, neither of us is at a loss for words, but tonight had been the U.S. Olympics of Awkward.

Nancy recovered first. "*You* certainly made a hit," she said sardonically.

"Come on now." I gripped her hand, trying to comfort her. "You saw what Didi was doing, even if Arnold didn't. She was being rude to you because she'd figured out that you're the one her father's interested in."

"We passed being 'interested' months ago." The edge was gone from her voice, replaced by pain she didn't try to hide.

Nancy Cummings, rising star in corporate law, had been born beautiful, rich, and smart. She also came equipped with the kindest heart of anyone I'd ever met. But her kind heart made her vulnerable.

Tonight Didi Rose had taken an ax to it.

THE CAB CAME to a stop in front of the Dakota, the nineteenth-century Gothic landmark on the corner of Seventy-Second Street and Central Park West where I have a co-op on the third floor.

While I was paying the driver, Frank, the building's night security man, opened the door and helped Nancy out, then offered his arm to me. Before he retired from the ring and joined the Dakota's staff, Frank (as "Frank N Steen") had been a favorite character on the World Wide Wrestling circuit. Although he told me that he'd lost many more bouts than he'd won, his comic antics had earned him fans. Once or twice a year, I'd see him scribbling his autograph for someone who'd recognized him.

"Thanks, Frank," I said as the soles of my boots touched the pavement.

"You've got mail in the office, Mrs. Tyler. Want me to get it for you?"

I glanced at Nancy, who was already at the entrance to the courtyard, pacing back and forth impatiently. This was not the time to stop for my usual heavy pile of scripts, catalogues, and bills.

"Just hang onto it," I said. "I'll pick it up in the morning."

Nancy was in the courtyard. She passed the central fountain at such a brisk clip that I had to run to catch up with her at the entrance to my wing of the building.

I walked all over the city and used stairs whenever possible—it was my fitness routine—but I asked Nancy if she wanted to take the elevator.

"Too slow," she said. "I desperately need a drink, a comfortable chair, and a good cry."

Hurrying up two flights of stairs, our footfalls sounded like a tap routine from an old Hollywood movie musical. As soon as we reached my floor, I took the front door key out of my pants pocket.

Nancy usually spent a moment glancing with approval at the antique brass and crystal sconces (converted decades ago from gaslight to electric) that provided the hallway's illumination, and she'd long admired the polished wood paneling on the walls. Not tonight.

I opened the door to see that my seven-month-old black kitten was sitting a few feet inside the front door. He greeted me with a blink of his big green eyes and a loud meow.

As soon as Nancy saw him, she smiled and reached down to pick him up. "Hi, Magic. How are you, little guy?"

He rubbed his head against her chin, and the tight muscles in her face relaxed. "He's getting bigger and bigger," she said as I was hanging my coat in the foyer closet. Magic began to squirm in Nancy's arms. With a sigh, she put him down gently. "Take care of the little boy," she said. "I know where the red wine and the glasses are. Meet you in the den."

Magic trotted behind me and then scooted ahead as we made our way to the kitchen, which was in the rear of the apartment. Its window looked down onto the courtyard, while the living room, den, and bedroom faced Central Park.

When I'd returned to the Dakota this afternoon to change clothes, I made sure Magic hadn't turned over his food or water dishes. I'd scooped out his litter box, and then we'd had a lively game of chase-the-feather-on-the-end-of-the-wand.

Now I opened a small can of Dick Van Patten's Natural Balance. His front paws kneaded the floor and his tail swished with anticipation as I scooped it into a dish. He started to eat as soon as I put it down on his dinner mat.

I joined Nancy in the den. She'd taken off her boots, sunk into one of the pair of oversized club chairs that faced the windows onto the park, and propped her feet up onto the shared ottoman between the two chairs. She'd opened a bottle of merlot and was already halfway through a glass of it. I took the matching chair and poured the Diet Dr Pepper I'd brought from the kitchen into a wine glass. Nodding at my soda, she said, "Good. That leaves the wine for me."

Nancy leaned her head against the back of the chair. "What am I going to do?"

"Be patient," I said. "When she gets to know you she won't be so hostile."

"Easy for you to say." Immediately, her tone became soft, contrite. "I'm sorry. I don't mean to take this out on you."

"It's okay," I said. "Tonight was rough. Didi plays her father as though he's a flute and she's James Galway."

Nancy refilled her glass and took a healthy gulp. "It's not that I expected her to love me instantly. I know life isn't like *The Sound of Music.*"

"For one thing, you can't sing." It wasn't much of a joke, but it made her smile.

"Do you know anything about Didi's mother?" I asked.

"Her name's Veronica. She's from Boston and her family has money. That's really all I know. Arnold doesn't talk about her, and I haven't wanted to pry. He was devastated when she took Didi and moved back to Boston after their divorce. He flies up there every weekend that he can, and has Didi down for a visit when Veronica allows it."

We gazed out at the white diamond sparkle of lights in Central Park. There was something tranquilizing in that lovely view. Many a night I've curled up in this spot, to think up plot complications for the characters on the show—or to try to sort through my own tangled emotions about the intriguing men in my personal life: steady, grounded Matt and Chet. And Philippe, who appeared and disappeared like a mirage . . .

"I love him, Morgan," Nancy said softly. "I would never interfere in his relationship with his daughter, or try to take her mother's place. I'd just like to be Didi's friend."

I patted Nancy's hand to express my support silently. I didn't want to give voice to my concern: Arnold's daughter was going to be trouble. *Big* trouble.

Chapter 7

I DIDN'T SEE the woman in the blue coat outside the studio when I arrived. Link wasn't supposed to work today, but I didn't think she could have known his schedule, so I took her absence to mean that the painful scene last night had discouraged her.

Several times during the morning I'd gone to the window behind my desk and looked down. No dab of blue.

At eleven o'clock I called Link at his apartment in Greenwich Village, and told him there hadn't been any sign of the woman outside the building this morning.

"I haven't seen her around my neighborhood either," he said, sounding relieved.

The implication of that startled me. "She doesn't know where you live, does she?"

"I hope not," Link said. "But a few days ago I was in the Village Bookstore when I spotted her across the street. I left the store through the back way. I haven't seen her since."

"Good."

"Forget about her," he said. "I'm sorry that she was so hurt last night, but it probably killed her interest in me." A teasing tone came into his voice as he added, "If that doesn't work, I'll go to Plan B."

"I'm afraid to ask, but what's Plan B?"

"I'm going to introduce her to Walt Willey," he joked, naming the tall, handsome blond actor and stand-up comic who played the role of Jack Montgomery, the resident hunk-for-connoisseurs on *All My Children.*

I told Link to go study his lines. I added, "Keep an eye out for her for the next few days, to make sure she's given up on you."

Betty Kraft opened the door and came in, carrying a gift-wrapped box about the size of a container of boutique facial tissues. "It's for you," she said.

As I took it from Betty, I felt my heart lurch inside my chest. The paper was slick and expensive, royal blue; the bow was white satin ribbon. No indication of the store from which it came. No card on the outside, but I guessed who it was from. My nervousness must have shown on my face.

"What's the matter?" Betty asked, frowning in concern. "Are you all right?"

"Yes," I said. My voice sounded a little too bright. I untied the ribbon.

"What did he give you?"

I stopped, my hands about to remove the paper. "*He*? Did you see who left this?"

"I was just coming out of the copy room and caught him. He asked me to give it to you." Betty made impatient fluttering motions with her hands. "Go on, I'm dying to know." Unfolding the paper, I wished that I was alone, but there was no way I could get rid of Betty tactfully. Besides, she'd seen *him*, and I wanted to know how he got up here, through our supposedly tight security.

"Wow." Betty leaned in close to get a better look. "Bal a Versailles. Five ounces, and it's the *perfume*, not the cologne!"

The perfume was exquisite, but it was the little white card underneath that interested me more. I turned it over and read: "From your grateful Gareth."

Gareth? I started to laugh. At myself, because the joke was on me.

"He's a nice guy, that Parker," Betty said, referring to Parker Nolan, the actor who played Gareth. "He told me in the lunchroom the other day that he's crazy about the new stuff you're putting into the Gareth–Jillian storyline, and he likes the way you have Gareth costumed now—in those cashmere turtlenecks and Brioni suits."

I'm dressing him the way Philippe dresses.

"Oh," Betty went on. "I meant to tell you how much I *loved* that scene in the swimming pool—when Jillian pulls him in fully dressed, and she's in the water, looking naked. Whew!" Betty fanned herself comically. "Where did you get that idea?"

"From life." My tone made the answer sound like a joke, but I was telling the truth. The scene Betty liked so much, and that the chat rooms were buzzing about, really did come from my own life, from something that happened a few months ago, with Philippe Abacasas. The only other person who knew my secret was Nancy, but her workload was so heavy she hadn't had time to watch the show in over a year. I didn't think she'd approve of my putting bits of Philippe into the Gareth–Jillian storyline, but she wanted me to get him out of my system. I told myself that was what I was trying to do: diminish Philippe by turning him into fiction.

I took a sheet of personal stationery out of the top left-hand drawer of the desk and started to write. "This is a note to Parker, thanking him for the perfume," I told Betty. "He's doing a wonderful job as Gareth. He doesn't need to give me a gift."

Betty fingered the gracefully curved bottle. "You're not giving it back, I hope."

"No," I said as I folded the note and handed it to Betty. "It's one of my favorite scents. I've been meaning to get some."

Betty looked horrified. "A woman should *never* buy her own perfume!"

"I've been buying mine for years."

"That's probably why you're still alone," she said. "There's such a thing as being too independent. You've been a widow for five years, but it took being investigated for murder last winter for you to finally start dating."

I leaned back in my chair and looked at her, surprised at the seriousness in her voice. She held my stare for a moment, then smiled. "I'm speaking from my twenty years' experience as a psychiatric nurse."

"Before you turned in your stun gun and came to work with the real nuts in network television."

"I didn't need a stun gun," she said. "I controlled the locked wards with the force of my personality."

I'll bet you did, I thought fondly.

Chapter 8

A LITTLE BEFORE noon, Tommy Zenos burst into the office.
A huge grin of triumph was on his face and a "WHOOP" ex-
ploded from his mouth.

"I did it!" he exclaimed, punching the air. He dropped his
bulky pigskin suitcase on the floor. "Dance with me!"

Laughing, I put down the script I was editing, got up, and
let him whirl me around our office. Even though Tommy
was—according to his doctor—more than fifty pounds over-
weight, he was a very good dancer. But there was too much
furniture crowded into our office for dancing to be a safe ac-
tivity. After he dipped me so low my hair brushed the carpet, I
righted myself and stepped away.

"Let me guess," I said. "Your trip to Las Vegas went well."

He was as animated as a boy who'd just hit the home run to
win his Little League championship. His eyes glowed with the
pride of accomplishment. In spite of having too many chins

and too little hair, in that moment Tommy looked ten years younger than his thirty-five years.

"Oh, Morgan, I wish you could have seen me! I made us the deal of a *lifetime*. Got us all rooms at the newest hotel on the strip, The Mount Olympus. *And* I got us use of their outdoor stage facilities for our Daytime Stars on Broadway show. Great sound—I tested it myself—and audience seating for three thousand fans. We're going to have the best Super Soap Weekend any show ever put on."

"That's wonderful."

"It's even better than that," he said. A grin as wide as the Cheshire Cat's split his face. "Except for plane fares and the per diems, it's not going to cost the network a penny."

"*Free*? How in the world did you pull that off?"

Tommy proudly strutted around the desk; he was practically dancing again. "I told them that they could film our show's event and make a promotional documentary for the hotel. I'll fix it with the unions," he said.

"Tommy, you're a deal-making genius!" For all of his quirks—his terror of authority figures, his four broken engagements, his tendency to go to pieces in the presence of an injured person or animal—he had the most inventive business mind I'd ever encountered.

"I guess that's *my* talent," he said modestly. "You create characters and keep the stories hot, and I take care of the behind-the-scenes stuff. We're a good team."

"There's nobody I'd rather work with," I said sincerely.

Tommy collapsed into the antique wingchair behind his side of the desk. "How have things been going here?"

"Taping is on schedule, but something's happened that could be a problem." I filled Tommy in on Link Ramsey and his obsessed fan. He winced as I described Lena pounding on the back of the taxi as we were trying to pull away from her.

"What should we do? Call the police?"

"Link refuses to let us. And no bodyguard. He's sure this Lena is harmless, but I've alerted building security that no one of her description is to be allowed in."

"Okay, good, you're handling it." Tommy sighed with relief, opened the top drawer on his side of the desk, and pulled out a large menu from the 21 Club. "I'm going to have a big celebration lunch. Come with me."

I shook my head. "Not today," I said. "I have an appointment." I took my red wool cape from our coat tree in the corner. "Just bring me back a sandwich. Anything that looks good to you."

Leaving the Global building, I turned uptown and began my brisk, nine-block hike to the Dakota. I had an appointment with Magic's veterinarian to get the last of his series of kitten inoculations.

Three months ago, on the street outside a crime scene, a hungry kitten jumped out of a garbage can and came up to Homicide Detective Matt Phoenix. The little creature rubbed against Matt's ankle and meowed insistently. When he questioned neighbors, Matt was told the kitten was a stray that came around begging for food. Not able to leave the kitten in the street, Matt picked him up, tucked him inside his jacket, and brought him over to my apartment.

I was about to protest, to explain that I'd never in my life had a pet. Then I held the kitten in my arms, listened to him purr, and fell in love with a skinny little bundle of black fur. We determined that he was a boy, and I named him Magic.

The next afternoon I bought a blue canvas and mesh carrying case. On the enthusiastic recommendations of the Upper West Side cat owners in our *Love of My Life* company, I took Magic to see Dr. Jeffrey Marks. The veterinarian had impressed me immediately with the kindness and tenderness he showed his patients.

Dr. Marks gave little Magic, who weighed four pounds on that first visit, a thorough checkup, pronounced him "a healthy little guy," and began Magic's series of kitten inoculations.

Before I'd walked two blocks, I felt a chill that had nothing to do with the dropping temperature. It was the creepy sensation that someone was following me.

My first thought was that it was Link's unhappy fan. I glanced back over my shoulder but I didn't see her. Nor did I see anyone else who seemed to have taken an interest in me. I told myself that my sense of unease was simply my imagination at work. I kept walking with my usual fast stride.

Still, I couldn't shake that feeling.

At the corner of Sixty-Eighth and Central Park West, I stopped. Pretending to search for something in my handbag, I leaned against the stone façade of an apartment building and covertly scanned the street.

I still didn't glimpse anyone who might be following me.

Telling myself firmly that what I was feeling was just a by-product of throwing *Love*'s characters into so many dangerous situations, I continued toward Seventy-Second Street.

But I turned around at each corner to look behind me.

I spent only a few minutes in my apartment, greeting Magic and putting him into his carrier, with a soft towel around him to keep him warm. Back on the street, I once again surveyed the area, but didn't see anything to be concerned about. I decided to forget about weird fans and just concentrate on being a responsible cat owner.

THE MARKS VETERINARY Clinic was located in a brownstone on West Seventy-Fifth Street between Columbus and Broadway. I carried Magic (who seemed to get heavier by the block) up the three steps to the first floor of the brownstone and pushed the bell. Almost immediately, I heard a responding buzz and opened the door.

The reception area and the examination rooms were on the first floor. The large, well-equipped, and immaculate operating room, the recuperation cages, and the bathing and grooming facilities were located in the basement.

On my first visit, Dr. Marks had given me a tour of his hospital. I'd been warned by *Love*'s experienced pet owners not to take Magic to a doctor who wouldn't let me see how the animals in his charge were cared for. I was relieved at the high quality of what I saw, and at the gentleness with which his assistants treated the hospital's patients.

As I came in, a woman with a cute but dirty little Pomeranian was handing him to one of the assistants. She was leaning over, making kissing noises at him, and assuring him that he wouldn't mind his "itty bitty bathy."

If anybody asked, I would admit that I talked to Magic every day. However, I'd made a silent vow on our first night together NEVER to subject him to baby talk.

Dr. Marks' pretty, blond wife, Mari, stood behind the waist-high counter that separated the office area from the waiting room. She was reading information from a chart to the hospital's secretary, who was typing it into a computer. Mari looked up and smiled in greeting when I came in.

"Right on time," she said, leaning over the counter to look through the mesh screen into Magic's carrier. "How's he doing?"

"Everything seems perfect," I said. "I had no idea what great company he'd be."

Dr. Marks emerged from an examining room and greeted me. An attractive, energetic man with a boyish face and thick, dark hair cut short, he picked up Magic's carrier. "Come on in."

In the brightly lighted, immaculate exam room, Dr. Marks took Magic out of his carrier and cuddled him for a moment before he lowered him gently onto the cradle-like digital scale.

"Seven pounds, eight ounces," he said. "That's a good weight for seven months."

I felt a surge of pride. Apparently, I was doing all the right things.

Later, carrying Magic down the steps to the sidewalk, I heard a familiar voice.

"Hello there, Red Riding Hood. Big Bad Wolf is back."

Chapter 9

I SMILED WITH delight when I saw the tall, athletic figure of Chet Thompson leaning against the side of his green Range Rover. A teasing grin was on his sun-tanned face. The tan was testimony to his having spent the last few weeks in California, doing research for his new book on genocide and war crimes.

"How did you know where I was?" I asked.

"Your secretary. Glad to see me?"

"I'd hug you, but my hands are full." I was gripping the cat carrier.

Chet leaned down to peer through the mesh. "Ah—it's the young monster who jumped on my back when I kissed you." He straightened up, grasped the carrier, and held it in one hand while he pulled me tight against him.

Chet's a little over six feet tall, and my head came up to the bottom of his chin. He was casually dressed, in a yellow crewneck sweater, a beige suede jacket, and brown wool slacks.

I pressed my face against the butter-soft suede and hugged him. He smelled pleasantly of fresh air and piney woods.

"Did you miss me, gorgeous?"

"Much to my surprise," I joked, moving back a step.

Chet laughed, opened the rear door of the Rover, and placed Magic securely on the seat.

AFTER WE PUT Magic back into my apartment at the Dakota, Chet drove me down to the Global building. Pulling over to the curb, he said, "I've got to spend this evening with my editor, but are you free for dinner tomorrow night?"

"Absolutely."

"Shall I get tickets to a show?"

"No! I want to spend a long evening hearing about your new book."

"Good answer." He turned in the driver's seat, put his hands on my shoulders, and drew me toward him. "I've missed you," he whispered. I leaned into his embrace and closed my eyes. His lips brushed my eyelids, then his mouth found mine. He kissed me lightly at first, testing my response. My own lips parted, our tongues touched, and our arms tightened around each other.

When we came up for air, he whispered, "Remember where we were."

"If I forget, you have my permission to remind me."

Chet reached across me to open the passenger door. "Go up to your studio and bring excitement and turmoil into the lives of your millions of viewers," he said. "You've brought a hell of a lot into mine."

I climbed out onto the sidewalk. As I watched, Chet gave me a wave, nosed the Rover back into the line of traffic, and was gone.

Smiling, still enjoying the sense memory of his lips on mine, I turned to go into the Global building when suddenly I heard an angry voice.

"Morgan Tyler you should be ashamed!"

Turning around, I saw the woman in the blue coat—and realized with a jolt that she now knew my full name.

She planted herself directly in front of me, blocking my path. If I'd taken another step we would have collided.

"I saw you kissing that man," she screeched. "I'm going to tell Link!"

How do I get myself into these situations?

Her voice fell back to its colorless monotone. Now she was talking as much to herself as to me. "He's going to be hurt, but better that he finds out what type of a girl you are! I'd never kiss another man." She shuddered; a scowl of distaste twisted her thick features. "When he knows the kind of person you are, he'll want me again."

"Lena—that's your name, Lena?"

She narrowed her eyes and nodded warily. I noticed that she was gripping a black quilted purse with both hands. Hands that were in thin black gloves today, not the thick blue ones she'd been wearing last night. Suddenly, I was struck with the irrational fear that she might have a gun in that purse.

I scanned the front of the building, hoping to spot one of our security officers who'd come outside to take a smoke break. No such luck. But one sight registered with me: the coffee shop on the ground floor of the building next door.

"Lena, have you had lunch?"

She shook her head.

"Neither have I." I gestured toward the coffee shop. Painted in black and gold letters on the front window was the name Central Park Café. "Let's get in out of the cold and grab a bite. My treat."

With more guts than sense, I stepped around her. My back to Lena, my pulse pounding, I started walking toward the door to the cafe. Reaching the entrance, I glanced back. After a moment's hesitation, she followed me.

It was a little past the lunch hour, so most of the booths were empty. I headed for the one closest to the front window. I took off my cape, slid into one side of the leatherette booth, and folded my wrap over my handbag.

Slowly, her limbs moving as though she was wading through water, Lena slipped into the booth on the other side of the table. She kept her coat on, but she released her hold on the purse. When she put it down beside her, I let out a little sigh of relief.

I extracted a one-page menu encased in plastic from its holder on the table, glanced at it quickly, and then handed it across the table to Lena. Trying to make this encounter seem somewhat normal, I smiled at her, saying "They have pretty good sandwiches, and very good vegetable soup that they make right here."

A waitress with platinum curls piled onto the top of her head and fastened with a pair of large tortoiseshell combs ambled over to us. Her nametag identified her as "Grace."

"Know what you want, girls?"

"I'll have an egg salad sandwich on whole wheat, and a cup of coffee," I said, then lifted a quizzical eyebrow at my companion.

Lena hadn't bothered to look at the menu. She said, "I'll have the same."

As soon as Grace departed, Lena fixed me with a penetrating stare. "Why are you being nice to me?"

"Because I don't want to see you hurt," I said truthfully. "You're attracted to Link. A lot of women are, but you shouldn't waste your time hanging around to see him. You should make real friends—"

"I love him," she said simply. For just a moment, I was struck by the thought that she sounded like Nancy telling me how she felt about Arnold Rose. But Lena wiped away the memory of my conversation with Nancy when she said, "Link and I were married a few months ago. Secretly." Her eyes burned with a feverish light, but her voice remained soft and her manner wasn't threatening. "We had to keep it a secret, because I was still sick. Link loved me anyway, and he kept on loving me. I know it because he sent me messages through the television set every day. While I was in the hospital."

I felt little hairs begin prickling the back of my neck, but I kept my voice light and sympathetic as I asked, "Hospital?"

Lena reached for her handbag and I flinched. I reached out for something I could use as a defensive weapon and my hand closed around the heavy glass sugar dispenser.

I didn't need a weapon. All she pulled out of her purse were two folded typewritten pages.

She studied the top page for a moment before she passed them to me across the table. "Read this," she said. "It proves I'm all right now."

I took the papers. On the letterhead of Franklin Woods Hospital, Westport, Connecticut, the first page was titled **Exit Mental Health Report**, and dated, February twentieth of this year. I read:

Name: Lena Jolene Cooper

Age: 24

Place of birth: Scarsdale, New York

Reason for Referral: Ms. Cooper was referred to this psychiatric facility because she showed romantic and sexual overtures to her college literature professor, Wade Maitland, who was not interested in her as a lover. She pursued him vigorously even after he explained that he was not interested in her romantically and that her overtures made him quite uncomfortable. Professor Maitland noted that Ms. Cooper has an exceptionally high IQ. He regarded her intelligence as near the genius level. Professor Maitland said he encouraged her to take challenging academic courses, but claims he stressed to her that he and Ms. Cooper could never have a romantic relationship.

Clinical Interview and Course of Treatment: A mental status examination revealed Ms. Cooper to have no indications of hallucinations, delusions, sexual deviations, or other abnormal thought patterns. She did indicate an obsessive desire to possess this man, Professor Wade Maitland, and a compulsive need to have him love her in return. These feelings and desires indicate an Obsessive-Compulsive

Disorder. The fact that she said she "would do anything" to make him love her indicates an Antisocial Personality Disorder raising the concern that she could be a danger to any man who, she believes, is spurning her. She underwent three hour-long sessions of verbal therapy per week for twelve weeks.

Diagnosis:
1. Obsessive-Compulsive Disorder
2. Antisocial Personality Disorder
3. Paranoid Personality Disorder

Conclusions: Ms. Cooper is diagnosed as having an Obsessive-Compulsive Disorder and an Antisocial Personality Disorder. However, she has responded well in verbal therapy so both conditions are seen as cured and she is no longer perceived as a danger or threat. Accordingly, she is being released on this date.

Joseph H. Melville
Exiting Mental Health Worker

I'd barely finished reading when Grace returned with our sandwiches and coffee. I'd lost my appetite. Lena ate hungrily while I sipped my coffee.

Between bites, she said, "Tell Link that it's all right to let people know about us. Now that I'm completely well, we're going to start our life together."

As she ate, I tried to persuade her that she had "misunderstood" (to put it gently) her relationship with Link, but she didn't reply. Realizing that her eyes were focused on something in the distance that was invisible to me, I guessed that she had retreated into a world of her own. It was a place where I couldn't—and emphatically did not want to—follow.

Chapter 10

AS SOON AS she finished eating, Lena pushed her plate away, stood up, grabbed her handbag, and walked out of the Central Park Café, without waiting for me to pay the check, without saying good-bye. By the time I'd taken care of the bill and was out on the street, she'd disappeared. I hurried first to one corner and then to the other without getting a glimpse of her. I refolded the pages she'd given me, shoved them into my handbag, and went into the Global building.

My thoughts of Lena were interrupted as soon as I got off the elevator on the twenty-sixth floor. Betty Kraft hailed me. She was usually unflappable, but now I saw worry lines etched deep in her face.

"You just missed the paramedics," she said.

My heart lurched. "What's happened?"

"Francie James was camera-blocking when she started having terrible back pains," Betty said. "The nurse looked at her and immediately called an ambulance. When Tommy saw how much pain Francie was in, he keeled over."

"Oh, no! Is he all right?"

She nodded, her gray corkscrew curls bouncing. "He's very sensitive to other people's suffering." She said it kindly, but with a wry smile; we shared knowledge of Tommy's vulnerabilities. "I put a cold cloth on his head and got him to lie down in the infirmary. I was just about to dial you on your cell."

"Where'd they take Francie?"

"St. Monica's, over on Columbus—"

"I know where it is. Thanks." I was about to reverse direction and head for the elevator when I had a thought. "With Francie out of action, we'll lose at least half a day of taping. Would you put together a package of our next five scripts and have somebody bring them over to me at the hospital? I have to figure out how to tape around her, to whatever extent we may have to."

"I'm on it," Betty said. "Go."

ST. MONICA'S, A four-story private hospital on Columbus Avenue between Sixty-Sixth and Sixty-Seventh Streets, was so convenient to the Global building we used it for medical emergencies that occurred during work hours. Luckily for those who needed its services, St. Monica's had an excellent staff.

It would have been an easy stretch of the legs if I'd had the time to indulge myself in the exercise, but I had no time to waste. I flagged down the first empty cab I saw. Less than five minutes later I pushed through the double doors of the Emergency entrance.

Actor Rod Amato was already there. Rod was Francie's love interest on the show and—according to Tommy's gossip hot line—had become her significant other in real life, too.

Rod saw me as soon as I entered the small reception area

and rushed over. He was shaking. "They think she's having a kidney stone attack," he said. He was trying to stay calm, but it was obvious he was frantic with worry. The irregular features that gave him an offbeat, idiosyncratic appeal were tight with tension, and sweat was running down his cheeks, cutting little rivulets through his TV makeup.

I winced. My expression must have alarmed Rod, because his fingers tightened.

"What? My God—is she going to *die*?"

"No." My tone was sharper than I'd intended, so I softened it. "I'm sure she'll be all right," I said. "But I had some experience with a kidney stone attack."

"You had one?"

"Not me." I took a deep breath and decided to share something from my past that might give him comfort. "When I was nineteen I married a wonderful wildlife photographer, Ian Tyler, and went with him to live in Africa. One night we were in Northern Kenya when Ian had a kidney stone attack. I'd never seen anybody in such agony—and we were a hundred miles from the nearest doctor. He was in so much pain I was sure I was going to lose him. Miraculously, a little after dawn, the stone passed and the pain was over. An hour later we were in our Land Rover, bouncing over bad roads, heading south toward Mombasa. He said he felt as though nothing had happened."

I couldn't bring myself to tell Rod the rest of it. While I hadn't lost Ian that time, three years later, our vehicle blew a tire and careened into a dry riverbed. I suffered only a broken wrist. Ian was killed instantly.

Before Rod could ask me anything else, a man in his thirties with a red buzz cut came through the door marked Authorized Personnel Only and approached us. He wore blue scrubs, with a photo badge that identified him as Mark Owen, M.D.

"Are you with Ms. James?"

Rod's voice was hoarse with apprehension. "How is she?"

"It's a kidney stone," the doctor said.

I put a hand on Rod's arm as I asked Dr. Owen, "What can you do for her?"

"She's had morphine, but that doesn't do much for a kidney stone—just makes her feel drunk, takes a little of the edge off. I hope we can break it up with ultrasound, but she's going to have a rough time until this is over."

With the back of one hand, Rod brushed a jagged lock of ash blond hair from his eyes. "Can I—can *we*—be with her?" His words were a plea.

"The distraction might help a little, but you'll have to wait a few minutes. We're about to move her to a private room up on two."

FRANCIE'S FACE WAS pale and her golden brown hair was dark with perspiration, but even in terrible pain she looked lovely. Four months ago, Francie had nearly been fired by a network executive because she'd gained weight and was no longer the slim beauty she had been when she started playing the role of Dinah six years earlier. To keep one of the best actresses in daytime drama on the show, I devised a fitness program for her. It was working. Without feeling deprived, or suffering on a fad diet, Francie had lost over twenty pounds in the past four months. Her figure might be fuller than it was when she began on the show, but she was beautiful, and up to this moment, healthy.

Francie wasn't the only one who'd benefited from the plan. I'd incorporated her fitness program into her story line and now, according to the e-mails that were pouring in, women in our audience were losing weight along with Francie—and we'd acquired a significant number of new viewers.

As Dr. Owen made notes in Francie's chart, a nurse adjusted the IV bag that dripped medication into Francie's vein. Her breath was coming in agonized little huffs as she twisted and contorted on the bed. I felt a stab of recognition: Francie was trying desperately to find a comfortable position, just as Ian had tried to do. But there was no position that would lessen the horrible pain.

When she saw Rod and me come into her room, she tried to smile. "I don't know . . . why people . . . take morphine for *fun* . . ." she gasped. "It's making me want to puke . . ."

"It's only a pleasure drug when you don't need it," the doctor said sardonically.

Francie reached for Rod's hand. "I wouldn't . . . mind the . . . pain so much . . . if I was going . . . to have . . . a baby . . . when it was over . . ."

Rod leaned over and kissed the hand that gripped his. "You're gonna be okay, honey. Hang on. It'll be over soon."

Rod's prediction of "soon" turned out to be six hours away, but he never left her side. I couldn't do anything medical for Francie, so I settled myself at the corner of a sofa in the waiting lounge and concentrated on reworking our taping schedule so we wouldn't go overbudget.

When I finished, I called Betty.

"How's Francie?" she asked.

"In a lot of pain—it's a kidney stone—but she's getting good care. Rod's with her, and that seems to help."

"He's a sweetie," she said. "I'm glad he's catching on with the audience."

"Me too. Have you got a notebook?"

"I pick up pen and paper whenever I hear your voice. Call me Pavlov's secretary."

After I'd dictated the schedule changes to Betty, she said, "I'll print this out and get it to everybody. Are you coming back to the office today?"

"Probably not. I can't leave here until I know Francie's going to be okay, and I don't know how long that will be. How's Tommy?"

"Up and functioning again. He's handling things here, so why don't you just go home when you can. Give Francie our love. Tommy's ordered a *forest* of flowers for her. When they're delivered, you'll need a machete to hack your way into her room."

That image made me laugh and I said goodbye to Betty.

Not knowing how much longer I would be at the hospital, and too concerned about Francie to want to read a magazine, I took a pad out of my handbag and started outlining future episodes.

Before I'd finished the first page, a deliveryman passed me, heading toward Francie's room. He was steering a dolly that held a flowering tree in a tub. At the base of the tree were piled what looked like a dozen bouquets of roses. Two orderlies and a young nurse's aide trailed the dolly, carrying vases. Betty hadn't exaggerated Tommy's generosity.

I'd finished outlining two episodes and was well into a third when I looked up to find the nurse I'd seen earlier in Francie's room coming toward me. Smiling. "You can see Ms. James now," she said, "but just stay a few minutes. She's worn out."

Quickly stuffing the outlines into my bag, I hurried down the corridor to Francie's room. Rod was sitting beside her, holding her hand and grinning like a lottery winner. Tommy's spectacular tree filled one corner of the room and vases full of roses covered every surface.

"How are you feeling?" I asked.

"I can be in the studio tomorrow morning," Francie said.

"But Dr. Owen wants her to stay overnight, for observation," Rod added.

I dismissed them with a wave of my hand and a smile. "The taping schedule's been rearranged. We won't need *either* of you until Monday." I gestured toward the tree and the flowers. "Your biggest problem is going to be how to get all that home."

Francie smiled weakly at my joke, and I gave her hand a gentle squeeze. "I'm so glad you're okay," I said. "Now get some sleep."

Rod walked me to the doorway. "I could fall in love with you," he whispered, "but I'm already crazy in love with her."

I hoped with all of my heart that this was a romance that was going to last.

From the e-mails we were getting, and the conversations in the Internet fan chat rooms we monitored, the audience liked the chemistry between Rod and Francie. I made a mental note to write some lively love scenes for them to play—sexuality mixed with comedy. That was a delicate combination, but I suspected they were up to the challenge.

Chapter 11

WHEN I GOT home from the hospital, there was a message from Penny on my voice mail. I called her.

After we exchanged greetings, she said, "Matt and G. G. are returning from Washington on Saturday. I'm going to give them a little welcome home party Sunday night. Will you come? It'll just be the five of us: you and Matt, and Brandi and G. G. and me."

"Count me in," I said. "Can I bring anything?"

"Not a thing, but thanks." She paused for a moment. "I wanted to ask Nancy to join us, but then I would have had to ask Arnold, too."

"Don't you like him?"

"Oh, I *do*—very much. Arnold and Nancy are a wonderful couple, but you know how much G. G. hates defense attorneys. He gets red in the face whenever he and Arnold are in the same room. This is his and Matt's welcome home party, and I want G. G. to relax. He's been down in Washington with the FBI—and he hates them too. I'll have Nancy and Arnold over again soon, and then G. G. will just have to behave himself."

Magic ate dinner with his usual enthusiasm while I edited a script. Later, I scrambled eggs for myself. While I dined, Magic took the opportunity to fastidiously groom his whiskers.

After he had used the litter box and I'd brushed my teeth and moisturized my hands, Magic settled himself on the pillow next to mine and went to sleep. Overflowing with affection, I watched the gentle rise and fall of his round little tummy. Magic filled a hole in my heart that I hadn't even known was there. What I felt for this adolescent kitten was forcing me to face the fact that there was another hole in my heart that hadn't been filled.

I wanted to be part of a *couple* again.

Years ago I read about a widow who said she felt like "half a pair of scissors." That did *not* describe me. I didn't feel like half a pair of anything. Yet in the last few months I'd come to realize that I missed that matchless feeling of loving and being loved without restraint.

THE PHONE RANG, jangling me out of a deep sleep. I opened my eyes in the darkness and squinted at the inch-high red numerals on my bedside clock.

I grasped the receiver and mumbled, "Hello?"

"Morgan—thank God you're home!" It was Tommy Zenos, sounding frantic.

"It's 2:14 in the morning, Tommy."

"I know—but something terrible is about to happen!"

"About to . . . ? What—"

"I couldn't sleep, so I went out to get the bulldog edition of the papers. That's how I found out! It's in tomorrow morning's *New York Post*—on the gossip page."

I knew the column Tommy meant. Even though it was called *Page Six*, it was usually located on page twelve or page fourteen. Lots of secrets were revealed in *Page Six*, and most of them turned out to be true. I sat up and switched on the lamp.

"I'm awake, Tommy." Beside me, Magic squinted, squirmed, and turned around so that he faced away from the light. "Tell me."

On Tommy's end of the line, pages rattled. "It says 'In an economy move, the Global Broadcasting Network is planning to cut a contract player from each of its three soaps: *Love of My Life* and *Trauma Center*, taped in New York, and *Dare to Desire*, which tapes in Hollywood.'" Tommy took a breath and, in a desperate tone, rushed on. "Our show is the best run of any on the net. We don't have any fat to cut!"

That was true, but Global's three daytime dramas were owned by the network. While Tommy and I were in charge of *Love* on a day-to-day basis, Global Broadcasting had the real power.

Tommy was distraught. "I love all of our people and everybody in the cast is material to the stories you're telling now."

I agreed. "Losing anybody is going to cause a lot of rewriting. Not to mention that an item like this could devastate cast morale. We've got to find a way to keep our group intact."

"The big *Page Six* story is about a rock star's plastic surgery," Tommy said, his voice suddenly full of hope. "Our piece is at the bottom. Maybe nobody will see it."

EVERYBODY SAW IT.

Even though I got to the studio earlier than usual, I was met with cast members close to hysteria. Actors not working that day telephoned to ask who was being fired. I told everyone that nothing had been decided, and that Tommy and I were trying to prevent any cast changes.

When Tommy came into the office at ten, the first thing he noticed was that our wastebasket was filled to the top with crumpled Kleenex.

"Same thing down at *Trauma Center*," he said.

"Everybody's so nervous, the taping is an hour behind

schedule," I said. "We've got to put this fire out now. Call a meeting—let's assemble the cast and crew in Thirty-Seven."

"What are you going to say?"

"I don't know," I admitted.

Studio Thirty-Seven was still dressed as Greendale Park, so there was plenty of room to sit on the benches and Astroturf. Tommy sat behind me, on a stool next to Camera One.

"What was in the paper this morning was just a rumor," I said. "It wasn't an announcement. Firing any one of you doesn't make creative sense."

The response was a dissatisfied grumbling. I couldn't blame them; what I'd said sounded weak, even to me.

Actor Parker Nolan, who had given me the perfume, spoke up. "*Post* items are right more often than they're wrong."

"I promise you all that Tommy and I will find a way to keep everyone on salary."

"How?" asked Clarice Hill, the young beauty who played Jillian.

"We have a plan," I said, making my voice ring with conviction. Behind me, I hoped that Tommy was playing along. That "plan" would be news to him. It was news to *me*.

My words calmed the troops. Everyone got up and went back to work with revived good spirits.

In our office a few minutes later, Tommy closed the door. "What's your plan?"

"I'm co-executive producer, so I made an executive decision. I lied."

Tommy blanched. "There isn't any plan?"

"There will be," I said firmly. "We just have to think of one."

We were getting hourly reports that the Internet chat rooms we monitored—the ones devoted to the daytime dramas—were buzzing about nothing else. Fans were afraid that their favorite characters were about to be axed, or they were making bets about who would be leaving.

* * *

IT WAS MIDNIGHT and I was getting ready for bed when the phone rang.

"They're not going to make us fire anybody." Tommy said.

"Wonderful! But, Tommy, how—"

"That thing in the *Post* was a fake, a plant by the network PR guys. They got this idea that if they start the rumor that somebody from each of the shows is going to lose his job, the fans will get upset and start campaigning for their favorites. They figure it'll make the shows' ratings go up."

"That's cruel! Our actors, and *Trauma Center*'s, are sick with the fear of losing their jobs. This awful day was caused by a stupid publicity stunt?"

"I don't like it either, but we can't tell anybody the truth," Tommy said. "We've just got to let it play out. We can't embarrass the network."

"So we have to let innocent, hard-working people worry unnecessarily—"

"Only six weeks," Tommy said. "At the beginning of the May Sweeps they're going to put out the story that because of the *overwhelming* response of the fans, the network has decided to retain the actors it had planned to let go."

"Whatever happened to truth in advertising?" I asked.

"I dunno," Tommy said with a sigh. "Whatever happened to 'Do unto others as you would have them do unto you'?"

What Tommy said made me realize what I had to do. "I'm telling our people what's really going on. I'll swear them to secrecy, but I won't let them suffer for six weeks."

"Okay," Tommy said slowly. "But tell them, too, that if the piece is exposed as a publicity stunt, it's our heads that'll be on the chopping block."

The next day, Friday, the actors were a lot happier when I told them that no one was going to be fired after all. They agreed to keep the secret, even from their loved ones and their agents. Taping went so well that we finished nearly an hour early.

Only one thing kept the day from being perfect. Looking out the window during the lunch break, I saw a familiar dab of blue. I beckoned Tommy over to take a look.

"I don't see anything blue," he said.

When I looked again, I didn't see it either.

THAT NIGHT I was enjoying a delicious Italian meal and the company of Chet Thompson. We were on Mott Street in Little Italy, at a charming family restaurant called Dante's. Chet had been telling me about the book he was writing on war crimes.

We were halfway through my linguine puttanesca and his rigatoni fra diavolo when he said, "Don't get me wrong, because I think you look *great*—I really like that black, sort of riding-type thing you're wearing—but I've never seen you in anything except pants suits. Do you ever wear dresses, or skirts?" His tone was conversational, but I didn't believe this was a casual question, and I don't like to play games.

"What are you trying to say?"

"I wonder why you always wear pants outfits," he said. "I'm interested in everything about you." The expression in his eyes was warm and kind. He seemed so sincere that I paused to consider his question.

"I was going to say that slacks are more practical than skirts for work," I said, "but then I realized that I'm not crawling through jungles anymore to take pictures. I suppose dressing like this has become a habit."

Chet studied me quizzically.

"Okay, Dr. Thompson, expert in the criminal mind, I sense you don't believe me, so what's your theory about how I dress?"

"It's nothing so formal as a theory, just something I noticed when we first met."

"What?"

"You've got a very good figure, but you were wearing clothes that were too big for you. I thought then that you were hiding inside them for some reason. Then you started wearing things that fit well. You're showing your shape now, but I think wearing pants all the time is still a form of hiding."

I didn't want Chet, or anyone, analyzing me. I tried to

cover my irritation with a joke. "Just what do you think I'm concealing—a wooden leg? Bad legs? No ankles?"

He grinned at me. "I'm sure your legs are fine. I'd like to see them sometime."

We were interrupted by the ringing of my cell phone. Chet said, "Don't answer it and I'll give you a thousand dollars."

"I can't be bought." I fished the phone out of my bag and pressed the answer button. "Hello?"

"We got big trouble, boss lady." It was Link.

I sat up straighter. "What's the matter?"

"When I got home tonight, I found that nut Lena in my bed!"

Chapter 12

"I HAVE TO get over to Link Ramsey's," I told Chet as I ended the call. "An obsessed fan has broken into his apartment."

"Did he call the police?"

"He refuses."

Chet was already signaling for the check. "I'm not letting you go alone," he said. "Where does he live?"

"Carmine Street, between Bedford and Bleecker."

LINK OCCUPIED THE ground-floor garden apartment at 135 Carmine, an old but well-maintained six-story building in the West Village. Bundled up in a navy peacoat, he was pacing outside when Chet's Range Rover pulled into a parking place two spaces down from the entrance.

As soon as he saw me get out of the Rover, he hurried forward. His frown of concern turned into one of anger when he saw that I wasn't alone. Indicating Chet with a brusque nod, he said rudely, "I didn't want you to bring that cop."

Chet smiled with good-natured amusement. "I'm not 'that cop'—I'm 'that *writer*.' He extended his hand to Link. "I'm Chet Thompson. Morgan has more than one man seeking her favor."

Link shook Chet's hand, then looked at me as if he was going to comment on my social life. That was the last subject I wanted to discuss. "Chet's also a psychologist, specializing in the criminal mind," I said.

The tension in Link's face eased a bit. "I could use one of those," he said, opening the front door for us. I noticed that it wasn't a security entrance; anyone could come in.

Link led us down the hall to his apartment. When we reached his door I looked at the lock and was surprised to find that it was an ordinary, basic device—the kind that practically anyone who'd ever seen a caper movie could pick.

Link inserted his key.

"Get a better lock," I said.

"I've lived in the neighborhood even before I could afford this place. Everybody knows everybody. I always thought it was safe." He opened the door. "I'll go in first." Just past the threshold, he scanned the room. Seeing no one there, he beckoned Chet and me inside.

The lighted brass table lamp cast a warm glow over the burgundy leather sofa and matching club chair. A mahogany bookcase against one wall reached nearly to the ten-foot ceiling and was filled with old-looking leather-bound volumes. No contemporary dust jackets, no paperbacks; it was the library of a collector. It also appeared that Link collected old magnifying glasses, too. About a dozen were displayed on the coffee table, on the end tables, and on the glass shelves in an antique curio cabinet next to the bookcase. Some were quite beautiful with handles of ivory, amber, and lapis lazuli.

Link, Chet, and I stood still for a moment. Cautious, listening.

"I left her in my bed," Link said in a low voice.

Chet followed Link, and I brought up the rear as we moved

quietly toward the closed bedroom door. I don't think any of us were sure what we were going to encounter.

Link reached for the knob, turned it, and eased the door open. I heard his sharp intake of breath. As he pushed the door all the way open, Chet and I crowded in behind him. The scene that greeted us made me gasp.

Link's king-size bed was a disaster area. The linens had been sliced into ribbons and some clear liquid—I *hoped* it was water—had been poured onto the mattress, soaking it so thoroughly I was sure it would have to be scrapped. Across the room, the closet door was open and Link's clothes pulled out and dumped into a pile on the floor.

Chet indicated the closed door to our left. "Is that the bathroom?"

"Yeah."

They started toward it.

"Be careful," I said. "She must have a knife, or a box cutter."

Lena wasn't in the bathroom. She was gone, but she'd left devastation behind her. Everything in the medicine cabinet had been swept out onto the floor. A white powder (talcum, by the scent of it) covered everything like a blanket of snow.

Chet knelt, picked up some pills. "Did she get any drugs?" he asked Link.

"I don't take anything except vitamins. My body is my temple." His tone was wry, but I could see the anger in his eyes.

"How did she get in?" I asked.

Link answered by striding to the far wall. He yanked at the cord on heavy, dark brown velvet drapes, revealing French doors to the garden. They stood open.

Link turned on the garden lights, illuminating a large, attractive patio enclosed on three sides by a six-foot brick wall. I couldn't imagine the woman I had met scaling that wall on either side, but then I saw a wooden gate in the corner, partially concealed by large terra-cotta pots full of plants.

"I'm so used to that gate I forget it's there," Link said.

The gate's hinges had been worked out of the brick, leaving an opening just large enough for someone to squeeze into the garden from the alley behind the building. "That's how she got in *and* out," Chet said.

Link was staring back into his vandalized bedroom. Suddenly it seemed as though the anger had drained out of him, replaced by anguish.

"You can't stay here," I said. "That gate has to be replaced by something a lot stronger."

"I've got a big apartment on Waverly," Chet told Link. "You can stay with me until you get this place fixed up, or move."

"Thanks," Link said. "I'll toss a few things in a bag." He clapped Chet on the shoulder in a gesture of appreciation. "I owe you."

Link went back into the bedroom, and Chet turned to me. "Your actor owes me more than he knows. I was hoping we might have our first hot night together."

Before I could reply, Link appeared in the garden door. "No cops," he declared firmly. "I don't want them pawing through my things, looking for clues."

"You have to file a complaint," I said. "There's no telling what she might do next."

"*No cops*! I mean it," he said. "I gotta have my privacy."

Chapter 13

CHET'S APARTMENT TOOK up the entire first floor of 155 Waverly Place, an elegant four-story brick-front building that
might have been a private mansion a hundred years ago. Link
and I followed Chet in as he unlocked his door and switched
on the lights.

In surprising contrast to the old-world stateliness of the ex-
terior, the décor of Chet's apartment was modern, featuring
lots of stainless steel, glass, and marble. Handsome, but not
my taste. Even though I've yet to replace the mostly bland and
no-period furniture that came with my Dakota co-op, I know
that I prefer old pieces that have stories to tell.

Link put down his duffle bag and glanced around. "Nice,"
he said. Referring to the painting over the fireplace, he asked,
"Is that a real Mondrian?"

"Supposedly," Chet said. "I sublet this place." He turned to
me. "What do you think of my secondhand pad?"

"It's very nice," I said politely.

Link glanced from Chet to me. "Haven't you been here be-fore?" he asked.

"I'd *hoped* she'd see the place tonight," Chet said. "Any-way, that was my plan."

"I crashed your party," Link said with a wicked smile. "Sorry about that, man."

Chet picked up Link's duffle. "Come on. I'll show you the guest room and check that there are sheets on the bed."

"I'll make us some coffee," I said.

An hour, a pot of coffee, and a bottle of wine later, Chet and Link were thoroughly bonded. On the surface they could hardly have been more different: Link was a self-educated high school dropout and Chet had a PhD, but they discovered they followed the same sports teams and liked the same music, ranging from rock to Bach.

When Link had relaxed, Chet skillfully brought the subject around to Lena. Sipping coffee, his shoes off and his feet up on a marble-top coffee table, Link told Chet essentially the same story he'd told me: that he'd never seen Lena until nearly two weeks ago; he'd thought she was just a fan, only a little more persistent than most. The scene she'd staged out-side the Global building, when she started yelling and pound-ing on the taxi was the first hint he'd had that she might be unstable.

"But I still didn't think she was anything more than the girls you see screaming and fainting at rock concerts."

"What I witnessed tonight was more serious," Chet said. "I think she's dangerous."

"Wait a minute," I said. "I've got something." I put down my coffee and crossed the room to where I'd left my purse. Then I realized, "It's home, in another handbag."

"What is?" Chet asked.

"Lena cornered me outside the GBN building, just after you dropped me off," I told Chet. "She saw us and was upset because she thought I was betraying Link."

Link shook his head. "This sounds like one of our story lines."

"She wanted me to tell you that she was 'well now.' She showed me her discharge papers from a hospital—a psychiatric facility. It was a report saying she was 'cured.'"

"I'd like to see that," Chet said.

"It's at home. I'll go get it and bring it back."

"No, it's too late for a round trip. I'll put you in a cab and when you get home, fax it to me." He scribbled his fax number on a pad beside the telephone on the table next to him, then he stood up. "Do you mind if I don't drive you home?"

"Of course not. I'd rather you two keep talking."

Link got up and leaned over to kiss me on the cheek. "Sorry I got you into this."

"Remember that when it's time to renegotiate your contract," I replied.

ALL THE WAY uptown, I thought about Link's situation.

In a professional way this was my problem, too. Link insisted he wasn't in physical danger, but I couldn't base my decisions on what he believed. Until we *knew* how this real-life drama would play out, I was going to have studio security increased—and do whatever else I thought necessary to protect Link, whether he liked it or not.

Magic was waiting for me at the door when I let myself into the apartment. I scooped him up in greeting, then hurried down the hallway to the bedroom, to find the handbag I'd carried the day I had that bizarre lunch with Lena. I was angry at myself for having forgotten about them, but a lot had happened in the last few days.

The discharge papers were at the bottom of my bag, below some script notes.

Because I did late-night and weekend writing at home, I'd set up a library table with a computer, a printer, and a fax machine in the bedroom, against the wall between the door to the walk-in closet and the windows facing Central Park. I took the number Chet had scribbled for me out of my jacket pocket and faxed the pages to him.

As the fax was transmitting, I kicked off my shoes and draped my jacket over the back of my writing chair. I propped myself against the headboard. Magic jumped up into my lap, kneaded my upper thighs with his little velvet paws, and then the phone on the nightstand rang. My roommate leaped up onto my left shoulder and draped himself over it, with his long tail hanging down my chest. I leaned forward, so he wouldn't bump his face against the headboard.

"Hello?"

"This report is total BS," Chet said. "Joseph Melville sounds like an incompetent; I think he wrote this drivel just to get rid of her. I'm sorry to say I've seen this sort of thing before."

I was so shocked that I had to make sure I understood him. "Do you mean you don't think Lena should have been released?"

"For this Melville to say she's *cured* is ridiculous. If it had been up to me, Lena Cooper wouldn't be running around loose. Her recent behavior—the hysterical fit outside your building, and the rage she exhibited in Link's apartment—indicates to me that this is a dangerous woman. Melville saw her for weeks; he must have—or he *should* have—spotted something that concerned him."

"But what if she didn't do anything like this before?"

"Unfortunately, we don't know what she's done before, except that she'd stalked one of her professors, and she was disturbed enough to be hospitalized. Her earlier behavior could have predicted these later actions. Melville should have known that if she found another target for her obsession, she'd escalate."

"So you think we've got some big trouble here?"

"Potentially. Link says he doesn't have to work until Wednesday, so I'm taking him up to Greenwich, to stay with me for the next few days. We're leaving in half an hour." Chet sighed, then lowered his voice and changed his tone. "I wish it was the two of *us* going to Greenwich. I want you to see my house. And meet my German shepherds. You like dogs, don't you?"

"I like all kinds of animals," I said.

After Chet and I said good night, I lifted Magic off my shoulder, put him down on the bed next to me, and leaned back. As I thought about the situation with Lena Cooper, it occurred to me that there were two things I could do. For the first one, I picked up the receiver and dialed Matt's cell phone number.

Matt Phoenix and G. G. Flynn, his partner at the Twentieth Precinct, were still in Washington, D.C., at an FBI seminar. They'd be home tomorrow evening, but I was too worried about the Lena situation to wait another twenty hours to talk to Matt.

Chapter 14

MATT ANSWERED ON the third ring. "Morgan?"

"How did you know?"

"Caller ID." I heard concern in his voice. "Are you okay? What's wrong?"

"I'm fine," I said, reassuringly. "But I need your advice. Can you talk?"

"Wait 'til I get Cameron Diaz off my lap."

"Very funny," I said.

"What makes you think I'm joking?"

His voice was warm, his tone amused, but still that response gave me pause. Why *did* I assume there wasn't a beautiful woman in his room? He was thirty-eight, single, very attractive, smart, and funny . . .

His tone turned serious. "You wouldn't call me in D.C. unless it was important. Talk."

And I did.

When I finished, he asked, "Who's the actor?"

"It's Link Ramsey, but he's adamant that he won't make a complaint. Even though he's upset about her getting into his apartment, and angry at the vandalism, he doesn't believe she's really dangerous. He'll be furious if I tell him I talked to you about this."

"If he won't press charges, there's nothing I can do. You must know that, so why did you call me? Not that it isn't nice to hear your voice."

"I wanted your take on this situation," I said.

"All right, here it is. Ramsey's refusal to report her makes me suspicious. Are you *sure* he doesn't know this woman, that they didn't have some kind of prior relationship, before she started following him around?"

"He insists not, and I believe him."

"You probably also believed in the Tooth Fairy."

Ignoring his sarcasm, I said, "I haven't given up trying to persuade Link to press charges. Tell me *what* she could be charged with."

"Assuming Ramsey's telling the truth, this woman is the classic 'stranger stalker,' one who targets somebody famous. If she hasn't been previously convicted of stalking, then what she's doing is called stalking in the fourth degree, a class B misdemeanor. She could also be charged with breaking and entering and destruction of personal property, but putting all those together, if she got a good lawyer and promised restitution for the damage she'd probably be let go with a warning. Unless—"

"Unless what?"

Matt's tone was ominous as he said, "She does something worse."

I felt a stab of fear. "Could Link get a restraining order?"

"He *could*, but if this Lena's really obsessed with him, the RO wouldn't be worth the ink in the judge's signature."

"Don't you have any suggestions at all?" I heard frustration in my voice.

"At the moment, I just have one," Matt said. "Outside the studio, keep far away from Link Ramsey."

"That won't be hard, at least for the next few days. He's gone out of town . . . to stay with a friend."

"Good." I heard Matt stifle a yawn.

"Sounds like it's time for you to go to sleep," I said.

"Yeah. It's been a long day here in the land of the super-size egos." He stopped talking. Listening intently, I could hear him breathing.

I lowered my voice to a whisper. "You haven't gone to sleep yet, have you?"

"No . . . I was thinking about something."

There was a strained note in his voice; it made me sit up straighter. "What is it?"

"Sunday night, after Penny's dinner party, I'll take you home," he said. "There's something we have to talk about."

"You sound serious."

"I am. We've got a problem."

One more problem—that's all I need. What I said was, "Let's talk about it now."

"Not over the phone, Marmalade."

I hated the nickname—he'd tagged me with it because he said my hair is the color of marmalade. Because he used it with affection, I responded with lightness and humor. "You called me 'Marmalade' so how bad can the problem be?"

His response was silence. That was so irritating I challenged him. "When it comes to talking about your feelings, you might as well be bricked up behind that wall in Poe's 'The Cask of Amontillado.' "

"Never read it."

Now *he* sounded irritated. Thinking I might be getting through to him, I pulled out the heavy artillery.

"Matt, you are the most self-protected human being I've ever met."

"Yeah? Look in the mirror!"

"Is this your idea of a discussion, throwing what I say back at me?"

He took a deep, calming breath. "Okay, I admit I don't put my feelings out on display. In this job I can't afford to. But you don't let me know you, either. We almost made love, but you've never told me anything about where you grew up, what your folks were like, if they're even alive. When we're together we talk about everything *but* you. I don't even know what your name was before you got married. Out of respect for your privacy I haven't tried to find out."

I fought hard to keep my voice steady, not to betray the shock he'd given me. "There's nothing much to find out," I said. That was the *truth*, but it was only the word "much" that kept it from being a lie. "Fine," I said, hoping to steer him back to the present. "We shouldn't discuss whatever our *problem* is over the phone."

When we said good night, I tried to lighten the mood by saying that I looked forward to seeing him Sunday night. His response was a grunt, so I put the receiver back in its cradle. Magic climbed into my lap, circled three times, and settled down again.

I stroked his head, and rubbed him beneath his ears and under his chin as I thought about Matt Phoenix.

To be fair, Matt was right; I was in no position to criticize him about guarding himself. After Ian's death, when I came back from Africa to stay with Nancy and figure out what to do with the rest of my life, I'd buried myself in work. But now the wall I'd built around my own feelings was finally coming down, one brick at a time. Ironically, meeting Matt because a colleague at the Global Broadcasting Network was murdered had started the process. Weird that it took being suspected of murder to jump-start my desire to have a romantic life again. The trouble is that I am terribly torn over whom to have it *with* . . . I've never liked to dwell on problems; I like to *solve* them. Gently lifting Magic, I repositioned him on the bed, got up, and went to my library table desk, where I'd left Lena's release papers.

I sat down, turned on the computer, and Googled the Franklin Woods Hospital, in Westport, Connecticut, where Lena had been a patient.

The top of their home page featured a photograph of a two-story white building that looked vaguely colonial. In the foreground was a green front lawn, with flowers growing along either side of a long driveway. Below that picture was a strip of three photographs of the same young woman. The first was a close-up that showed her in tears. In the second, she was sitting in a chair and looking up at something beyond the camera, a slightly hopeful expression on her face. The last picture showed her smiling as she walked down the driveway, away from the Franklin Woods psychiatric facility. Not a very subtle ad, but effective. I clicked on the "About Us" link.

According to that information page, "At least one out of five people will experience a mental health problem during his or her lifetime."

That's a pretty grim thought.

It went on to say, "When problems are severe, and a protective and supportive inpatient treatment setting is needed, Franklin Woods Hospital's adult psychiatric programs provide excellent individual services, crucial to support and recovery. A distinguished team of mental health professionals work to restore patients to the highest level of functionality. The Franklin Woods approach to treatment stabilizes and reverses acute psychiatric conditions. Our patients' needs are met in a number of ways, including psychiatric evaluation and treatment, individual counseling, medical evaluations, and therapeutic activities."

The last item was a list of the adult psychiatric disorders they treated: affective disorders (depression and mania), anxiety disorders, mental illness and chemical addiction, personality disorders, psychotic disorders, schizophrenia, self-harm behaviors, and suicidal and homicidal thoughts and behaviors.

A pretty chilling menu.

"Franklin Woods," it went on, "is accredited by the Joint Commission on Accreditation of Healthcare Organizations, licensed by the Connecticut Department of Public Health."

To the left of the text were various links for further information. I clicked on "Meet Our Staff." The "mental health professionals" listed had color pictures next to their names and a brief paragraph about their backgrounds. Scrolling down, I found Joseph H. Melville. He looked to be about fifteen years old. Under a thick helmet of surfer-blond hair, he was *grinning*. Either this was a very old picture, or he was a very new mental health professional. The paragraph that accompanied his picture didn't tell me much. He hadn't attended the top schools, and if he'd published any papers in medical journals, or articles anywhere, they weren't listed.

Maybe Chet was correct in thinking that Melville was incompetent. Or maybe he was just inexperienced. Even though it seemed the least likely answer, in my heart I hoped that Melville was right, and that Lena was well enough to be out of the hospital.

Next, I Googled the object of Lena's previous obsession, Professor Wade Maitland.

Wade Thorston Maitland was the author of three nonfiction books. The first, published eighteen years ago, was *Against the Odds: Nineteenth-Century Women Novelists.* The next, published ten years ago, was *Alice James: Henry's Forgotten Sister.* Wade Thorston Maitland's most recent book, published five years ago, took on a twentieth-century subject: *Zelda Fitzgerald: Gifted Artist, Destroyed by Love.*

I sensed a theme here: women as victims. Ironic, considering that Maitland himself became the victim of stalking by Lena Cooper. Reading further in Maitland's bio, I learned that for the past twelve years, he had been teaching literature at Trinity College, in Hartford, Connecticut.

I switched from Google to Amazon books and typed in the title of the Zelda Fitzgerald book, hoping that it would offer "a look inside," which usually included front and back covers. It did. The picture of the author on the back showed that Wade Maitland—with a full head of dark hair, a close-cropped dark beard, and intense, piercing eyes—was an attractive man. He looked rugged, in a plaid, lumberman's-style shirt, leaning against the rough bark of a tree. It was easy to see how a female student might develop a crush on him.

As I studied the picture, I realized that while it appeared to be a casual shot, it actually had been carefully posed and artistically lighted. A thought occurred to me, and I quickly typed in the title of his first book, the one published eighteen years earlier. Yep, as I suspected: on the back of that book was the *same photo*. It told me a little something about Wade Maitland's ego.

I called Connecticut information and got telephone numbers for the Franklin Woods hospital in Westport and for Wade T. Maitland in Hartford.

Chapter 15

ACCORDING TO MAPQUEST, the Franklin Woods Hospital in Westport, Connecticut, was exactly 51.05 miles from the West Eighty-First street garage where Nancy Cummings kept her sky blue Mercedes sports car.

"Of course you can borrow it," she'd said when I called her early Saturday morning. "I'll call the guy at the garage and tell him you're coming."

So at a little after ten o'clock I was on the Henry Hudson Parkway, watching the signs, about to merge onto I-95 toward the Cross Bronx Expressway. According to MapQuest, the trip should take one hour, but because this was Nancy's treasured car—a gift from her father the day she passed the New York State Bar Exam—I was driving with particular caution. Conservative speed and the fact that I was traveling an unfamiliar route, would, I figured, add another twenty minutes to the time, but I'd still be a little early for my 11:30 appointment with Joseph H. Melville.

When I'd called the hospital at eight o'clock that morning, I was put through to Lena Cooper's "exiting mental health worker." On the phone he sounded more grown-up than his picture on the Web site. Maybe, like Maitland, he used an old picture.

"My name is Morgan Tyler, Dr. Melville. I'm calling because I understand you knew Lena Cooper while she was at Franklin Woods."

"Stop right there." His voice was suddenly tight. "I can't tell you anything about Lena Cooper. I can't even say whether or not she was ever a patient."

"It's no secret she was there. She gave me her release papers. You signed them."

"That may or may not be my signature," he said defensively.

"I can fax the page to you."

"Don't bother. I'll confirm nothing." He sounded beyond nervous. Sensing he was about to hang up, I decided to use flattery.

"Lena told me that you're a *wonderful* doctor," I said. "I wouldn't dream of asking you to compromise your ethics. She praised you so highly I wanted to ask your advice about something. I can be there any time you name."

"No," he said. His voice had hardened; I'd lost him. Unless . . .

I lowered my voice and adopted a dramatic tone. "Dr. Melville, I'll tell you the real reason I need your expert advice, but this must stay just between us. Agreed?"

He was curious enough to agree.

"I'm the executive producer and head writer of a high-rated television series," I said. "We're developing a story about the young staff of a psychiatric facility. I thought perhaps you might—"

"Be your technical advisor?" He didn't sound rude anymore. During the five years I've been in show business I've discovered that few people can resist the lure of it. Melville was susceptible, but more practical than most.

"You pay for that—for advising—don't you?" he asked.

"Absolutely. Technical advisors are well compensated."

"Hmmm," he said, nibbling at the bait. "I've got a busy schedule, but I can spare a few minutes. How's 11:30?" He'd swallowed the hook.

"See you then." I said good-bye before he could ask more questions or change his mind. Playing the show business card wasn't something I was proud of, but it worked. I didn't know how much information I could pry out of Joseph H. Melville by distracting him with heady visions of being a technical advisor, but for Link's sake, I had to try.

It was nearly 8:30 when I reached Wade Maitland. His voice was a deep, rich baritone. I introduced myself and apologized for calling him so early on a Saturday morning.

"No need," he said pleasantly. "I've been up for hours. I'm working on my new book."

"Professor Maitland, I wouldn't have disturbed you unless it was urgent. I need to talk to you about a former student of yours—Lena Cooper?"

I heard a deep sigh on the other end of the line. "Lena Cooper. Who are you?" he asked suspiciously.

"Morgan Tyler. I write for television, but I'm not going to write about her. This is entirely personal."

"What program? What is the program for which you write, Ms. Tyler?"

"*Love of My Life.* It's a day—"

"I know that program." His voice warmed several degrees. "I am one of your most passionate viewers. In fact, I must confess that before TiVo came into my life, I arranged my class schedule so that I could have lunch with my friends in your town of Greendale."

"Really? I'm pleased to hear that." *Surprised* to hear it was more accurate.

"Your lovely Jillian—I *fear* for her. That Gareth is a dangerous man. I'm sure he will imperil her life and then break her heart. But I must tell you that last Friday's and this past Monday's episodes were the most *lyrical* erotic scenes I've ever witnessed. When Jillian pulled Gareth—fully dressed—into the swimming pool with her, where she was naked . . . and then when they made love . . . Well! I confess that I required a cold shower before I could return to my work."

"I'm delighted you're so interested in the story," I said, keeping any hint of clashing emotions from my voice. It was one thing to write that scene, but it gave me a queasy feeling to hear it described as a kind of visual Viagra. I turned the conversation back in the direction I needed it to go. "To hear praise from a distinguished writer"—I was laying it on a little thick—"to hear that *you* watch our show is a great compliment."

"Popular entertainment is nothing to be ashamed of," he said.

Ashamed? It never occurred to me to be ashamed of daytime drama. I held onto my temper and parried—pleasantly—with "Shakespeare wrote for the groundlings. Perhaps we can discuss this at length one day, but now could we talk about Lena Cooper?"

"I haven't seen her since—I haven't seen her for many months. I can't imagine what possible use it would be to talk to me." The tone of his voice implied that while he was reluctant to talk, he wasn't exactly refusing.

"Professor Maitland, Lena's become obsessively interested in a friend of mine. Someone I work with. I'm concerned, and I really need to know whatever you can tell me. I'll be in Westport later this morning. I could come to Hartford—"

"No—don't come here. By a fortunate coincidence I am going to the Westport Playhouse this afternoon. We could have lunch . . ."

"Perfect. But please let lunch be my treat. Where shall we meet?"

His voice warmed again. "The Westport Inn. Charming place, wonderful food—12:30. It's on Post Road East—"

"I'll find it. See you then."

* * *

IT WAS A few minutes past eleven when I reached the coastal town of Westport, Connecticut. Westport is so clean and attractively designed it might have been a movie set. Early American touches everywhere, in the museums I passed, and in the surprising number of churches. I noticed houses of worship of all denominations.

Using MapQuest as my guide, I followed Post Road all the way to Old Road. A quarter of a mile up Old Road I came to a freshly painted, two-story, classic white colonial-style building, set back against thick woods. In front of the hospital, a wide lawn that was just beginning to show signs of spring grass swept down from the colonnaded entrance to the road. A discreet oxidized bronze sign on one of the stone pillars flanking the mouth of the driveway identified the place as Franklin Woods Hospital.

I realized that the hospital must have been named for Benjamin Franklin when I saw the larger-than-life statue of the man standing in front of the small private hospital. Franklin was one of my favorite historical characters; he was a writer, an inventor, and a diplomat whose brilliance contributed to the founding of a new nation. Also, reputedly, he was very popular with women. An improbable man—just my type.

There were very few cars in the lot, which was a surprise. I thought Saturday would have been a busy visiting day, but maybe I was a little early. I parked Nancy's Mercedes well away from any other vehicle; I didn't want to return it to her with chipped paint because some other driver was careless opening a door.

I was only a few yards from the hospital's entrance when a blond man, carrying a bag of golf clubs, rushed out.

"Joseph Melville?"

He braked to a stop like a felon who heard the police yell, "Freeze!" His shoulders slumped in a "caught" posture, his bag of clubs bumping against his rear. Beneath his mass of unruly blond hair, Joseph Melville had the face of an evil baby.

"Dr. Melville, I'm Morgan Tyler." From behind him, at one of the hospital's ground-floor windows, a flash of bright red hair caught my eye. A woman in what looked like a nurse's smock was watching us. No time to wonder about that; I concentrated on Melville. "You and I had an appointment." I said.

"Yeah, well, I changed my mind." He went on the offensive. "I looked you up on Google—you're with a soap opera. I thought you were something important in *prime time*."

Prime time. Does everybody read *Variety*? I smiled as though I didn't want to punch him in the face. "Can't we talk, just for a few minutes?"

He shifted his clubs to his other shoulder. "No," he snarled. "You're in *soap opera*." He hurried toward a dirty silver gray sedan.

"We call it daytime drama!" I called to his back.

I glanced at the ground-floor window again. The woman was still there, but when our eyes met, she stepped away and disappeared.

Melville looked back to see what I was doing, so I strolled toward Nancy's Mercedes. Apparently satisfied that I was leaving, he put his golf clubs into the sedan, slid behind the wheel, and zoomed off, spraying gravel as he drove away too fast.

As soon as he was out of sight, I pivoted and hurried toward the hospital's entrance.

I had a hunch and wanted to talk to that nurse.

Chapter 16

THE FRONT DOOR opened onto a small reception room. Street scene murals covered the walls, giving the place a cheerful atmosphere. A waist-high oak counter some ten feet long stretched from the solid wall on the left to a pair of locked double doors. Each of the two doors had a small window set at about the height of my shoulders. The glass was double-sided, with a layer of steel mesh between. On my right was a living room arrangement. A deep sofa against the wall was covered in brown corduroy, and flanked by wooden end tables in a dark finish. In front of the sofa was an oval coffee table covered with magazines. The furniture looked expensive, but it was without character, like pieces in a department store display.

No one was waiting in the sitting area, but there were a man and a woman behind the counter. The man—large and muscular, wearing the uniform of a security guard—sat casually before a bank of four monitors, his chair tilted back against the wall. I couldn't see what was on the screens from my side of the counter, but I guessed they were hooked up to security cameras.

The woman at the end of the counter was the one I'd seen looking out the window: about my age, thirty or so, Technicolor hair, wearing a nurse's smock. She was making notes on a clipboard when I came in. From the expression on her face, she was startled to see me. I hadn't planned what I was going to say to anyone except Melville. Operating on instinct, I took a gamble. Nodding to the man with a brief, polite smile, I widened my mouth into the happy grin of an old friend and said to the woman, all in an excited rush, "Oh, what a miserable drive I had! When are they going to do something about the traffic! I hope I'm not too late for us to get some coffee! Callie said she'd positively *kill* me if I didn't tell you all about her wedding plans!"

The nurse picked up the cue. "Hi," she said, as brightly as though she'd known me for years. She turned to the security guard. "Harry, I'm going to take ten. We'll be in the front." She grabbed a jacket from the wooden coat tree beside the front door. Making inane conversation about the imaginary "Callie," we giggled our way outside.

She struggled into the jacket and steered me toward the right-hand corner of the building, over to an arrangement of four wrought-iron chairs surrounding a matching patio table. On the ground next to the table stood a metal cylinder about three feet tall with a bowl of sand on top that was used as an outdoor ashtray.

"Thank you for playing along with me," I said as we sat down at the table. "But why did you?"

She took a package of cigarettes from her jacket pocket. "I wouldn't have—except Joe Melville's been acting weirder than usual since he got a phone call this morning." She pulled a cigarette out of the pack. "Mind if I smoke?" It was a rhetorical question; she lighted up before waiting for an answer. "We were both in the staff lounge. Were you the one who called? About eight o'clock?"

"Yes."

"I wouldn't have paid any attention except I heard him mention Lena Cooper, so I listened in. At first he was all excited—he was acting like *People* magazine was going to name him one of the world's sexiest men. Later, when I went into his office to get a file, I heard him calling Lena's father. From the look on his face, I guess Daddy Cooper read him the riot act, because when he got off the phone, he was pretty shaken." She took a long drag on the cigarette. "You can't blame me for wondering what was up."

"Of course not. By the way, my name's Morgan Tyler."

"Hi. I'm Phyllis Howell."

"Where is Mr. Cooper?" I asked.

Phyllis shook her head. "When Lena was here in the hospital, he was in Paris, Other than that I don't know." Phyllis exhaled, saw that the slight breeze would carry the smoke in my direction, and quickly waved the pungent stream away from me. "Dr. *Prick* left so fast he practically whipped up a breeze. I was curious, so I looked out the window. When I saw you stop him, I figured you were the one who got him so stirred up."

"I can't imagine why I upset him."

"That's easy. Lena Cooper. How do you come to know her?"

I thought for a moment, unsure what to say. I decided on heavily edited truth. "I'm worried. Lena's become very interested in a friend of mine."

Phyllis grimaced. "You mean she's chasing some guy again." She stuck out her tongue to flick a stray piece of tobacco from it.

"She has been pretty hard to discourage," I said.

Phyllis nodded with understanding. "Lena was a tough case. Joe Melville doesn't like tough cases. They're too much work. So when a problem child gets *better enough* that he can sign them out, he does. He wants a Park Avenue practice. Until then, he'd much rather work with our substance abusers.

They make a big racket at first, but when they calm down, they're a lot less trouble than the really disturbed patients."

"Do you think Lena Cooper's one of those patients? Really disturbed?"

"I'm *just a nurse*, as Doctor Prick reminded me when I asked why he was letting Lena go home."

"Then you don't think she should have been released?"

Phyllis sucked on her cigarette, blew out a curl of smoke, and didn't answer for a while. I kept quiet. There are a lot of people who can't stand white space in a conversation. If I didn't say anything, maybe she'd keep talking.

At last she said, "Lena went to school with my little sister. She used to hang at our house—I felt sorry for her. Her father always seemed to be traveling."

"What about her mother?"

Phyllis shook her head. "Died when Lena was six."

"Who looked after her?"

"Servants. I went to the Cooper place once to pick up Cecile—that's my sis—and the door was opened by a butler, in a uniform—like in some old movie. I mean, we lived in Scarsdale, so we weren't exactly trailer trash, but the Coopers are really *rich*. Private planes and houses in Europe rich. Ever heard of the Cooper Building in New York City?" With her cigarette, she gestured behind her at the hospital. "It costs about thirty K a month just to sleep in this place—not counting lab work, meds, and psych services."

"The times I've seen Lena, she didn't give the impression of having money."

"Because she's dumpy looking and dresses like a cleaning lady? Don't let that fool you—the girl inherited pots from her mother."

Phyllis repositioned her chair so that the smoke from her cigarette wouldn't keep flowing in my direction. I saw genuine sadness in her eyes as she added, "For all the good that money's done the poor kid . . . Even when she was in high school, she was like that song about trying to find love in all

the wrong places. CeCe told me that when a guy she liked
backed out of taking her to the senior prom, Lena poured a
can of gasoline all over his new car and set fire to it. Didn't
even try to hide—she did it in front of a dozen witnesses."

"Was she arrested?"

"Daddy Cooper paid off the boy's parents. Lena was taken
out of school and sent away somewhere. That was six years
ago. I didn't see her again until she turned up here. She was in
pretty bad shape—every day, crying like her heart would
break . . ." Phyllis stubbed out her cigarette and stood up. "I
got to go back in."

"I won't tell anyone we talked. I don't want you to get in
trouble."

"Thanks, but I'm getting married next month, to a derma-
tologist. I won't be coming back here."

As we neared the hospital's entrance, Phyllis lowered her
voice. "I broke the rules because I'm hoping you care enough
about that friend of yours—the one she's after—to find a way
to get Lena the serious help she needs, before it's too late.
That poor kid never caught a break."

Chapter 17

EVEN THOUGH I arrived at the Westport Inn fifteen minutes early for our 12:30 appointment, Professor Wade Maitland was waiting for me in the lobby.

I recognized him immediately. Tall and long-limbed, wearing a red-and-blue argyle sweater beneath a mossy gray tweed jacket, with his dark beard and his carefully styled sable brown hair reaching almost to his shoulders, he looked—amazingly—like the picture on the back of his oldest book jacket.

When I came close enough to introduce myself and shake his hand, I saw that his hair and beard were all one color, and a bit too dark to be natural. Still, whatever his age, he was an attractive man.

"Thank you for meeting me," I said.

"I am absolutely delighted." Aiming a thousand volts of charm at me, he held my right hand in both of his. His manners were so courtly he might have stepped out of *Masterpiece*

Theater. I deal with actors every day, so I'm immune to studied magnetism, but I could see how Wade Maitland's charisma might dazzle inexperienced college girls.

Glancing at the gleaming leather wing chairs positioned around the lobby's fireplace, the casual arrangements of fresh flowers, the good antiques, and the numerous replicas of sailing ships, I said, "What a lovely place." Using a dollop of charm of my own, I added, "I'm so glad you chose it." When he smiled with pleasure, I saw how susceptible he was to subtle flattery.

"Shall we have lunch, Professor? You said you were going to the Westport Playhouse, and I don't want to make you late."

"If I must miss the play to be in your service, so be it," he said gallantly.

"I don't think we'll need that much time."

Maitland cupped one hand beneath my elbow and steered me away from the lobby and into the Early American dining room.

Few of the tables were occupied yet, so it was easy for the maitre d' to accommodate Maitland's request for a "a quiet table." We settled ourselves in a corner, well away from other diners. The maitre d' left menus and told us that a waiter would be over shortly.

"The inn has a surprisingly full wine list," Maitland said.

"I can't drink wine in the middle of the day, especially when I have a long drive ahead of me, but please, order some for yourself."

"Then so I will—as a reward because work on my new book went well this morning." He glanced at me over the wine list. Clearly, he was expecting me to ask.

"New book?"

"It's called *Next to Greatness: Women Who Married Extraordinary Men.*"

"That sounds interesting," I said sincerely. "I'll look forward to buying a copy when it's published."

Scanning the menu, I chose grilled salmon with dill sauce

and green beans. Maitland ordered a steak, baked potato, creamed spinach, and a bottle of merlot.

Half a bottle of wine later, after much small talk that consisted of me encouraging Wade Maitland to tell me about himself—not at all a difficult task—we got around to the reason I was there.

"Lena Cooper." He sighed, and poured himself another glass of merlot. "Sadly ill-favored in face and form, but ahhhh . . ." He tapped his forehead. "What a brilliant mind. Lena was painfully shy, but her essay papers were superb. Because it was so difficult for her to express herself in class, I made a terrible mistake."

"What do you mean?"

He finished that glass of wine and poured himself another. "I allowed her to do her verbal work in my office, with me privately. And I must say with pride that she blossomed. Unfortunately, she mistook my appreciation of her intelligence and thought that I returned the romantic attachment she'd formed. I tried to discourage her." He shook his head in frustration.

I said sympathetically, "It must have been flattering at first."

"It was. I'm only human." He sighed again. "But then she began to follow me everywhere. Twice I discovered her sleeping outside my home. The first time, it was raining, so I invited her inside to dry off and get warm." A rueful smile curved his lips. "I should have remembered my ancient legends. Did you know that a vampire must be *invited* into one's home, otherwise he—or she—cannot enter?"

"I did know that," I said.

"Well, I forgot it. With tragic consequences."

I was astonished to see his eyes glisten with tears. He clenched one fist so hard his knuckles turned white. "What happened?" I asked.

"Lena Cooper poisoned my dog. Alice, my beautiful, precious red setter."

"Oh, no!" I felt a wave of nausea.

"She's alive—the veterinarian was able to save her, but she almost . . ." He cleared his throat and took a deep breath. "I insisted on pressing charges, and raised such a furor that the police finally arrested Lena." He relaxed his fist and blinked back the moisture in his eyes. "Her father, a vile man named Mitchell Cooper, paid for Alice's medical treatment, but still I insisted that Lena be jailed. Finally we compromised. Cooper agreed to put Lena in a mental hospital, but I feared that she'd get out and try to harm Alice again. I took my beautiful red setter to Syracuse, to stay with my sister, Nora. Now Alice has a fenced yard the size of a park, and children who adore her. I make overnight visits twice a week. When I'm sure it's safe, I'll bring Alice home again."

"I hate to tell you this, but you have a right to know. Lena was released from the hospital a few weeks ago." His face lost color. "I don't think she'll bother you," I hastened to add. "She's pursuing an actor on *Love of My Life*. Link Ramsey— he plays Cody. Link resembles you a bit. He's about the same height and build, and has dark hair."

Maitland took a calming breath and finished the bottle of merlot.

"You referred to Lena's father as 'vile.' What did you mean?"

"Mitchell Cooper is the kind of man who, if given control of a country, would become a despot. One of the worst. In my observation, he is a man without a heart. He doesn't love Lena; truly, I think he might even hate her."

"That's a pretty shocking statement."

"I don't say it lightly, I assure you. Mitchell Cooper controls a huge fortune, and he craves power. That's a dangerous combination for those in his orbit." Maitland's brow creased in thought as he stared down at the tablecloth. I gave him the gift of patient silence. Finally, he looked up and went on. "Mitchell Cooper is as complex and as destructive as any villain you've ever had on your show. By withholding the tiniest shred of affection and approval, he's damaged his daughter— perhaps irreparably."

"Tell me about Lena. Anything you can."

"Lena Cooper has an exceptional mind, but, in my opinion, she's unbalanced. Whatever you have to do, keep her away from your actor friend." He reached across the table, took my hands in his, and leaned forward. "This Link Ramsey—is he your *gentleman caller*?"

"No. We only work together." I was going to leave it at that, but decided to add an uncomfortable fact. "Even though it's not true, I'm afraid Lena *thinks* we're involved."

Maitland scrutinized me with narrowed eyes. I heard concern in his voice as he said, "You must protect yourself, my dear. Whatever the reasons for her mental state, I truly think that Lena Cooper is capable of killing someone."

Chapter 18

I NEEDED SOME time to think about what I'd learned in Westport, so before going home I did something I hadn't done in a
long time: I went to a beach. One of the actors on the show
who lives in Connecticut told me about the Calf Pasture
Beach, in Norwalk. At a gas station in Westport, I picked up a
map and found my destination, on Calf Pasture Road, off I-95.
Officially, most beaches in Connecticut don't open until
Memorial Day. Perfect.

Taking off my shoes and walking in the sand, sitting and
watching the ocean was just what I needed. By the time the
sun started to go down I felt completely refreshed.

After refilling the gas tank, I returned Nancy's car to the
garage and went home. It was after seven o'clock. Magic was
not pleased that I'd been away for nine hours, even though he
had plenty of food and water. I apologized, and held him gently in my arms until he began to purr. Now that we were friends

again, I put him down, opened a fresh can of Natural Balance, and refilled his water dish.

I watched him eat while I checked my voice mail. Six messages. Two from Penny, urging me to call her, one from Nancy, urging me to call *her,* one from Chet, telling me that he and Link had played tennis, had gone to Chet's gym, and were having fun, but he missed me.

The fifth call was from Tommy Zenos, about the Super Soap Fan Weekend. "Shall we—you and I—stay together in the two-bedroom Zeus Suite? Or would you rather I share it with Link or Rod, and you share the Venus Suite with Julie or Francie? Of course, if we split us up like that, then it leaves a man and a woman to share a suite. I think Julie would *like* to bunk with Link, and Rod and Francie are—*you know.* But I want to keep our show's image clean. I mean, as clean as possible for a daytime drama. It's okay for you and me to share a suite because we're the producers. You can trust *me*—and I'm pretty sure you won't come knocking on my door in the middle of the night because I've seen the guys you go out with, they're in good shape." He took a breath and I wondered if this long message was ever going to end. I hate long messages.

Tommy went on, "Okay, your message thingy says I only have twenty seconds left. If you want to share the Zeus with me, then we can put the guys together in Apollo and the girls in Venus. I've got Sean, Parker, Clarice, and the staff placed, but I need to know who you want in Zeus, Venus, and Apollo." He lowered his voice to a conspirator's whisper. "Whatever bed-switching anybody does after lights out isn't our business, right? Call me." Click.

Who's going to sleep where in Las Vegas two weeks from now wasn't an urgent discussion. I decided to call Tommy back last.

The final message was no message at all; whoever called had hung up without saying anything. That was a little creepy.

Before I had a chance to think about it, the phone rang. I picked it up and heard Nancy's voice.

"Oh, Morgan! I knew you weren't home so I've been calling and calling on your cell. Didn't you take it with you?"

I plunged my right hand into the pocket of my jacket. "Ooops. I must have left it in the recharger," I said.

"You've got to be more careful. What if you'd had an emergency?" Nancy didn't wait for an answer. "Have you talked to Penny?"

"No, she called but I haven't had a chance—"

"Good, I wanted to be the one to tell you the great news: Penny's going to have *her own* cable television show!"

"Wow!" I sat down at the kitchen table and eased off my ankle boots. "I swear, I leave town for only a few hours and lives change."

"Remember, I'd asked her to come over to my office this morning? It was because I wanted her to meet a client of mine—Mickey Jordan. He's the one who bought the Better Living Channel."

I made acknowledging noises and stretched out my legs, getting comfortable. Nancy went on, "Penny had no idea why I'd asked her to come over; neither did Mickey. Before she got there, I told Mickey about her, about what an amazing cook and hostess she is, what a great imagination she has, about the flower jelly and on and on. Then Penny arrived and he saw how pretty she is. I thought his eyes would pop out of his head. But he wasn't all hormones; he tested her."

"How?"

"Mickey said, 'Make me something clever. Anything. But just out of stuff that's around *here*.' I thought we were dead, but Penny surveyed the office and went to work. She took half a dozen Hersey's Chocolate Kisses from that jar on my desk, then she pulled a sheet of pink foil from a box of candy Arnold gave me, and twisted pieces of the foil around the kisses, making them look just like pink rosebuds. Then she clipped off a few bits of greenery from the flower arrangement on my sideboard and—voila! She'd created a bouquet of pink rosebuds. Mickey was dazzled."

"So am I."

"I worked out a deal for Penny to have her own half hour five days a week on the Better Living Channel, starting mid-May."

"That's in two months! How can anybody launch a show so fast?"

"Because we have to. Mickey's got a big programming hole that has to be filled quicker than quick. He'll start his publicity machine going Monday morning, and he'll hire a producer. Penny's got to start planning her shows, what she's going to do. He offered to hire a writer for her, but she said no, she wants to talk to the audience while she demonstrates things on camera. He said he'd still hire a writer, to organize the show and do transitions, but he promised Penny she can choose what to make, and she can explain things in her own words."

"I'm thrilled about this," I said sincerely.

"Finding something new that you could do well brought you out of your widow's shell," Nancy said. "I'm hoping that being on TV and meeting a lot of people will do the same for Penny."

That was my hope, too.

Chapter 19

THE NEXT EVENING, Sunday, I got to Matt's narrow, red-brick town house with the white trim at a few minutes before seven. I noticed that Penny had placed elegant black iron pots filled with scarlet geraniums on either side of the black lacquer front door.

Shortly after I met Matt, he'd raved about his Aunt Penny's fabulous cooking, and invited me to his home to have dinner with them. When he gave me his address—East Sixty-Eighth Street between Madison and Park—I was so surprised that I fell into the trap of stereotyping. How, I'd asked myself, could a homicide detective on the NYPD afford such an expensive address?

I'm ashamed to admit that I suspected the worst: that Matt Phoenix, the first man who had interested me since Ian died, was a dishonest cop. It was an enormous relief to find out how wrong I was. The house had been Matt's family home for three generations, and his grandfather had left it to him.

My second surprise that night was meeting Penny. From what Matt had told me about his widowed aunt, I was expecting an elderly Julia Child type, but the woman he introduced me to looked more like a younger Sophia Loren. I vowed to find an indoor sport to replace conclusion-jumping.

Another of my new friends opened the door to greet me with a happy hug.

"Hi, girlfriend," said Brandi Flynn, wife of Matt's partner, dour detective G. G. Flynn. Grinning, she helped me out of my cape. "Our boys are back—whoopdeedoo!" As she opened the door to the hall closet and moved some coats aside, she lowered her voice. "I don't know about you, honey, but for me phone sex just doesn't cut it anymore."

The thought of G. G. Flynn having phone sex made my jaw drop, but I snapped it shut before Brandi caught the dumbfounded expression on my face. "Ahhhhhh," I said. Not much of a response, but it was all I could muster.

Brandi had big brown eyes surrounded by a forest of thick black lashes, the figure of a Barbie doll, and an explosion of bright curls in a color that she described as *I Love Lucy* red. Tonight, she was wearing tight velvet slacks in a leopard print, and a black off-the-shoulder sweater that further emphasized her voluptuousness. Some women would have looked like a hooker in such an outfit, but Brandi—with her soft, kind eyes and loving smile—came across as *flamboyant*.

Closing the closet door after she'd hung up my cape, Brandi grasped my hand. "Let's go give Matt a thrill," she said, pulling me down the hallway in her wake. "He's been looking at his watch every three seconds for the last fifteen minutes, and scowling like he wanted to arrest somebody 'cause you weren't here yet."

"I'm not late. It's just seven—"

"Give that story to the c-o-p," she said with a wink.

The first person I saw in the living room was the other half of the oddest couple I knew: Brandi's beloved, Detective G. G. Flynn. The homicide partners couldn't have looked less alike. Matt Phoenix had dark eyes and a wild mane of brown hair. He was tall, with the lean, muscular build of a long distance runner. G. G. Flynn, older than Matt by ten years, was shorter and bulkier and had a lot less hair. His neck and shoulders were thick, and he moved with a forward thrust that was more of a stomp than a stride.

G. G. half rose from his semi-sprawl on one of the deep, comfortable sofas that flanked the fireplace and saluted me with "Hiya."

Before I could return G. G.'s greeting, I felt a pair of strong hands cup my shoulders and give a gentle squeeze.

"Hello, Matt," I said, turning to face him. "Welcome back." He gave me a quick kiss on the cheek, and a whiff of the faint scent that I'd come to identify with him: part elemental *male*, part Irish Spring soap.

Matt emitted one of his vast repertoire of grunts. This was a soft one that I interpreted to mean "Hello yourself."

I realized that Brandi and G. G. were staring at us. So did Matt. He stepped back a foot and, in a casual tone, asked me, "Have you been keeping out of trouble?"

G. G. snorted. "She'll stay out of trouble when a duck sings at the Met."

Penny, her face pink and a sheen of perspiration from the heat of the kitchen along her hairline, opened the door to the dining room and said cheerfully, "I hope everybody's hungry."

Penny's dinner was, as always, spectacular. Individual Cornish game hens baked in clay with sliced vegetables, orange and cranberry chutney in peach brandy, and blueberry pie for dessert.

Tonight's theme—Matt's and G. G.'s return from Washington, D.C., and Quantico, Virginia—was "Welcome Home," which was spelled out in red, white, and blue streamers hanging from the ceiling, in front of the drapes. The centerpiece on the rectangular dining table consisted of water lilies floating in low crystal bowls. The bowls were arranged in a circle, in the middle of which was a little tourist replica of the Washington Monument.

G. G.'s first act upon sitting down was to pick up the statue of the Washington Monument and put it on the floor under the table.

Penny was amused, but Brandi was horrified. "Georgie, put that back!"

"It's all right," Penny said to G. G. "Matt told me you two didn't enjoy your time in the capital."

"What was the problem?" I asked.

"The Fffing Bureau of Idiots," G. G. growled.

BACK IN THE living room after dinner, the conversation turned to Penny's upcoming TV show.

"I've got to have a meeting with Mickey Jordan, tomorrow," Penny said. "To talk about details of the show, but I don't know what to say."

"Let's break it down into parts," I suggested. "Nancy said he's going to hire a producer to take care of the physical setup and the crew. Will you have a studio audience?"

"Yes."

"So you'll talk to the camera, and to the folks in the seats."

Penny nodded. "I want to show people how to make food taste good, using inexpensive ingredients, things they can afford—nothing with truffles!—and how to make any meal seem festive by setting the table with interesting little things you can find in junk shops and at moving sales. Elegance on a budget, like taking a bunch of flowers from the market, and making it into four or five smaller arrangements for all over the house."

"You'll need an on-camera assistant," I said. "Somebody who can chop, dice, and grind, and hand you things as you need them. Somebody you can talk to, while the audience watches." I glanced at Brandi, and saw that her eyes were bright with enthusiasm. Suddenly, I had a hunch. "How about Brandi?"

Brandi blinked. "How about me what?"

"You could be Penny's on-camera assistant," I said.

"Yes!" Penny clapped her hands with delight. "Oh, Brandi, we'll have such fun! We do that kind of thing anyway, when you come over to try out a new dish."

"Do a show about hot dogs," G. G. said. "I want somebody to tell me why the franks come six to a pack, but the buns come in packs of eight."

Matt's cell phone rang. "Sorry," he said. He got up and walked toward the hallway as he answered it.

"I want to learn recipes a person can make once, but that it lasts for two or three days if you heat it up," Brandi said.

"Stews," G. G. said. "I like stews."

Before we could throw any more ideas at Penny, Matt was back, and looking like a cop.

Penny saw his expression too. "Matt? What's happened?"

G. G. sat up straight and buckled his belt. "Was that the house?" he asked, meaning their station house, the Twentieth Precinct.

Matt nodded at G. G. but spoke to me, all business. "You were with a man named Wade Maitland at the Westport Inn yesterday?"

"I had *lunch* with him there," I said. "Why?"

"Your name and the time and place of your meeting is in his date book."

"How do you know that?"

"Because he was found dead last night, behind a dumpster up in Westport."

"Dead? How?"

"Blunt force trauma. That's all I know right now. According to the ME he was killed shortly after you two had lunch."

While I was trying to take in what Matt was saying, G. G. focused on a practical matter. He asked Matt, "If the guy bought it up in Westport, why are they calling *you*?"

"Stan Shelly caught the case. We were at the academy together. He recognized Morgan's name from the story in the papers about our homicide last winter." Matt turned to me. "What did you do after you had lunch with Maitland?"

"I drove out to a beach in Norwalk. I wanted to think without any interruptions. There isn't much chance to do that, even at home. When I'd had enough peace and quiet, I came back to the city." Matt was frowning. "Don't tell me I'm going to need an alibi again!" I said.

"Did you talk to anybody at the beach? Meet somebody who'd remember you?"

"It's off season. The beach was empty," I said stiffly. "And if anyone saw me there, I didn't notice."

Penny eased herself between us and put a hand on Matt's arm. "You can't possibly think that Morgan had anything to do—"

"Of course I don't," Matt snapped. He softened his tone and added, "I'm just trying to anticipate questions that will be asked."

"That's a *good* thing," Penny said, giving my hand a squeeze. With a cheerful smile, she asked, "Now who'd like some more coffee and dessert?"

Chapter 20

AT THE FRONT door of his town house, Matt helped me put on my cape. "I'm too tired to walk you home tonight," he said. "I'm not as young as I used to be."

"You deteriorated seriously in two weeks? You're only thirty-eight."

He smiled, but it was more of a muscle reflex than an indication that he was amused. "My car's outside."

Matt had parked his unmarked NYPD Crown Victoria near his front door. A printed card proclaiming Police Business, held against the windshield by the visor, kept him from getting a ticket.

It was a few minutes before midnight. Most of East Sixty-Eighth Street appeared to be asleep; only one other house showed lights on inside.

Matt turned north, and at East Seventy-Second Street he turned west, taking the transverse through Central Park. As far as I could see out the window, nothing in the park was stirring.

Probably even the field mice were asleep. I relaxed and leaned back against the worn plastic seat. On any other night, after a delicious meal with friends, and tossing ideas back and forth with Penny about her coming TV show, I would have enjoyed a companionable silence, but there was nothing especially companionable about the atmosphere in Matt's car tonight.

"I can't stop wondering if my meeting with Wade Maitland had any connection to his death," I said.

Matt glanced at me. "We'll have a better idea tomorrow, when Stan Shelly comes down from Westport to talk to us."

"Us?"

"I'm not going to let him question you alone."

That startled me. "Do you think he suspects I had something to do with Maitland's murder?"

Matt shrugged. "He doesn't know you, that you're some kind of magnet for homicides. Irritating, but innocent."

"I'm *irritating*?"

Matt didn't reply, which *was* a reply.

We were nearly through the park, almost to the Dakota, when I asked, "What is this *problem* you say we have? That thing you didn't want to talk about on the phone."

We emerged from the park on a green light. Matt slowed, pulled over to the curb a few yards beyond the Dakota.

"Do you want to come upstairs?" I asked.

"No." He turned in his seat, rested his left arm on the steering wheel, and looked at me. His expression was so serious that I felt a cold lump of anxiety form in the pit of my stomach.

"What is it?"

"Marmalade." He reached toward me with his right hand and twined a lock of my hair around his fingers. "You interest me more than any woman I've met in the last few years, but I've got to ask you a question."

"Ask me anything," I said, hoping the question was one I could answer.

"By my calculations, in twenty-one days you're going to be eligible to collect that inheritance—seven or eight million dollars. I need to know if you're going to take the money."

So that was it. But *what* was it? "I've had almost six months to think about this. Yes, I am going to accept it."

He released the lock of my hair and dropped his hand. "I figured that."

"You sound as though I shouldn't take it."

"It's up to you—but that's the problem."

Confused, I shook my head. "*What* is the problem?"

"You're rich. I'm not."

"You've got an eastside town house!"

"Which keeps me almost broke," he said. "It's the family home; I can't let it go."

"You shouldn't. But what are you saying to me? Please, spell it out."

"I can't see you, like I want to *see* you."

"Just because I'm going to have a few million—"

"*Eight* million—"

"Whatever! I probably make more on my show than you do as a detective—"

He gave a short, mirthless laugh. "You got that right."

"Why wasn't *that* a problem?"

"Because you could lose your job at any time, and you've got a hefty mortgage on your co-op. Financially, we weren't very far apart."

"I don't care about money. I never have."

"You care enough to take the eight mil!"

"I don't believe we're having this conversation," I said.

"And I don't marry for money!"

Marry . . .

The word sat between us like the proverbial elephant in the room that nobody wanted to mention. I could tell by the way he drew back, farther away from me, closer to the car door on his side, that he wished he hadn't uttered that word. When I felt the passenger side door handle poking me in the back, I realized that I'd move away, too. I was as afraid of that word as he was. I wanted to say something witty, to break the tension, but I sensed this wouldn't be a good time.

Before I could think of anything safe to say, Matt got out of the car and came around to open the door on my side. His face was frozen in one of his homicide cop non-expressions. Instead of helping me out of the car, he stood back.

I guess he thinks that since I'm almost rich I don't need a helping hand.

Standing on the curb, I pulled my cape tight against the late night chill. "Which one of us is supposed to say, 'I hope we can still be friends?'"

"You've got a smart mouth," he said. The way he was looking at my mouth I thought in spite of what he'd been saying he might kiss me. But he was made of tougher stuff. He resisted the impulse as he was resisting me.

"You're strong in your medieval righteousness," I said softly.

"That's me—chain mail under my clothes."

"It must be uncomfortable to sleep in chain mail."

He bit into his bottom lip. "Stan Shelly's coming to the Twentieth tomorrow at three. Will you be there?"

"Yes." I added a parting shot: "I'll have the chauffeur polish the golden limo."

Chapter 21

MANHATTAN'S TWENTIETH PRECINCT, home base of Detectives Phoenix and Flynn, is located on West Eighty-Second Street between Columbus and Amsterdam Avenues. It's a short, square building, and about as graceful-looking as a sumo wrestler in a squat. Two pale gray stone upper decks rest on a base of bricks that have turned charcoal gray with the decades. I call its architecture style "no-frills institutional." Of course I don't say that to Matt or G. G. To them, it's "the house," but it's not even remotely like a home.

It was a brisk Monday afternoon—slightly cloudy, with patches of sunlight—a few minutes before three P.M. I'd been in my office since seven that morning, so I'd walked up from the Global Network building, some twenty blocks to the south and a long block and a half to the east. I needed exercise, I wanted natural (not "conditioned") air in my lungs, and I wanted to see *real* grass and trees instead of the Astroturf and fake bark of our Greendale Park set back at the studio.

The slender trees that lined West Eighty-Second were bursting with newborn leaves. An errant sunbeam glinted off the identifying metal letters and numbers affixed to the front of the Twentieth Precinct building. I would have enjoyed these sights, if I hadn't been on my way to discuss a murder.

A few feet to the left of the entrance as I came in, four unhappy-looking people were sitting on a bench. From my previous visits, I knew they were waiting to tell their stories or give their statements.

The nearest occupant was a scowling woman with a missing front tooth. She wore a torn, dirty sweater, a long skirt, and tennis shoes that were slit along the sides next to her toes. Beside her sat a pair of disheveled men in zip-front jackets and low-slung jeans. They reeked of alcohol and body odor. Further down the bench, separated from them by as much space as possible, was a well-dressed man in his fifties. He held a pair of broken gold-rimmed glasses in one hand, and with the other used a white handkerchief to dab delicately at an ugly bruise on his cheek. An alert young policeman who looked newly minted stood opposite the bench, watching over them.

A husky sergeant with seen-it-all eyes, a salt-and-pepper crew cut, and a pale gouge scar on his left temple presided over the front desk.

"I'm Morgan Tyler," I told him. "I have an appointment with Detectives Phoenix and Flynn."

He checked a note on the desk. "Yeah, I see." He nodded toward the wooden stairs on his right and said, "Second floor. Want me to have somebody take you up?"

"Thanks, but I know the way."

He grinned. "Yeah, I've heard about you—you're Phoenix's dead body gal."

"I'm not anybody's 'gal,'" I said with heat. I wanted to object to the "dead body" label, too, but there was a certain amount of truth to that. In the last few months I had stumbled across more than my share of homicide victims.

With one stubby forefinger, the sergeant tapped the nametag

on his shirt and said with a smile, "If you ever need an alibi, my name's Weems."

"I'll remember," I said, returning his smile.

The detectives' squad room on the second floor was a big, open bull pen, illuminated by long tubes of fluorescent lighting on the ceiling; some of the tubes had burned out. The room was filled with about a dozen battered old desks and chairs. Nothing matched. Most of the desks were shoved together in pairs, face-to-face, used by the detectives who worked as partners. The desks were equipped with modern phones, but the computers on them were relics from the previous decade. Three of the desks were occupied, with detectives in shirtsleeves, jackets hanging from the backs of their chairs, talking into phones or going through file folders.

At the far end was what I had learned was the private office of the squad's lieutenant. The slatted blinds over the window that looked out into the squad room were open. I didn't see anyone inside.

The pair of desks used by Matt and G. G. stood against the far wall, near a stand that held a large American flag and the banner of the State of New York. G. G. was bent over, talking into his phone, and glowering.

Matt was half standing, one hip perched on the edge of his desk, talking to a sandy-haired man whose back was to me. Like Matt, the other man was dressed in slacks and a sports jacket. Matt had a good body, and clothes fit him well; off-the-rack looked tailor-made on him. By contrast, the sandy man was wearing clothing that even from the back seemed to be a little too large, as though he'd lost weight recently and hadn't had his clothes altered, or bought new ones.

Matt spotted me, straightened up, and came forward. Watching him walk, I had the same impression I always did: he moved like a lion on the hunt. Behind them, G. G. finished his call, got up, and joined us.

"Morgan, this is Stan Shelly," Matt said. "Westport PD."

From the front, Detective Shelly resembled a young Elvis

Presley: a lock of hair falling over a thick eyebrow, eyes with heavy—almost hooded—lids, and slightly fleshy lips.

I extended my hand. "Hello."

"How's it goin'?" said Shelly. He may have looked like a southern good ole boy, but his voice and accent were pure New York. He gave my hand three quick pumps and let go.

"Interview rooms are full." G. G. aimed a thumb toward the empty, glassed in office. "The Loot said we can talk in there."

Steering me in that direction, Matt asked, "Want some coffee, or a soda?"

"No thanks, I'm fine."

The lieutenant's office was furnished with a desk, a filing cabinet, and three chairs. Realizing we needed a fourth chair, G. G. grabbed one from the nearest empty desk. He positioned it beside the door, lowered himself into it, and tipped back until the front legs were off the floor and his head rested against the wall.

Detectives Phoenix and Shelly sat next to each other. I was the point of their triangle, and the focus of their attention.

"How well did you know Wade Maitland?" Shelly asked.

"Barely at all. I'd never seen him before we met for lunch."

"But you'd talked to him before that," Shelly said. "When?"

"About 8:30 that same Saturday morn—"

Matt held up a hand to stop me, turned his head, and spoke to Shelly. "Why don't we let her tell us her story, then we ask questions?"

Shelly chewed his lip for a moment. "Yeah. Okay." To me he said, "What's your story?"

I began with the call from Link Ramsey telling me that a fan had broken into his apartment. I left out the fact that I was having dinner with Chet. I wasn't going to lie about it, but I didn't want to volunteer it.

After telling them about the damage Lena did to Link's bedroom and bathroom, I opened my handbag and took out

Lena's discharge papers from Franklin Woods Hospital. While Matt and Detective Shelly studied the report, G. G. lowered the front legs of his chair to the floor and joined the conversation.

"Where's Ramsey?"

"He doesn't have to work until Wednesday, so he's staying out of town until then."

Matt looked up from the hospital report. "Where?"

"In Greenwich, Connecticut."

"The head of your network, Winston Yarborough, has a house in Greenwich," Matt said. "Is that where Ramsey is?"

I braced for an argument, or as much of one as Matt would allow himself to have in front of other people. "No. He's staying with Chet Thompson."

The first flash of hostile fire came from G. G. "Your *friend,*" he said, his tone heavy with sarcasm. "The hotshot writer. Were you with him when Ramsey phoned?"

"We were having dinner at a restaurant downtown, not far from Link's apartment." I turned to Detective Shelly. "His name is Kevin Chet Thompson. Ten Millpond Road, Greenwich." Shelly took a small notebook from his pocket and wrote down the address.

"Let's get back to Wade Maitland," Matt said, in a tone that could have frozen beef. "Why'd you arrange to meet him?"

I gestured at the hospital report in his hand. "Lena stalked Maitland before she fixated on Link. I wanted to find out from him whatever I could. I hoped I'd learn something that would make Link press charges against her."

"What'd you find out?" Shelly asked.

I recounted the Lena–Maitland story just as Maitland had told it to me, ending with Lena being sent to Franklin Woods Hospital.

Matt was studying me. His voice was now so casual that I knew he was laying a trap. "Since you were up in Westport, I'm surprised you didn't go to the hospital to talk to this doctor."

"I did," I said, keeping my voice calm to conceal my anger at his treating me like one of his perps. "I cornered Joseph

Melville in the parking lot, but he wouldn't tell me anything."
I shrugged, to imply a period on that statement. Matt was acting like such a *detective* I wasn't about to mention my conversation with Phyllis Howell. Even if she was going to quit her
job soon, there was no reason to cause her trouble. By talking
to me, she had tried to help Lena; she didn't deserve to be put
through a third degree.

Shelly consulted his notes. "You and Maitland met at the
Westport Inn a little before 12:30 and had lunch. What'd you
two do after lunch?"

"I left Westport. Wade—Professor Maitland—said he was
going to see a show at the Playhouse."

"He never made it," Matt said.

"There are some things I'd like to know," I said to Detective Shelly. Without waiting for him to agree, I asked, "How
and when did Wade Maitland die?"

"Hit on the back of the head with a claw hammer. We
found the weapon next to his body; no prints. Maitland might
have lived if he'd gotten to a hospital, but he bled out. According to the ME, he died where he was found, behind a dumpster
in an alley not far from the inn. Because we know when,
where, and what he ate, the ME fixed his time of death at between 2:00 and 2:30 P.M."

"I left him just before two." The horror of the timing struck
me, and suddenly my mouth was dry. I swallowed and tried to
clear my throat.

Matt voiced what I was thinking. "Whoever killed him
could have been watching the two of you."

"Good thing you got the hell out of Dodge when you did,"
G. G. said.

A heavy silence enveloped the room as the three detectives
stared at me.

The ringing of my cell phone broke the tension. I took it
out of my jacket pocket and saw the calling number.

"It's Nancy," I told Matt.

"Go ahead, answer it."

I moved over to the far side of the office. "Hello, Nancy?"

"I'm glad you remembered to carry your phone." Her voice was unnaturally bright, but before I could ask what was wrong, she said, "There's somebody here who wants to talk to you."

"Okay . . ."

"Hi, Morgan!" It was Didi, sounding excited. "This is important, so I really, *really* hope you're not busy! Oh, please don't be busy!"

I glanced up at Matt and said, "I think I'm just about finished with what I was doing."

Matt nodded. He, Detective Shelly, and G. G. stood up.

Shelly closed his notebook. "I may want to talk to you again," he said.

I nodded and turned my attention to the phone. "What's going on?" I asked.

"I'm at the Woodburn stables, on West Eighty-Sixth Street," Didi said. "Can you come over and see me ride? It's really, really *super* important."

"I can come for a little while, but then I'll have to get back to my office."

"Great!" she said, disconnecting the phone before I could ask to speak to Nancy.

Chapter 22

IT HAD GOTTEN colder while I was inside the Twentieth Precinct. The sky had darkened and it had begun to drizzle. The Woodburn Riding Academy, on Amsterdam Avenue and West Eighty-Sixth Street, was only four blocks north of the precinct, but I wasn't dressed for rain, so I hailed a cab.

Amazingly, we caught all green lights, and reached the yellow stone three-story building on the corner of Amsterdam that housed the Woodburn Academy less than ten minutes after Didi's phone call. I paid the driver and dashed through the wide-open barn door entrance.

The first thing that hit me was the powerful aroma of horses, and their by-products. It wasn't unpleasant—I like horses. In Kenya, I did some riding with Ian, who was a superb horseman, but all I can claim is that I managed to stay on. I never got the feeling that the horse and I were one. At best, I managed an uneasy alliance.

Twin girls who looked to be about fourteen or fifteen years

old were on horseback on the far side, in the smaller of the two riding rings that consumed most of the building's dirt and sawdust ground floor. They were steering their horses rather tentatively, under the supervision of a thin, wiry woman wearing a blue Woodburn sweatshirt, jeans, and riding boots. Her steel gray hair was held back from her face by a bright yellow headband.

"Morgan! We're over here." It was Nancy's voice. Turning to my left, I saw Nancy standing next to a large dark brown horse. She was wearing a sweater set, slacks, and flat shoes, and was doing something I never expected to see: cinching the horse's saddle. On the far side of the horse, I saw a pair of black riding boots. At the same moment, Didi raised her head and waved at me. The wave looked a little awkward; I realized she was using her left hand.

"Hi, Morgan!" Didi called.

"Hi." I waved back, reaching Nancy just as she gave the cinch strap a final tug and fastened it. "That's a beautiful horse," I said admiringly.

Didi came around from the other side of the big animal. She was dressed in pale yellow jodhpurs, a black riding jacket over a white shirt with an ascot collar, and black boots. Her brown curls were topped by a black safety helmet. She stroked the horse's nose with affection. "This is Moon Glow, my favorite. Mrs. Woodburn always saves her for me when I'm in town." She turned to me. "Nancy said you spend every day in your TV studio, so I thought you could use a little break." Didi threw a brief glance at Nancy, just enough to indicate she knew Nancy was standing beside her. "Do you ride?" she asked me.

"Badly," I said. "I haven't been on a horse in a long time, but Nancy rides."

Didi flashed Nancy a phony smile. "Oh," she said. "Maybe we should ride together. Sometime."

Didi picked up a stool that was just outside the ring, put it down next to the horse, and from there vaulted easily into the saddle.

"Put the stool back, Nancy." As an obvious afterthought, she added, "Please."

Nancy moved the stool safely out of the ring. A stranger would have thought that Nancy was fine, but from her stiff shoulders and frozen smile I knew that she was seething inside at Didi's arrogant princess act.

Nancy and I moved back, well outside of the ring, as Didi gripped the reins and signaled the horse with a click-click of her tongue. "Watch me, Morgan," she said. "You too, Nancy."

Didi leaned forward slightly and tightened her knees against the horse's sides. She started with a walk and eased the horse into a trot. I'd always thought the trot was the least attractive gait that a horse had, but that might be because I'd bounced when I trotted. Didi didn't bounce. She really did seem to be one with the horse.

The trot became a graceful canter. Didi leaned farther forward as the horse stretched her legs out. Didi leaned closer to the horse's neck, moving her lips. The horse began to go faster and faster.

The sound of the flying hooves attracted the attention of the wiry woman in the yellow headband. "Hey that's too fast! Slow down."

Either Didi didn't hear her or she pretended she didn't. The horse was going around the ring in a full-out gallop now. Nancy and I had to jump back to avoid being hit by the clumps of earth and sawdust churned up by the horse's hooves as it raced past us.

Suddenly Didi cried out. Simultaneously, the horse's saddle slid over to one side and Didi went flying off, to crash into a heap in the middle of the ring. The horse ran a little farther. Before it stopped, I was kneeling at Didi's side. The girl was unconscious, but her body wasn't twisted in an alarming way that would suggest she had broken her neck or her back. The woman with the headband came running over.

"Don't anybody touch Didi," I said. Snatching the cell phone out of my jacket pocket, I dialed 911.

As I told the dispatcher that we needed an ambulance, and

gave the address, the woman with the headband went over to examine the horse, and the saddle that had slid over to one side of its belly.

"Who the bloody hell didn't tighten this cinch!" she demanded.

I looked at Nancy, who stood frozen, staring at Didi's unconscious form, her fingers pressed against her mouth. She was whispering, over and over, "Oh dear God, oh dear God . . ."

As soon as I was sure that an ambulance was on the way, I dialed another number—and asked for Arnold Rose.

Chapter 23

ARNOLD MET NANCY and me in the Emergency Room of Manhattan Orthopedic Hospital. I'd called him again, this time on his cell phone, to let him know where the ambulance was taking Didi. I'd assured him that Manhattan Orthopedic, on Sixty-Ninth Street and West End Avenue, was the best hospital of its type in the city, and told him that Nancy had had to threaten the ambulance company with a lawsuit in order to force them to take Didi to a facility that was just outside their normal territory.

Arnold, his hair and his topcoat speckled with raindrops, nodded at me and grasped Nancy's hand as though it was his lifeline. His normally ruddy face was white with worry. Nancy's face, too, had lost all of its color.

"Where's Didi?"

"Doctors are examining her."

"Did she lose consciousness?"

"Yes, but only for a few seconds," I said. "She was talking by the time the ambulance got to the stable."

"My God, how did this happen?"

"It was an accident," I said. "Her saddle slipped—"

"No." Nancy shook her head to silence me and pulled her hand from Arnold's. "It's my fault. I'm so *sorry*—I must not have pulled the cinch strap tight enough."

"You didn't—!" Sports of red flamed on Arnold's cheeks. "How could you make such a stupid—"

"Hey," I said. "Stop it! Nancy feels terrible enough."

Arnold's face was a portrait of rage. "There's no *terrible enough* if she's harmed my child."

A young doctor with white-blond hair came through double doors marked Authorized Personnel Only and approached us. The picture ID clipped to the pocket of his white lab coat identified him as "Richard Campbell, M.D." Dr. Campbell looked at the three of us and asked, "Who are Mr. and Mrs. Rose?"

"I'm Arnold Rose. How's my daughter?"

"Nothing's broken. She's probably going to be fine."

"*Probably?*" Arnold repeated, as though he was in court nailing a hostile witness.

The young doctor flinched, but steadied himself quickly. "What I mean is that all of the signs are good. Your daughter is healthy and well-conditioned. She was wearing a helmet, and she fell on a surface with some give to it."

"Is she in pain?" Arnold's tone was muted, but he was still wound tight.

"No," the doctor said with a reassuring smile. "Her shoulder may be a little sore tomorrow—that took the force of the impact. I don't like to recommend medication for someone her age, unless absolutely necessary. Hot showers should reduce any discomfort. I really don't see anything to worry about, Mr. Rose. She's checked out just fine."

Arnold expelled a sigh of relief. "Will Didi have to stay in the hospital tonight?"

"She can go home in about an hour. I'd let her go now, but to be absolutely sure she's okay, another radiologist is study-

ing her X-rays. Not that I expect any problems to show up."
He took a card from the pocket of his lab coat and offered it to
Arnold. "But just in case anything develops tonight—and
that's highly unlikely—for your peace of mind, here's my
pager number."

Arnold took the card. "Thank you, Dr. Campbell. I appreciate it." He turned to Nancy and me. "You two go home. I'll
wait for Didi."

Nancy's smile was full of hope. "It's good news, Arnold,
what Dr. Campbell said about Didi's physical condition. It's
probably her gymnastics training before she started riding."

Arnold nodded, but didn't reply. Worry had etched deep
lines in his face.

"Call me later?" Nancy asked him. "Let me know how
she's feeling?"

"All right," Arnold said. He patted Nancy's hand, and gave
a flash of what he might have thought was a smile.

Nancy was holding herself together with great effort: back
straight, chin up, hands clasped in front, but she couldn't conceal from me the distress she was in. I wanted to shake Arnold
for not realizing that Nancy was hurting, too.

The doctor had gone only a few feet toward the double
doors when he stopped and turned back to us. "I almost forgot. Mr. Rose, your daughter asked me to give you a message.
She said, 'Please don't be mad at Nancy.' "

IT HAD STOPPED raining while we were in the hospital. I
hailed a cab outside Manhattan Orthopedic and gave the
driver Nancy's address, on West Eighty-First and Central Park.
Because it was rush hour and the streets were clogged with
traffic, a journey that would have taken less than ten minutes in
off-peak hours took close to thirty. During that whole time,
Nancy never said a word. Although she was staring out the side
window, I knew she wasn't looking at anything we passed.

I used the quiet time to think about what had happened that
afternoon, to go over every detail that I could recall since I got

to the Woodburn stables. Most of my memory was clear; I could describe in detail the twins having their lessons, the wiry woman in the Woodburn sweatshirt, the rich brown color of the horse named Moon Glow, and Didi's expensive riding habit. There was another image at the edge of my consciousness prodding me, tauntingly just out of my grasp.

When the cab finally stopped in front of her building, Nancy didn't seem to realize it. She turned to me, a look of surprise on her face.

"We're home," I said.

Nancy automatically fumbled in her handbag, but I was already paying the driver.

The evening was cool and damp, and smelled fresh-washed from the afternoon's rain. Getting out of the cab and taking in a breath of clean air revived Nancy enough to greet her doorman: "Good evening, Grady." Her voice was steady; only someone who knew her very well would realize how upset she was.

Nancy's building, known as the Bradbury, was one of the most elegant on the Upper West Side. Relative to the Dakota, the Bradbury was a young building, constructed in the 1930s. The art deco lobby was one of the best examples of that style still standing. Entering it, I always half expected to see Fred Astaire and Ginger Rogers do "The Continental" across its polished marble floor.

Most of Nancy's apartment on the tenth floor faced the park. When I came back from Africa, I was a twenty-five-year-old widow with a shattered wrist and a broken heart. Nancy's home became my sanctuary. She turned her den into a bedroom for me and insisted that I stay until I was thoroughly healed and had figured out what I was going to do with the rest of my life. I was with her for nearly a year.

Nancy opened her front door and we stepped into a quiet world that seemed far away from New York City. Her exquisite country French décor merited a spread in *Architectural Digest*, but Nancy had refused the offer. "This is my home," she'd said. "It's not for display."

"I'm going to plug in your coffeemaker," I said, "then fix you something to eat."

Nancy couldn't help smiling. "*You're* going to cook?"

"That isn't funny."

"I know," she said. "I'm sorry."

"You wish Penny was here. So do I. We need comfort food. But I can open cans, heat soup. Even boil water and make spaghetti, if you have something to put on top of it."

"Let's do what's easiest," she said.

I filled her Mr. Coffee with water, spooned ground beans into the paper-lined basket, and flipped the switch to On. Nancy stood staring into her well-stocked pantry; she seemed unable to decide.

Gently, I eased her aside and reached for a large can of Progresso Minestrone. "We need mugs for the coffee, bowls for the soup, spoons, and napkins," I said.

Having a task brought Nancy out of her near stupor. By the time she had everything in place, the coffee had perked and the soup was bubbling hot.

When we sat down at her kitchen table, I saw that Nancy's eyes were filled with tears. "I'm never going to forgive myself for being careless with that cinch strap."

"You weren't careless. I saw how hard you pulled before you fastened it."

"Morgan, Didi could have been seriously hurt. The cinch was loose and that was my fault!"

Suddenly the fuzzy image in my head cleared and I glimpsed what it was that I had been trying to remember.

I leaned forward, my elbows on the table. "What if it wasn't your fault?" I asked.

"Stop trying to excuse what I did. You're not helping."

"Listen to me. When I came into the stables, Didi waved at me—with her left hand. I noticed because the gesture looked awkward. She's *right*-handed, isn't she?"

"Yes, she's right-handed, but what—?"

"So what was she doing with her *other* hand?"

"I don't understand what you're asking."

"Didi was on the far side of the horse while you were tightening the cinch strap," I said. "What if she had her right arm between the strap and the horse? No matter how hard you pulled, when she removed her arm, the cinch would be loose. Loose enough for the saddle to slip. You said she'd been a gymnast, so she'd know how to fall without hurting herself."

"Are you saying that *Didi* . . . ?" Nancy gawked at me. "That she made sure the strap would be loose enough to . . . ?" As the full implication of what I'd guessed hit her, she gasped. "But she knocked herself out. Would she take that kind of risk?"

"Didi's only twelve—she probably didn't think it through." We sat there while our soup grew cold, considering the kind of girl who could pull such a cruel trick in order to damage the relationship between her father and the new woman in his life.

Finally, Nancy said, "Awful as it is, I think you're right."

"When I tell Arnold, he won't be angry at you—"

"No!" Nancy was vehement. "You absolutely will *not* tell Arnold about this."

It was my turn to gawk. "But—"

"It will break his heart to find out. We can't tell him."

"If he doesn't know the truth, he'll keep thinking you were careless."

"Accidents happen. If he won't understand that, then no matter how much I love him, I'll know he's not the man for me. This is the first bad thing that's happened to us as a couple. Losing him will just about kill me, but if we can't get through this together . . ."

"Arnold loves you, and you two probably *will* weather this little storm, but—"

"I know what you're thinking," Nancy said. "What if Didi tries something *else*?"

Actually, I was afraid it wasn't a matter of "if," but *when*.

Chapter 24

TUESDAY MORNING I was up at 5 A.M. Too early for Magic. My little prince opened his beautiful green eyes halfway, squinted, then closed them again, curled up tighter, and went back to sleep.

While I drank a super-size mug of coffee, I read the major Connecticut newspapers on the Internet, searching for stories about the death of Professor Wade Maitland. I learned a lot of trivia about the man but not much about his murder. The Westport police declined to comment about their "ongoing investigation."

Several fellow faculty members at the college in Hartford were interviewed. All praised Maitland as an instructor, but none mentioned having a close relationship with him. The students interviewed were all female; it was clear that at least two of the young women had developed major crushes on their literature professor. One enterprising reporter had looked up Maitland's books on Amazon and found that they were out of print. Contacted in New York, his last publisher declined to discuss whether or not Maitland had a deal for the book he was supposedly writing.

Looking for some reference to his sister, I found it at the end of his obituary in the *Hartford Times*. "Professor Maitland is survived by his sister, Mrs. Gordon Stoddard of Syracuse, New York, and three nephews."

The last name of his married sister, Nora, was what I wanted to know. I dialed Syracuse Information and got the telephone number of Gordon Stoddard. I planned to call her later that morning.

By the time I had showered, performed the rituals of basic female upkeep, and dressed for the office, Magic was waiting for me on the kitchen counter, beside his breakfast bowl. As I opened one of his favorite cans, he swished his tail and purred.

With Magic taken care of, I retrieved the morning papers from outside my front door, made a fresh pot of coffee, poached a couple of eggs and eased them onto a piece of whole wheat bread that I'd toasted and crumpled up. Not fancy, but nourishing.

While I was finishing my breakfast, Nancy called. She didn't sound like her usual upbeat self.

"What is it?" I asked. "There's nothing wrong with Didi, is there?"

"No, she's fine. Arnold called to tell me that last night, but we had the world's shortest conversation." Before I could respond, Nancy hurried on to another subject. Forcing a bright tone, she said, "I'll be working on Penny's cable show deal today. I'm probably as excited about this as Penny is—it's the first TV show I've had a hand in."

"More than a hand," I said. "You made it happen."

"I don't know who the producer's going to be yet, but if we need a daytime star to guest on the first show, could you supply us with one?"

"Absolutely. When you know, give me the tape date and time."

"Great. I can cross that off my to-do list. Now I've got to

start getting dressed. I want to look *fabulous* at the office to-day."

I chuckled. "That's the spirit—show Arnold what he could lose."

Nancy said, "You know me too well," and hung up.

JUST BEFORE I left for the office at eight o'clock, I dialed the number in Syracuse. A woman answered the phone. Her voice was pleasant, without any discernible accent, but she sounded subdued. In the background I heard the voices of children—and some spirited barking.

"Mrs. Stoddard? My name is Morgan Tyler. I met your brother and wanted to express my sympathy. I hope I'm not calling too early."

"No." I heard fatigue in her voice. "We're up, but I suppose you can hear the racket." She covered the mouthpiece and I heard a muffled, "Quiet down in there!" When she removed her hand the noise had abated.

"I don't want to take up too much of your time, Mrs. Stoddard, but I was wondering if there's going to be a funeral for your brother."

I heard her sigh. "No, Ms.—I'm sorry, but what did you say your name is?"

"Morgan Tyler. Please call me Morgan."

While she was polite, her tone was strained, as though she'd answered this funeral question too many times. "My brother didn't want a church service, Morgan. When his—when the authorities have finished—I mean . . . No. My brother wanted to be cremated without any ceremony. I'm go-ing to follow his wishes. Are you asking because you would have come to a funeral?"

"Yes. I didn't know your brother very well—I only met him once—but I wanted to express my condolences."

She was silent for a moment. "Morgan Tyler . . . your name—oh, you're the woman he was going to have lunch with in Westport."

"He told you about our lunch?"

I heard new warmth in her voice. "He called Saturday morning to tell me that he was meeting the woman who writes *Love of My Life*. Wade and I watch—I mean he did and I do watch your show just about every day."

"That's nice of you to say. Mrs. Stoddard, is there anything I can do, or *send*? Did Professor Maitland have a favorite charity? I'd like to give a donation in your brother's honor."

"Well, he loved dogs. I have his Alice—you might have heard her playing with my boys. Anyway, he always gave any extra money he had to a place that supports abandoned animals until they find good homes. Just a minute." I heard her pulling out a drawer, and the sound of papers being moved about. She came back on the line and gave me the name and address of an animal care foundation. I wrote it down.

"Morgan, I just thought of something. Perhaps you *could* help us."

"What is it? I'll do whatever I can."

"Did Wade tell you he was writing a new book?"

"He mentioned it," I said, "but he didn't go into any detail."

"It's here. The manuscript. He brought it over when he brought Alice. He worked on it here when he came to visit every week. I don't know anybody in the book business. Could I send it to you? Maybe you know a publisher?"

This was about the last thing I wanted to hear, but I couldn't be ungracious to the sister of the man who was murdered shortly after he'd had lunch with me. Then I realized that I might really be able to help her. "I have a friend who writes books," I said. "Kevin Chet Thompson. Perhaps Chet's publisher might be interested in Wade's manuscript. It's worth a try."

"Oh, thank you!" she said. For the first time in our conversation, she sounded happy. "This is so good of you."

"Not at all. If I can help, I'll be glad to." I gave her my home address and she said she'd send the manuscript as soon as she gathered the pages together.

"I don't know how often you come in to Manhattan," I said, "but if you ever want to visit the set of *Love,* you could watch some filming and meet the actors."

Her reaction surprised me. "Oh, *no*—but thank you," she said. "I mean, I do appreciate the invitation, but it would be like finding out how a magician does his tricks. I'd like to keep my illusions." She gave a short, slightly sad laugh. "I don't have many of them left."

I EXITED THE Dakota into the crisp morning air. It had rained again during the night, leaving the streets looking freshly washed, and the new leaves on the trees sparkling with little crystalline drops.

In spite of the beauty of the morning, I felt a stab of unease as I reached the corner of Seventy-Second and Central Park West, and turned south to walk the nine blocks to the Global Broadcasting building. Again, it felt as though someone was watching me. I whirled around, but I didn't see anything unusual. Or anyone I knew.

I was relieved *not* to see Lena in a blue coat.

The faster I walked, the more distance I seemed to put between me and the creepy feeling that hit me when I left my building. Maybe I was becoming paranoid. Then I remembered the old joke about paranoids having enemies, too.

I didn't see Lena Cooper in front of the Global building. Nor, according to the guard at the front desk, had anyone of her description tried to get in.

Getting off the elevator on twenty-six, I smiled and greeted people all the way across the floor to my office. The door was closed, but Betty was at her desk, holding an accordion file folder. Her lips were pressed together in a thin line, and she looked tense. She saw me approaching and stood up.

"We've got a problem." Betty handed me the file. I looked inside and saw several letters, but before I could take them out, Betty nodded at them and said, "Link's getting death threats."

Chapter 25

IN THE SECOND-FLOOR squad room at the Twentieth Precinct, phones were ringing, rough characters who looked as though they were probably guilty of *something* were ushered into the interview rooms, and citizens on both high and low rungs of the social ladder were giving statements to detectives.

Approaching Matt and G. G. I asked, "Don't you ever have any quiet time around here?"

G. G. snorted. "Our busy season is twelve months a year."

"Here's what I told you about on the phone," I said, handing Matt the accordion file.

G. G. commandeered the last unoccupied chair in the room, brought it over, and placed it for me next to Matt's desk. I thanked him and sat.

Matt and G. G. slipped on thin rubber gloves, removed the letters from the file, carefully took them out of their envelopes, and spread everything faceup across the cleared surface of Matt's desk.

"How many people have handled these?" Matt asked.

"My assistant, Betty Kraft, gave them to me. When she told me what they were, I put on gloves before I read them. You'll find her fingerprints on them, and also Jim Sales's; he works in the mailroom. It's Jim's job to open all letters addressed to the actors and read them."

"You don't give the actors their own mail?"

"Not until it's read by Jim first. Most ask for autographed photos, and we send them out. If there's something sweet or touching in a letter, we'll give it to the actor to answer, if they care to. If they don't want to answer, they give it back and a network secretary answers for them, to keep fan relations good." I gestured toward the letters on Matt's desk. "The nasty ones don't get to the actors; we don't want to upset them unnecessarily."

G. G. looked over at me, frowning in distaste at what he was reading. "You get a lot of stuff like this?"

"Most actors at one time or another get hate mail, or letters with obscene pictures in them. We have a filing cabinet full, going back years. If someone threatens to come to the studio, we alert security."

G. G. read aloud, " 'Link, I'm going to shoot your balls off and watch you die.' That's from one sick bastard."

I agreed. "I know the police won't do anything without— without 'an overt act.' Meaning that the letter writer has to actually hurt the actor physically, or at least try to."

"That's the law," Matt said. "We don't make preemptive arrests in this country."

"Wish we could," G. G. growled. "The problem with all this freedom is it protects the skanks an' leaves the decent citizens on their own."

This wasn't the time to debate the Achilles heel of democracy, so I got the discussion back on track. "I brought these over because the woman who's been stalking Link broke into his apartment and destroyed some of his property. I suspect she wrote most of these."

With gloved hands, Matt moved the two that were handwritten to one side of the desk. "Do you have a sample of her handwriting?"

"No, but—"

"Then what makes you think any of them are from her?" G. G. asked.

"The handwriting is different in these two notes," Matt said, "and the ones typed on computers use different fonts."

"I saw that, but I think all but one of these letters are from the same person."

"You're an expert in document comparison?" G. G.'s tone was mocking.

Ignoring his sarcasm, I stood and leaned over Matt's shoulder. I pointed toward the envelopes, but was careful not to touch them. "Look at the postmarks. These four were all mailed in the same week, from Manhattan and upstate New York." I indicated the open letters. "Different pieces of stationery, but you can buy those anywhere. About the handwriting—it *seems* to be different, but in both cases the person makes their *o* with a little curl at the top. That's very distinctive—I don't believe it's a coincidence. And in four of the letters there's the phrase 'you're all alone'—even though in two of them the word is misspelled as 'your.' "

"Lots of people make that mistake. Why are you so sure that these four were written by the same person?"

"By the same *woman*," I said. "Not the one about shooting Link's balls off—that's something a *man* would say. Look, I make my living writing drama. I know the subtle differences between how women and men express themselves. These four letters were all written by the same woman, but she's trying to make it seem as though Link is in danger from several different people."

"Why?" Matt asked.

"I tried to figure it out as though I was writing her character for the show. Her motivation would be to scare Link, scare him so much he'd accept her, instead of rejecting her."

"That's a nutty theory," Matt said.

"These people *are* nuts," G. G. said, surprising me. He added, "I'm not saying I buy it, but *maybe* you got somethin'."

Matt and G. G. studied the letters more closely.

"Professor Maitland told me that Lena Cooper has a brilliant mind," I said. "That was his word—*brilliant*. He was a big man, in good shape, but he was afraid of her. And now he's dead."

"You think one person wrote four out of these five?" Matt said. "Forget the 'balls' line. We've collared women who talk as rough as men. Is there anything else that makes you believe that letter is the only one not written by whoever wrote the others?"

"The font," I said. "It's an old style called Algerian. I recognized it because it was the favorite typeface of the head writer before me. He used it for all of his personal letters, then when he upgraded Windows several years ago, Algerian vanished—been retired, the company said. Harrison was so mad he cursed Bill Gates for a week."

G. G. pursed his lips in thought. "So this one was written on a machine with old software."

Pointing to another font, I said, "And this one wasn't available until the most recent Windows upgrade."

G. G. grunted. "What about this last whachacallit?"

Matt answered. "Arial. It's a basic."

G. G. frowned as he peered at the letters again. He and Matt exchanged a silent communication, Matt nodded agreement, and the two of them focused on me. "We shouldn't try to get so smart we overlook the obvious."

"What obvious?" I asked.

"That these letters could have been written by that mailroom guy," G. G. said.

"That's ridiculous. Jim's worked at Global longer than I've been *alive*. He's a devoted grandfather who brings his grandchildren to the network's holiday parties, and he's a former professional baseball player who spends his weekends coaching kids in the projects."

"Gotta be careful of those guys who sound too good," G.

G. said, but there was a twinkle in his eyes that signaled he was making one of his rare jokes.

"We'll forget him, at least for now." Matt stood up, rotated his neck to loosen tight muscles, and said to me, "Okay. Have Betty Kraft and Sales come in today so we can print them for elimination. We'll run any other prints through the system to see if we get a match."

"It's a long shot," G. G. said.

"I understand." I said good-bye, and added, "Say hi to Brandi for me."

G. G.'s face burst into one of his *Brandi smiles*. The only times I saw that big grin were when he was with his wife or talking about her.

A uniformed officer, whose nametag identified her as S. Robles, interrupted us. "Detective Phoenix?"

Crowding close behind Officer Robles were two people who had caused a dozen heads in the squad room to swivel toward them. Actually, it was the female half who commanded the attention. Eurasian, in her early twenties, her chin-length black hair was cut to emphasize her prominent cheekbones and large dark eyes, features that dominated the exquisite oval of her face. With her long legs, slim figure, and haughty carriage she might have been a high fashion model striding down a runway in Paris or Milan. Crossing the second floor of the Twentieth Precinct, she looked neither to the left nor the right, seeming to have no curiosity about her surroundings.

The young woman was as tall as Matt, who just topped six feet. The man beside her was half a head shorter, with a broad face, broad torso, thick, super-size hands, fleshy cheeks, and unnaturally dark hair. It was obvious he was old enough to be the woman's father, but the possessive way he held her arm was far from fatherly.

"This gentleman wants to see you," Officer Robles said.

"I don't *want* to see anybody here. It's a necessity." His glare speared G. G. first, and then Matt. "Which one of you is Phoenix?"

Matt raised his hand. "And you are?"

"Mitchell Cooper, here to make sure that my daughter, Lena, isn't railroaded into prison."

Lena Cooper's father. It was easy to spot the family resemblance: same stocky build, large hands, and slightly bulging pale blue eyes. He wore several thousand dollars' worth of carefully tailored Armani, but he still looked like a day laborer dressed in somebody else's wardrobe.

It was his voice that was decidedly *unlike* Lena's, and it didn't fit his coarse features and bulky frame. Cooper had the rich, modulated intonation of a trained actor. If my eyes had been closed and I'd only heard that voice, I would have expected it to be reciting blank verse, or singing a baritone role in an opera. Unless she was shrieking, Lena's voice was a colorless monotone. My guess was that somewhere along the line Cooper had taken speech lessons. I wondered why—and why he hadn't bought some vocal polish for Lena.

There was no time to mull the Cooper contradictions. Matt told Officer Robles that she could go, and then he introduced Lena's father to G. G. Flynn.

Cooper didn't offer his hand to either detective. Instead, he shot a rude glance at me and said to Matt, "Where can we speak in private?"

Ignoring his arrogant behavior, I extended my hand. "My name is Morgan Tyler, Mr. Cooper. I've met your daughter several times."

A glint of recognition lit his eyes. "You're the one with that television show."

"Yes, I am."

"Don't sound so proud of it," he snapped.

Before I could respond, G. G. nodded toward a partly open door in the corner and said, "Let's go in the coffee room."

As G. G. led the way, I noticed that the expression on the face of the young woman with Cooper had not changed. She hadn't reacted with so much as a flicker of awareness to the admiring gawks from some of the men in the room. If this exotic beauty was typical of the women in her father's life, Lena must have felt like an ugly duckling. No wonder she was so hungry for love that she went to extremes to get it.

The coffee room was a kitchenette furnished with an old table that had a folded matchbook cover wedged under one leg to keep it from tilting, and four mismatched wooden straight back chairs. Along the side wall was a small, hotel-room size refrigerator. A shelf above it that held a hot plate with a tea kettle on it, and a forty-cup coffee maker that looked as though it hadn't been washed since the beginning of the new millennium. Hanging from hooks above a water-stained sink were a line of mugs, most of which were chipped.

Matt asked, "Coffee? Soda? Water?"

Everyone declined, including the woman with Cooper, whose first sign of communication consisted of a tiny sideways movement of her head.

"This is not a social call, Phoenix," Mitchell Cooper said. Taking a small gold case from his cashmere topcoat, he extracted a business card and handed it to Matt. "This is my lawyer. I've already given his name and number to your chap in Westport."

"Do you mean *Detective* Shelly?" Matt was keeping his voice level, but I saw a muscle at the corner of his left eye twitch in annoyance.

Cooper switched gears to become just a hair's breadth more pleasant. "You have to understand that I'm very worried about my daughter. Lena is a troubled girl." He shrugged and said ruefully, "Not exactly the daughter I had imagined my late wife and I would produce."

If that comment was meant to elicit sympathy, it didn't work. Matt and G. G. stared at him, their mouths set in hard lines.

I fantasized forcing Cooper to drink an entire pot of the Twentieth's coffee.

G. G. said, "So what you're telling us is that you know, or you *think,* that your daughter killed Professor Maitland."

"I said no such thing."

Cooper didn't deny it, I realized; he only denied that was what he'd *said*.

"Business is taking me out of town today," Cooper said. "I went to Westport and then came all the way down here to make sure that when Lena is apprehended she says nothing without our lawyer being present." He made a brusque gesture toward the card in Matt's hand. "If you're familiar with his name, you'll know that he's one of the most formidable criminal attorneys in the country."

"The *whole* country?" G. G. said in an exaggerated tone of awe.

Matt ignored his partner. "When we find Ms. Cooper, we'll be sure to notify her attorney."

"Immediately."

"As immediately as we get around to it," G. G. said, stifling an exaggerated yawn.

Mitchell Cooper aimed a fierce scowl at G. G. "Police Commissioner Nelson is a friend of mine," he said. "My next stop will be his office. If you arrest Lena, our lawyer will know how to reach me."

With that, Cooper tightened his grip on the arm of the young woman with him—the woman he hadn't bothered to introduce—and stalked out of the coffee room.

"Poor Lena," I said softly.

G. G. countered with a snort. "She wasn't the one who got bashed in the head and left behind a dumpster." He turned to Matt. "Who's his ambulance chaser?"

For the first time, Matt looked at the card in his hand. His eyebrows lifted, and he glanced at me before he replied, "Arnold Rose."

I was relieved. Whether Lena Cooper was guilty or innocent, Arnold would give her skillful representation. I said, "I'm going back to the office, where I have some control over what happens to people."

"Yeah." Matt's tone was sardonic. He lowered his voice so

that only I could hear him add, "You certainly don't want to lose control."

Refusing to take the bait, I told Matt, "Let me know when there's a Mr. Congeniality contest at the Twentieth—so I can come up and cast my vote for *G. G.*"

Chapter 26

AS SOON AS I was out on the street I called Nancy on my cell phone. After she told me she could talk for a few minutes, I asked her how things were with Arnold.

"Warmer. He realized that I'd never intentionally hurt Didi."

"Good." I was relieved that things between Nancy and Arnold were better. "Now, I've got something to tell you," I said. "Remember the young woman who's been following Link?"

"The one who attacked our cab. What about her?"

"Her father is one of Arnold's clients, Mitchell Cooper. Do you know him?"

Nancy groaned, but she tried to keep distaste out of her voice. "Arnold and I've had three or four dinners with Cooper and his flavor of the month."

"What's he like?"

"Very smart. Big ego. Always insists on picking up the

check. He thinks he's charming, but he's not somebody I'd spend time with for fun."

"Why does he have a criminal lawyer?"

"Uh-huh," Nancy said. "I can't answer that."

"Of course not. Sorry I asked. Can you have dinner later?"

"Didi went back to Boston this morning, so I'm seeing Arnold. Why don't you join us?"

"Some other time," I said. "But thanks."

Late that afternoon I was rewriting some dialogue at my desk when Betty buzzed.

"Detective Phoenix is on line one," she said. I heard her heave an exaggerated sigh. "That man gives *great* finger-print."

I thanked Betty for using her lunch hour to give a sample of her prints.

"Don't mention it," she said. "Jim Sales and I had a couple pieces of pizza on the way back, but it was worth missing a real meal to have Detective Hunk hold my fingers for a few seconds."

"Glad you enjoyed it." I pressed line one. "Hi. Did Cooper get his friend the police commissioner to fire you? Are you calling from the unemployment line?"

Matt laughed. "Not yet, but thanks for your concern. I've got the fingerprint report."

"What did you find out?"

"Not much. One useable print on the letter you don't think came from Lena Cooper. After eliminating Ms. Kraft and Mr. Sales, everything else was too smudged to be useful."

"But you have one good print. Do you know who it belongs to?"

"He—or she—isn't in the system."

"Meaning?"

"The person hasn't been arrested, or had to give prints for any other reason, like certain kinds of employment, or military service. But that print is on file now."

"That's something, at least. Any news from your friend in Connecticut?"

"The Westport police are investigating," Matt said, mocking the style of a radio newsreader. He added abruptly, "Promise me you're not going to go up there and try to be helpful."

I didn't like his tone, so I was quiet for a moment, letting him stew. "All right," I said at last, stretching out the words, pretending to agree with reluctance. Then I added in a rush, "But I didn't promise not to go to Maitland's house in Hartford!" I hung up before he could reply. While I had no intention of going to Hartford, I wasn't going to let Matt Phoenix think he could dictate what I could and couldn't do. Let him worry.

Pressing the intercom to talk to Betty, I said, "If Detective Phoenix calls back, tell him I said I can't talk to him because I'm getting driving directions to Hartford, Connecticut."

"When are you going to Hartford?"

"Probably never, but don't tell him that."

"Oh, I see." Betty said. "You're using that old female technique."

"What technique?"

"The one that goes: 'If you treat the man you want the way you treat the men you *don't* want, you can have any man in the world.'"

"I've never heard that saying."

After speaking to Betty, I sat thinking. Making a decision, I reached for the phone and dialed the number of someone who had become one of my favorite people.

"Robert Novello, Discreet Investigations," announced a cheerful tenor at the other end of the line.

"Hi, Bobby. It's Morgan."

"Ah, my best-looking client this year. Last year, too, come to think of it. You in some kind of jam I can help you out of? Or is that just wishful thinking on my part?"

I laughed. "I need you to check something out for me, Bobby."

I heard his comic heh-heh-heh; he was intentionally sounding like the villain in an old melodrama. "Come down to

my web and let's play a little spider and the fly." Then he re-
verted to his natural voice. "Unless you're still going out with
that big guy writer."

"Chet's in Connecticut at the moment, but yes, I am. What
time are you free?"

"Ms. Morgan, you of all people should know I'm not
free—not after that bill I soaked you with a few months ago.
Can you be here at six?"

BOBBY NOVELLO LIVED on MacDougal Street, in the Village,
in a neat four-story apartment building with a brick façade,
built during the fading lights of the nineteenth century. It's
right in the middle of the grid I call Literary Old New York,
surrounded by the landmarks where Edgar Allen Poe wrote
The Raven, where Louisa May Alcott created *Little Women*,
the gate on Grove Street that inspired O. Henry to write *The
Last Leaf*, and the house where Edna St. Vincent Millay
"burned [her] candle at both ends."

I pressed the outside button for One B, and heard Bobby's
teasing voice through the building security intercom, "Is this
who I hope it is?"

"You bet your birdies," I joked. He buzzed me in immediately, and had opened his door at the rear of the ground floor
before I reached it.

"Hi, cutie," Bobby said, looking up at me with a big smile
on his handsome face.

The first time I met Bobby Novello, I hadn't expected what
I saw. Bobby's a Little Person, about four feet tall. When I got
to know him, I realized that if one measured him by his brains
and his charm, Bobby Novello could play center for the New
York Knicks.

Stepping back to let me in, Bobby ran a hand through his
tangled thatch of rosy gold hair. I saw that it was wet.

"Hope I didn't spritz you," he said. "I just got out of the
shower."

Coming into his living room, I smiled with pleasure to see

that his huge antique cages were once again filled with chirping exotic birds.

"Oh, Bobby, they're beautiful," I said enthusiastically. My genuine pleasure at the magnificent feathered creatures before me was tempered by guilt. Bobby had lost his previous collection of birds—and almost his life—because of a job I had hired him to do. He must have known what I was thinking.

"It's okay," he said. "Actually I got two of my old gang back. They were perched on the windowsill, waiting for me when I came out of the hospital. I think the others are living in sin in Central Park, mating with the doves and pigeons."

I didn't know whether Bobby was saying that to make me feel better or if he really believed it. I knew that I wanted to believe it.

"While we talk business, can I take you out to dinner?" he asked. "Or shall I order in?"

"That's sweet of you, but I can't stay very long. I've got a script to rewrite tonight, and I have to get home to take care of my cat."

Bobby's eyes widened in feigned horror, and he made frantic shushing motions at me with his hands. "No, no! We don't use the *c* word in this house. It upsets the birds." He removed a stack of newspapers from the red leather client chair for me. Except for the cages, Bobby had made his office a replica of Nero Wolfe's as described in those books we had both grown up reading.

I sat down and Bobby scurried around behind his desk, stepped up onto an antique stool, settled himself in his high back chair, and heaved an exaggerated sigh of resignation.

"Well, since you have one of those furry . . ." He scrunched up his face. "The *c* word, I guess we're not destined to ride off into the sunset together."

"How much will it take to heal your broken heart?" I took out my checkbook.

"Depends. What, besides my handsome self, lures you to Casa Novello?"

"Two things. The first should be easy. The other one, not so."

"That's why I get the big bucks." He leaned forward attentively. "What's bothering you?"

"First, would you check out something called The Archie Foundation? It's supposed to be an organization that takes abandoned pets and keeps them comfortable until appropriate homes can be found. If it's legitimate, if they really do take good care of the animals and are careful about who they let adopt them, then I want to send them a donation in honor of someone." I gave Bobby the piece of paper on which I'd written the information that Wade Maitland's sister had given me.

"Should be easy enough. You want pictures?"

"That's a good idea. Yes."

"What's next?"

I told Bobby about Lena Cooper, beginning with Link telling me that she'd been following him, through her breaking into his apartment and Link's going to stay with Chet in Greenwich. I told him about her time at the Franklin Woods Hospital in Westport, what I'd learned about her wealthy and arrogant father, about my meeting with Wade Maitland and his subsequent murder. And about the death threat letters I'd turned over to the police—three that I was sure Lena had written.

"I have no idea where Lena is now, but I believe she poses a real danger to Link. It's possible she may have murdered Wade Maitland."

"Your Lena sounds enchanting," he said. "So my not-so-easy assignment is to find her?"

"Yes."

"And then what?"

"Contain her." As soon as the words were out of my mouth, I realized how idiotic that sounded.

Bobby did, too. He laughed. " 'Contain her.' In *what*?"

I had to admit I hadn't thought that far.

"I charge more when the client doesn't have a plan," Bobby said with a wink.

Chapter 27

I'D JUST COME out of the shower at 7:30 the next morning when my telephone rang. It was Matt.

"Are you dressed?" he asked.

"Is that an official inquiry?"

"I'm downstairs at your reception desk, with a box of Penny's fruit muffins. Right out of the oven."

My salivary glands sprang to life. "Come up."

In the minute that it took Matt to reach my front door, I pulled a NY Knicks sweatshirt over my head, zipped up my jeans, and gave my hair a couple of swipes with the brush.

"Coffee's just made," I told Matt as I let him in. "Mm-mmm. Those smell great."

Magic was having his breakfast as Matt and I came into the kitchen. He stopped eating and looked up as Matt put the box of muffins on the table and sat down.

Noticing Magic, Matt said, "Hi, fella." He turned to me. "He's gotten bigger."

"He's not a kitten anymore, he's an adolescent."

As I filled two mugs with coffee and put plates and napkins on the table, Matt said, "The cat's staring at me. Do you think he remembers?"

"That you're the one who rescued him? I wouldn't be surprised. He's very smart." I opened the box of muffins and sighed with pleasure. "Blueberry and raspberry. Everything Penny bakes looks like a magazine cover."

"She's practicing for what she's going to do on her TV show," he said.

"Lucky us, to be her guinea pigs."

Matt reached for a blueberry muffin and I took a raspberry. It tasted even better than it looked. We were silent, savoring Penny's creations.

Matt finished his blueberry and took a raspberry.

"What progress has there been on the Maitland murder case?" I asked.

"They haven't caught the killer yet." His tone was casual, but what he said next was anything *but*. "Did you go up to Maitland's place in Hartford?"

"No, I didn't. Why?"

"Somebody tore his house apart."

I put down my coffee mug and stared at Matt. "He was robbed?"

"*Burglarized*," Matt said. "It isn't a robbery unless the victim's present."

"Don't give me a lesson in police semantics, tell me what happened."

"Somebody got in by smashing the window beside the back door. TV, DVD player, and a laptop were in the bedroom, along with an expensive camera and some jewelry. Stan was there with the Hartford cops. He said that the mattress, the overstuffed chairs, couches, and pillows were ripped apart, drawers pulled out, the contents dumped on the floor, freezer emptied, mirrors and pictures taken down. The backing from a painting was ripped off. All of the furnishings were trashed."

I refilled our mugs. "Whoever broke in was looking for something," I said, "but I'll bet he, or she, didn't find it."

Matt looked at me. "What makes you think that?"

"When people get what they want, they stop looking. From what you describe, it sounds like *everything* was ripped up and destroyed—but saleable things that a normal thief might have taken were left behind."

"Stop trying to play detective," Matt said. "Stan and his partner are staying on the case. They're getting a lot of help. Murder's a rare occurrence in Westport. Nobody wants this one to go unsolved."

"Have they found Lena Cooper?"

"Not yet. That father of hers went to France; he's at a hunting lodge in Elbeuf, Seine-Maritime. Stan contacted the Surete—the French police. Cooper was with a young woman when they interviewed him. He claims he hasn't heard from his daughter in several months, but he said that it wasn't necessary for her to contact him because she has money of her own, from her mother."

"What if Mitchell Cooper was lying?" I said. "Could that young woman have been Lena? The French police wouldn't know Lena by sight."

Matt chuckled. "No chance. His companion wasn't the Asian beauty he brought to the station, either. From the description Stan got, the one at the lodge sounds like a Swedish Playmate of the Month."

"It must be very hard on Lena, with that kind of competition for her father's attention." I took a blueberry muffin. "What happens now?"

"Westport's working the case. You keep out of it."

"I can't ignore the fact that Link could be in danger!"

"Hire bodyguards," he snapped.

I was about to tell Matt to take the rest of the muffins and go, but I never got the words out because Magic suddenly jumped up onto his lap, rubbed his little head against Matt's abdomen, and started to purr.

"I guess he *does* remember me," Matt said softly.

Chapter 28

IT WAS A week before I heard from Bobby. He telephoned me at the office.

"It's an old joke, but it's true. I've got good news, and I've got bad news." Without giving me a choice as to which I wanted to hear first, he went on. "Good news wins. Your Archie Foundation is legit. Two women in their late sixties run it, and they spoil the animals like they were their grandkids. It's harder to adopt a pet from them than it would be to get a human baby. You and I should be looked after so well."

"That's a relief. I'll send them a donation today."

"Save some money for my bill," he joked. "Now for the bad news. Does your office face Central Park?"

"Yes."

"Go to the window and look down."

Keeping the phone in my hand, I got up and moved around behind my desk chair. Staring down onto Central Park West,

I felt my heart lurch inside my chest. Near the entrance to our building I spotted a familiar dab of blue.

"She's back . . . Where are you, Bobby?"

"You probably can't see me for all the cars, but I'm across the street from her, leaning against my chopper, talking to you on my cell."

"It's the same shade of blue as her coat, but are you sure that's Lena Cooper?"

"Yep. I got her picture from Motor Vehicles. Her license has been revoked, by the way—too many tickets. Speeding, reckless driving, etc. Anyway, on a hunch this morning I went back to Ramsey's place on Carmine Street, to talk to the super again. That's when I saw her. She was outside with the super, slipping him money."

"She's trying to find out where Link has gone!"

"Elementary, my dear Morgan. How much does the guy know?"

"Link paid him to sublet the apartment; he didn't tell him where he was going."

"What about the mail? Ramsey must be having it forwarded."

"He rented a P.O. box."

"The super scribbled something on a piece of paper and gave it to her. Probably the box number. She won't have any problem finding it, and she'll wait for him there."

"I'll arrange for one of our security men to pick up Link's mail."

"Okay, that's good. Now I've got to tell you some worse news," Bobby said.

"What?"

"*You're* being followed."

It felt as though something hard had whacked me across the chest. For a moment, I couldn't breathe. When I got my voice back, I asked, "How do you know?"

"I staked out your place for two days, thinking she might come to you. Early this morning I recognized a PI leaning against your building on the south side of Seventy-Second, pretending to read the paper, but he was really watching the entrance to the Dakota. When you came out, at exactly 8:07 this morning, he crossed over to the park side of the street, waited until you were half a block ahead of him, then started following you. He didn't have a car, or a waiting taxi, so he knows you walk to work."

"This detective. Who is he?"

"I only know him by sight."

"What does he look like?"

"Like a million other men. Don't try to spot him. Just go about your business. I'm sticking with the woman, but I've put one of the guys I use onto him."

This situation might have been funny, if an innocent man hadn't been murdered. "What a world," I said. "Now detectives are following other detectives."

"It's a living." His voice lost its casual tone. "Gotta go. She's moving away from your building."

"What do you want me to do?"

"Keep writing those sexy scenes, like that one in the pool. I'll keep in touch." He disconnected. I looked down onto Central Park West, but I couldn't see Bobby.

And the dab of blue was gone.

LINK WAS ADAMANT. "I don't care if you saw her outside. I won't have an effing bodyguard!"

"Link, I'm pulling rank. I wasn't asking your permission. I'm going to hire protection for you. Live with it!"

He pursed his lips, expelled a few comical puffs, and fanned himself vigorously. "Ohhhh, you make me hot when you get tough." He switched tactics from stubborn to charming. "Boss-lady, stop worrying. I come and leave the studio through the connecting basements that lead out onto Columbus Avenue."

"Connecting basements?"

"I'll show you sometime," he said. "There's a whole world under the streets."

"You'd tell me, wouldn't you, if you saw her anywhere near Chet's place?"

"In a nanosecond. I'm *private*, not crazy. I don't want that broad dogging me any more than I want some hired bozo nipping at my heels. Anyway, we're off to Vegas in a few days."

"That's another thing," I said. "There's been a lot of publicity about the Super Soap Weekend and the Daytime Stars on Broadway Show we're putting on for the fans. Everybody who's interested knows you'll be there."

"Relax. Vegas is my territory. I've got pals," he said quietly. Something in his darkened tone set off an alarm bell in my head.

"What do you mean? What kind of pals?"

"The type that come in handy if you've got a problem the cops can't handle."

"Link!"

"Don't get bent out of shape," he said soothingly. "I won't let anybody hurt that poor delusional gal. But they won't let her hurt *me*, either." He grinned the devilish grin that made his female fans—including my own Betty Kraft—go weak in the knees and added, "Sometimes it helps to have friends in low places."

BOBBY CALLED JUST as I was getting ready for bed.

"I took your tail to dinner tonight."

"Lucky I read detective novels, so I know that 'my tail' is the private detective who's following me. What did you find out?"

"That he likes his steak rare and his wine red—and with dust on the bottle. Don't ask what it cost."

"Was it worth what I'll be paying?"

"Yep. He swore he didn't know the name of his company's client, and I believe him because of the way that firm operates, but he did say they were hired by a guy in Europe. Who do you know across the pond who'd want to keep tabs on you?"

Philippe Abacasas. The thought infuriated me. At least, anger was *one* of my emotions.

I didn't want to share this with Bobby, so I tried to cover with a joke. "Since Prince Charles is too old, and Prince William is too young, I can't imagine. But I'd like to 'shake that tail' before I go to Las Vegas."

"When are you leaving, and which airline?"

"Friday morning, on Delta." I gave him the flight number.

"Just go about your business for the next few days, Miss Morgan. On Friday morning, call me on my cell ten minutes before you're ready to come downstairs with your luggage."

"What are you going to do?"

I heard his impish heh-heh-heh. "Arrange a little diversion."

Chapter 29

THE NIGHT BEFORE I left for Las Vegas, I took Magic across town to stay with Penny for the few days I would be gone. Penny laughed when she saw what I brought with him: dishes, food, toys, litter, and a new litter box.

"Why'd you buy a new box?"

"When I bring him home on Sunday night, he might need to use it before I unpack." I handed her a typed list of his habits. "Be sure you know where he is when you open the door to delivery people, he's an indoor cat. And tell Matt to be careful, too!"

Penny listened to my nervous instructions with a patient smile on her face, while Magic explored her kitchen. His posture was cautious—this was strange new territory—but he seemed fascinated by all the places there were to investigate. I knelt down to say good-bye, and to assure him that I'd be back soon.

"Don't worry about a thing," Penny said. "I'll take good care of him."

I believed her, but it was hard to get to sleep that night, without my little companion curled up near me.

I WAS PACKED and ready to call Bobby Novello's cell number when my own phone rang.

"There's a small bit of news in the Maitland murder," Matt said. "I don't know what it means. Could be nothing."

"What is it?"

"According to Maitland's will, everything he owned goes to his sister. Stan arranged for her to collect any of Maitland's effects that she wanted. Among the things she took was his laptop. She called Stan last night to tell him that when it wouldn't work, her older son opened it up and discovered the hard drive was missing."

My pulse quickened. "Whatever the burglar wanted must have been on the computer."

"That's what I think," Matt said, "and whoever broke in tore up the house to throw the cops off about what they were really after."

I sensed there was something he was leaving out. "What's bothering you, Matt?"

"Stan faxed us pictures of the interior of the house. Whoever tossed the place did a thorough job. That takes time, and every minute they spent inside they were at risk of getting caught."

"Maybe they were looking for something else," I said. "They might have thought that Maitland backed up whatever it was on a floppy and hid it."

I heard the bark of G. G.'s voice in the background.

Matt told me hurriedly, "We have to go out on a call. Talk to you later." Before I could remind him that I was leaving for Las Vegas, or even say good-bye, he hung up.

A glance at my bedside clock confirmed that if I didn't phone Bobby right away, I was going to be late. He picked up immediately.

"You ready to go?

"Yes."

"Chet's taking you to the airport?"

"How did you know?"

"His Range Rover just pulled up at the entrance and parked," Bobby said.

"I told him not to come up, that I'd come down."

"Good. Now in *exactly* eight minutes, zip-zip out of the building, hippy-hop into the Rover, and take off. I guarantee that detective won't follow you."

My luggage for the trip consisted of a carry-on duffle and a tote bag, both of which I could handle easily without help.

Seven minutes after my conversation with Bobby, I was moving cautiously, flattening myself against the inside of the arched entrance to the Dakota's courtyard, out of sight of anyone who might be waiting for me to emerge onto West Seventy-Second Street.

Seconds before the digital numbers on my watch registered exactly eight minutes, I heard the roar of a powerful motor, coming fast from the direction of Columbus Avenue. I spotted a dark red and bright chrome motorcycle zoom past Chet's Rover, speeding toward Central Park West. A voluptuous young woman with long black hair streaming behind her controlled the machine with one hand; her other hand was at her side. She wore black leather pants and a hot pink bikini top, at least one size too small. She was just past the Dakota's entrance when she raised her free hand, pointed a large pistol at a man in slacks and a windbreaker—and *fired*!

Her human target screamed, but instead of taking a bullet, he found himself covered from face to waist in bright yellow paint!

The paint-covered man bellowed obscenities at the cyclist as she made her escape by jumping the curb and roaring away south on the sidewalk, scattering pedestrians.

People on both sides of Central Park West yelled at her. Brakes squealed as startled drivers swerved their cars to avoid collisions, in the process snarling north–south traffic.

With all the howling, running, and screeching of brakes, no one noticed me sprint the ten yards to the spot where Chet was parked with the motor running. I tossed Chet my duffle and tote, jumped into the vehicle, and ducked beneath the dash-board. Chet stomped on the accelerator and the Range Rover shot forward, just as I heard the wail of sirens. From my position crouching on my bags in the passenger well, I couldn't see anything, but it sounded as though a patrol car passed us, racing toward the bedlam.

Three blocks from the scene of the paintball attack, Chet said, "You two can sit up now. We're safe."

I squirmed my way up to perch on the front seat, and saw Link rising from the floor in the back, chuckling.

"First time I ever saw a drive-by paintballing," he said. As we buckled ourselves in, he leaned over and asked Chet, "Did you get a look at that sweet machine?"

"What was it?"

"A 2004 Honda Silver Wing—dark candy red."

Chet nodded with appreciation. "Ahh, with the 582cc liquid-cooled, four-stroke parallel-twin engine?"

"And the swingarm rear suspension. Dual hydraulic shocks and five-spring preload adjustability."

"Hey, guys," I said, "cut the Martian-speak. You've got an Earthling in the car."

Link gave me a comic leer. "We caught a good-looking one, too."

Chet glanced at me as he drove. "I like that red blazer, black shirt combo."

"Thanks," I said. Pulling the phone out of my jacket pocket, I dialed Bobby's cell. When he answered, I said admiringly, "That was quite a diversion."

"Happy to be of service."

"Ask him where he got the babe," Link said.

"Link wants to know about the woman."

"She's in my motorcycle club. An English teacher on spring break. To make extra money, she does odd jobs for me," Bobby said. "Bad luck for Ramsey—she's married."

I repeated the information and Link muttered, "If any of my teachers had looked like that, I'd have stayed in school." He settled back against the seat to watch the scenery flashing by.

"Have fun in Vegas," Bobby said. "Give my regards to the crap tables."

THE SIDEWALK IN front of Delta's curbside check-in trolley was swarming with travelers of all ages, chattering in a variety of languages and counting pieces of luggage before getting the appropriate tags and hustling through the doors into the terminal.

Chet skillfully maneuvered the Rover into a spot that was designated for the unloading of passengers and baggage and we got out. When Link and Chet unloaded the bags, I saw that Link traveled as lightly as I did, with a single well-worn duffle.

Production manager Joel Davies spotted me before I saw him. He shouted my name, waved his arms above his head, and muscled his way through the throng. Five feet nine, with a wrestler's build and an undercover vice cop's bizarre sense of style, Joel not only handled physical production problems at the studio, he was the expert "fixer" sent along whenever our people had to shoot scenes on location, or made group personal appearances. I'd experienced Joel's unflappable crisis-management skills a few months ago, in California, when a network executive and I had nearly been murdered.

I greeted Joel warmly. Joel and Link, old friends by now, tapped knuckles.

To Chet, I said, "This is Joel Davies, our combination production manager and miracle worker. Joel, this is Kevin Chet Thompson."

"Hey," Joel said. "I like your books, especially the one about the river murders." Joel hefted my duffle. "Check or carry?"

"Carry." I scanned the travelers around us. "Where's our group?"

"I sent the two-man camera crew to Vegas yesterday, with Tommy Z, so they can chart out the best places to film, while Tommy's making sure everything's on track at the hotel. I stashed the actors, the makeup artists, and the hairdresser up in the VIP lounge and came down to wait for you and Link."

"Is everybody okay?"

Joel glowered. "Depends on your definition. Sean's changed his seat eleven times, Francie and Rod don't care where they sit as long as it's together, Parker had a monster fight with his wife last night and he's started drinking again. Clarice smelled his breath, had a hissy fit and swears she won't sing their duet with him at the show tomorrow. Fifteen minutes ago Julie confessed she's got a gambling problem and wants me to lock her in her room when <u>she's</u> not onstage or at the autograph-signing table."

"In other words," I said, "it's just a typical day at the office."

"You can lock Julie in *my* room," Link volunteered.

Chet leaned against the side of his Rover and smiled. Our eyes met, and I realized we needed a moment alone together. "You two go on up to VIP," I said to Link and Joel. "I'll join you in a few minutes."

"Don't take too long to say good-bye," Joel said. "Going through the security check is a bitch."

As soon as Link and Joel were inside the terminal, Chet ignored the crowd of people surging by and drew me into his arms for a light good-bye kiss.

"I'll miss you," he said, "even though we haven't seen much of each other lately."

"You've been going steady with Link."

"He's a good guy; I like him. While you're gone, I'm going to help Bobby nose around, see if we can find Lena Cooper. Do you think she'll show up in Las Vegas?"

"Bobby's trying to prevent that. He's hired detectives to watch for Lena at airports, train and bus terminals in New York and New Jersey, plus he's been in touch with a private

detective firm in Las Vegas. He e-mailed Lena's picture to
them and arranged for men to watch all the planes, trains, and
buses from New York and New Jersey twenty-four hours a
day. There's even a team on the private airfield. They started
yesterday and they'll keep it up until after we're back in New
York Sunday evening. The network's paying for that private
army."

"Smart," Chet said. He leaned down and kissed me again,
this time just on the tip of my nose. "I love your nose," he
whispered.

"Yours doesn't exactly repulse me."

"When you come back, maybe they can get together for a
little quality time."

"I'd like that." I meant it, but inside my stomach I felt a familiar nervous fluttering. It was getting closer and closer to
the point when I would have to decide how serious a relationship I wanted to have with Chet. Specifically, was I going to
go to bed with him? In some respects, he was the perfect man
for me: single, attractive, smart, talented, witty, patient, and
successful. So far, his need to travel to research his new book,
and my involvement with murder investigations, had kept us
from spending more than three or four days in a row together.

Complicating the situation was my attraction to Matt
Phoenix. Matt and I had almost made love, but an attempt on
my life had stopped that. Now he'd declared there was no
chance for us as a couple if I accepted the inheritance that I'd
be eligible to collect in two weeks, forcing me to choose between a relationship with him or financial security: door number one, or door number two. *The Lady or the Tiger?*

Then there was Philippe Abacasas, the mystery man who
was absolutely wrong for me in almost all respects. *Almost.*
Even now, months later, I could recall every detail of the hours
we'd spent in each other's arms. Fearful of falling in love
again—really, afraid of losing control of my life—I'd held off
both Matt and Chet, but one crazy night I'd succumbed to
Philippe. Nancy believed that he was only my transition back

into the world of grown-up women. Philippe was a fantasy figure, all moonlight and no dirty dishes, Nancy had said; Matt
and Chet represented real life, and the responsibilities that
came with it.

The Lady or the Tiger?

Chapter 30

THE TWELVE-MEMBER *LOVE of My Life* expedition—consisting of seven actors, two makeup artists, a hairdresser, Joel Davies, and me—took up Delta's entire first-class section. I noticed that the attractive female flight attendants were giving a great deal of smiling attention to the desires of our four male daytime stars. Francie didn't seem to notice, but she was generally undemanding. Julie had that afraid-to-fly glaze over her eyes. Clarice, accustomed to being treated like a daytime princess, looked irritated; she'd had to signal several times before one of the flight attendants noticed and brought her the extra pillow she wanted.

As was usual on our airline trips together, Joel prearranged that he and I had seats in the first row. We were the perfect travel mates; Joel's preferred seat was next to the window and mine was on the aisle. I liked to read, and all he wanted to do was sleep.

Joel had selected seats for the rest of our party: putting the two makeup artists, middle-aged twins Mary and Molly Murray, across the aisle from us. Because Link and Rod were in the best physical shape, he'd put them next to the two first-class emergency exits, with Francie on the aisle beside Rod.

Clarice Hill, who played our emotionally fragile–romantic jeopardy heroine Jillian, wasn't currently speaking to Parker Nolan, her acting partner who played Gareth, the mystery man and Jillian's secret husband. Joel had switched their places and put Clarice next to Link.

In a keep-things-calm inspiration, Joel had paired nervous flyer Julie Lawson with Hugh Jefferson, our jolly, avuncular hairdresser, affectionately known as "Mr. Hairpiece." Sean O'Neil, who was as indecisive as Hamlet, had changed his seat one too many times and was now out of options, sitting in the last row of first class, next to brooding Parker Nolan.

The distance by air between New York and Las Vegas was 2,242 miles. Our estimated flying time in Delta's Boeing 757-200 was five and a half hours.

We'd been in the air for all of ten minutes when a problem arose.

Joel had just informed the nearest flight attendant that he didn't want anything to eat, drink, read, watch, or listen to. He didn't want to be disturbed at all, he told her, until ten minutes before our scheduled touchdown. After she agreed to pretend he wasn't there, he propped two pillows against the window, found a comfortable position while remaining seat-belted, and closed his eyes.

He hadn't taken more than three deep breaths when Sean O'Neil leaned over me to prod Joel awake.

"Hey, buddy," Sean said, "we got trouble back in the cheap seats."

Joel opened his eyes, "Sean, you're in first class with the rest of us, and you wouldn't think your seat was cheap if you had to pay for it."

Sean flinched. Intimidated by Joel's sharp retort, he took his arrogance down a notch. "Parker was already half blotto when we boarded. Now, even though they told him it's too early to serve, he's *hokking* the flying waitresses for booze."

Joel sat up and corrected his pronunciation of the Yiddish word, *hokking*. "You're Irish, Sean. Just say he's *bothering* them. Don't try to talk Jewish."

Sean, the shortest actor in our cast, drew himself up to his full five feet, four inches and said stiffly, "I can play Jewish. I was Shylock in *Merchant of Venice* at Loyola."

Joel muttered a phrase I'm not allowed to put in a script, squeezed in front of me, and lurched down the aisle toward Parker Nolan.

Sean was already slipping past me to buckle himself in to Joel's seat when he asked, "It's okay if I sit here, isn't it?"

"Sure," I said. My smile was pleasant but insincerity was in my heart; Sean loved to talk, and his favorite subject was himself.

"It's my good luck that Parker went back on the sauce." Seeing my disapproving frown, he quickly amended his statement. "Oh, it's not that I'm glad about Parker's situation—I bleed for the poor guy—it's just that I really needed to talk to you. In private."

Now what? "Is there a problem, Sean?"

"I'm worried about this fan weekend."

That was the last thing I expected to hear. Offstage, Sean O'Neil was an egotistical little backstabber who never thought of anyone except himself, but he photographed like early Robert Redford, and delivered his lines with great feeling. I suspected he didn't always understand what the lines *meant*, but that ambivalent quality gave interesting nuances to some of his speeches. Even though in the past year he'd lost two leading ladies on the show to more charismatic actors, he still had a fan following.

"There's nothing to be concerned about. You do well in interviews."

His head bobbed up and down, like one of those fake dogs on the dashboards of some cars. "Oh, I do, I do. In print, and on the radio—oh, yeah, oh yeah. And on TV where they let me sit at a desk or a table. But I'll be *walking* out on that stage tomorrow. The fans'll see I'm shorter than the other guys. Rod's not all that big, but next to Link and Parker, I'll look like a shrimp in a shark pool."

"A man's height isn't important," I said, meaning it. "Some of the greatest movie stars ever were sh . . . not tall. Humphrey Bogart, James Cagney, Alan Ladd. The public adored them."

"They're all dead."

"Tom Cruise is alive and making zillions."

Sean shook his head impatiently. "Camera tricks keep the fans from knowing I'm short, and the directors stage things so I'm not standing up near most of the other people." He added in a whine, "I had *two* acting partners who were shorter than me, and you took both the girls away."

"That was necessary to give you better stories, to write you a stronger role."

Because Sean had no romantic on-screen chemistry with the last two women we'd tried to team him with, it had forced me to turn his character, Nicky, into a bad guy. As a young-love hero, Sean hadn't clicked, but since I'd started creating rotten things for him to do, his fan mail had increased.

"I've got several ideas about how you can solve my problem," he said.

Oh, great. "What are they?"

He started ticking them off on his fingers. "One: I could already be seated on the stage when the curtain opens."

"No curtain," I said.

"I could arrive on horseback."

"No horses."

"I'm a good rope climber. How about I swing on stage like Tarzan?"

"We don't have insurance for that." One of my many duties as co-executive producer was to soothe the feelings of nervous actors or to build up their confidence when it was low. Attempting to make Sean feel important, I added, "You're too valuable for us to risk your safety."

Before he could come up with another idea, Joel returned. He was such a welcome sight I could have hugged him.

"*You* better go talk to Parker," Joel said. "This situation needs a woman's touch."

I unbuckled my seat belt and stood up. "Don't worry, Sean. I'll work something out so you'll feel comfortable on the show tomorrow."

Sean slipped into my seat as soon as I'd vacated it, and immediately a flight attendant hurried over to ask what she could bring him.

Making my way down the aisle, I saw Parker Nolan slumped in his seat.

"Parker?"

As soon as he realized I was standing next to Sean's empty aisle seat, he straightened his shoulders and flashed a smile at me. It was a good impromptu performance, likely to fool someone who didn't know what was going on in his life.

"What an unexpected pleasure," he said graciously. "Please, sit down."

I sat, and for the next two hours, I talked to Parker Nolan about the role of Gareth, praising particular strengths in his performance, and hinting at an exciting future story. I wouldn't tell him any concrete plot details, but what I *implied* seemed to ignite his enthusiasm.

"I'm not going to dance around this, Parker. Tommy took a chance on casting you when the word in the industry was that your drinking had made you unreliable. You told us you'd cleaned up your act and were in AA." My voice was firm, but there was sadness in my tone as I said, "The plain truth is that if you're going to keep drinking, we'll let you go and recast the part."

Parker rocked back as though he'd been struck.

"Think about it this way: *you're* the one with all the power," I said. "It's really *your* choice whether or not you'll continue playing Gareth."

After a moment, he cleared his throat and spoke. In the

warm baritone that made his dialogue such a pleasure to hear, he said resolutely, "This—today—was just a setback. A bump in the road, so to speak. I give you my word that it won't happen again."

"I'm very happy you've decided to stay with us, Parker," I said, meaning it sincerely. "When you see what I have planned for Gareth and Jillian, I'm sure you'll be glad you did."

Parker nodded in the direction of his romantic acting partner, who was sitting several rows ahead of us, engrossed in conversation with Link. "I'll apologize to Clarice. I was a swine this morning," he said. In an attempt to make light of the problem, he added, "I'll throw myself on her mercy and tell her that if she doesn't forgive me, I'm going to look rather silly at the show tomorrow, singing our love duet all by myself. The fans will think I have bad breath."

"Let me know if you want me to talk to her." I didn't want to do it, but if Parker didn't succeed in making up with Clarice—if the fans saw coldness between them—it could hurt the show. "Use all your charm," I urged.

What I *didn't* tell Parker was that I had enough problems on my plate already. The most serious was making sure that Lena Cooper didn't get close enough to Link to hurt him. Or worse.

Chapter 31

RATHER THAN GO back to my own seat and condemn Parker to Sean O'Neil's company for the rest of the trip, I'd decided to stay put. If Parker had to be strapped in next to Sean for a few hours I was afraid it might weaken his new resolve to stop drinking.

To my delight, Parker turned out to be an entertaining companion. While I saw him every day that he taped his scenes, I knew little about him personally. I enjoyed hearing about his training at England's Royal Academy of Dramatic Art, how he almost flunked Fencing, his funny mishaps onstage, and about his time in the navy, serving on a submarine. Although an American born in Idaho, he was so adept at doing foreign accents that he'd played many different nationalities convincingly. It made him the perfect choice to portray Gareth, our vaguely European man of mystery.

"Just before my first audition with Tommy," he said, "I asked him what kind of accent Gareth had. He told me, 'just play him down the middle.' I was so desperate to get the job, I was afraid to ask 'the middle of *what*?' "

"Sometimes Tommy needs a translator," I admitted with an affectionate laugh. "I know we haven't been specific in the story about where Gareth comes from, but what nationality *are* you playing? I can't quite decide."

"I call my accent 'Hollywood European.' Actually, I copied the inflections from an Italian actor, Rossano Brazzi, when he played the Frenchman in that old movie, *South Pacific*."

It was a little past three in the afternoon, Nevada time, when a male flight attendant turned on the public address system. He spoke briskly, as though he'd made his announcement so many times the information bored him: "Please return to your places and fasten your seat belts. We're about to begin our descent to McCarran Airport."

"My bags are under my seat up there," I told Parker, gesturing toward the front of the cabin.

"Go ahead," he said. "I've enjoyed this time together, Morgan." He lowered his eyes and added, "Thank you, for our talk. I won't disappoint you."

"I know you won't." I said, giving his hand a quick pat.

I passed Sean in the aisle. He didn't look happy.

"I saved you from a dull flight," he whispered. "Joel's idea of conversation is an occasional snore."

Joel greeted me with, "Did you get Parker to stop drinking?"

"Yes."

"Good. Ten more minutes with Sean and I would've started."

Another flight attendant picked up the microphone, this one female. In the cheery voice of a Miss America contestant, she said, "Last year, 28,214,122 passengers arrived and departed from McCarran International Airport, and so far this year passenger traffic is up 2.5 percent.

"McCarran has two terminals—we'll be arriving at number one. There are ninety-two gates in the two terminals, more than fifty retail shops and thirty restaurants, lounges, and snack bars."

"She should tell us how many slot machines there are, door-to-door," Joel muttered.

"Slot machines in the airport?"

"Everywhere," he said. "You'll see. They're even in the toilets. The slots are the casino's biggest profit producers, they're rigged to pay off at whatever number of plays the casino decides. The folks don't know when they'll hit, so they just keep pouring the money in."

"Like lab rats," I said, "pushing the buttons over and over again because every now and then they're rewarded with a food pellet."

OUR DELTA 757-200 touched down smoothly, and we deplaned into an air-conditioned terminal that was practically a city, populated by travelers and vendors.

A stocky, silver-haired man in a chauffeur's uniform stood at the rope separating the crowd of arriving passengers from those meeting them. He held a white sign with "Davies" printed on it in black marker. Joel raised his hand and called, "Over here."

The chauffeur folded the sign and stuck it in one deep jacket pocket. "The Mount Olympus, right, sir?"

Joel nodded and handed the driver his duffel and mine. I held onto my tote.

Like a 180-pound sheepdog, Joel rounded up our group and kept us together as we hiked through the terminal behind the driver.

Many of the people I saw coming toward us, heading for the departure gates, looked rumpled and heavy-lidded with fatigue. Las Vegas wasn't a place where tourists came to rest.

The Baggage Claim carousels were next to the glass walls separating the terminal from the street. I followed Joel's gaze and watched him survey the line of black limousines outside.

"The first five are yours," the chauffeur said.

I asked Joel, "Why do we need *five*?"

"Four for the passengers, and one for the luggage." Joel indicated the carousel with our flight number on it. Bag after bag was being pulled off and piled up around our *Love* troupe. Not everyone traveled as lightly as Joel, Link, and I.

The bags were sorted and the ticket stubs checked against the luggage tags by airport security at the door. I stepped outside and was hit with a blast of heat so powerful it felt as though I'd walked into the mouth of a furnace.

My second surprise was that the nearest casinos were close to the airport. Shading my eyes against the glaring sun, I could see the sign for Mandalay Bay Resort and Casino not that far away up Las Vegas Boulevard.

"Where's the Mount Olympus?"

"Other side of the Mandalay Bay," Joel said. "We could walk if it wasn't two hundred degrees." His reference to the temperature was an exaggeration, but it didn't feel like much of one.

As soon as the last bag was stashed in the rear car, Joel steered Link, Julie, Francie, and Rod into the second of the air-conditioned limos, the other actors into the third, and the makeup and hair staff into the fourth. He ushered me into the first car, climbed in and told the driver, "Onward."

A few minutes later, our caravan pulled up under the canopy that shaded the front entrance to the Mount Olympus. Positioned between the soaring Mandalay Bay and the huge, onyx-tinted pyramid of the Egyptian-themed Luxor, the Mount Olympus Hotel and Casino was as spectacular as its neighbors. Constructed in the style of an immense ancient Greek temple, flanking the grand bronzed glass entrance were ten-foot-tall statues depicting four Greek gods: Zeus and Apollo stood on one side, with Aphrodite and Eros on the other.

Joel had the rear door of our car open before we'd come to a full stop. He bounded out, gesturing to the five camera people (four men and one woman) who were lounging in front of the hotel. Responding to Joel's hand signals, they hefted video rigs onto their shoulders and aimed the cameras where Joel pointed: at limos two and three. As our actors emerged from the cars, each smiled into the cameras and waved.

I recognized two of the camera operators as part of the *Love* crew: Jimmy Blake and Jimmy Devane—known around the New York studio as Jimmy One and Jimmy Two. They'd arrived in Las Vegas the day before with Tommy.

As the actors were being filmed moving toward the hotel entrance, I joined Joel on the sidewalk and asked, "Who are the other three camera people?"

"They're shooting footage for the hotel's promotional film," he said.

I nodded, remembering the deal Tommy had made to get free accommodations; our Global crew was filming for future network promotions.

Joel and I—trailed by the makeup and hair artists, each of us being careful to keep out of camera range—followed the actors into the lobby of the Mount Olympus.

We entered a visual wonderland. Sky blue carpeting lay beneath our feet. Paintings of white cloud formations encircled us along the walls. The combination produced the dreamy illusion that we were walking among the clouds. The Mount Olympus of Greek mythology existed high above the earth. It was where the gods lived and played, and amused themselves by making trouble for the mortals below.

Tommy Zenos, dressed more casually than I'd ever seen him in a yellow polo shirt and brown cotton slacks, was waiting for us inside the entrance. Looming only a few yards behind Tommy, and reaching halfway to the three-story high ceiling, was a replica of the Parthenon, marking the entrance to the casino. It wasn't a perfect replica because instead of the eight Doric columns supporting the top in the original, here there were only six. The middle two had been removed to allow easy access to the gambling.

Adults of all ages and shapes, wearing outfits that ranged from sedate to gaudy, flowed through the lobby and into the casino. Some stopped to watch the video cameras filming.

Many in the crowd recognized the actors, nudged each other, and pointed. Waves of excited whispering swept through the lobby, competing with the noise from the gamblers and the machines in the casino.

Tommy greeted our group, grinning like a professional host. "Welcome, everybody. I've checked you all in, so nobody has to bother with Reception." He consulted a list he held and began handing out card keys. "You're in two-bedroom suites, so everybody's got privacy. If you want to switch suite mates, tell Joel first, because we need to know where everybody is."

I moved up to stand beside Tommy, facing our *Love* troupe. "Don't forget, the media interviews are scheduled from eight to ten tonight. Where will they be, Tommy?"

"In the private dining room behind the Lord Elgin Restaurant. I've arranged for the hotel to serve us dinner, because nothing warms up the press like free food and drinks." He waved genially at the cameras and got a laugh when he joked, "Don't tell them I said that."

I told Francie, Julie, and Clarice, "If you want to go swimming now, or go to the spa, you can get your hair and makeup done in the Neptune Suite beginning at six this evening."

"When the press interviews are over," Tommy said, "you're free to do whatever you want, until our big show for the fans tomorrow at one P.M."

"You all have the running order of the songs and acts in the show," I said. "We FedEx-ed your music sheets to the accompanist, so he'll be up on the songs. He'll be there at noon, during the sound check. You won't be able to rehearse with him, but make sure he knows your key, and alert him if you're doing anything special with your timing or transitions."

Tommy joined in, "Just a reminder: the *show* part of the show will last about an hour, then we'll have people with hand microphones circulating through the audience. The fans can ask you questions for the next ninety minutes. After that, we'll take a break, and then we'll reassemble in the Athena Ballroom at 4:30 for autographs. You'll be sitting behind a long table and the fans will come up to have you autograph . . . well, whatever they want you to sign. We're providing free photos. The hotel has *Love* coffee mugs, T-shirts, mouse pads, posters, and the rest of the stuff for sale in the gift shop. We'll have security at the signing, in case anybody gets out of hand, or wants you to autograph something . . . *inappropriate.*"

Tommy finished the instructions by reaching into his pants pockets and bringing out a big handful of hundred-dollar chips. He handed each person in our group two chips. "Have some fun on Morgan and me," he said.

Out of the corner of my eye, I saw Link gently remove the pair of chips from Julie's palm, fold her hand into his, and whisper something to her. She giggled, and they strolled off together. To my relief—given Julie's confession about having a gambling problem—they were going in the opposite direction from the entrance to the casino.

I thought wryly that it looked as though Link was going to give his "all" to keep Julie safe from the tables. I glanced around, fearful that I'd see a familiar face, with or without her blue coat, following him, but I saw nothing to concern me.

I told myself to stop worrying.

With Bobby Novello's detective colleagues watching the planes, trains, private airfields, and buses in New York, New Jersey, and Las Vegas, with instructions to detain her, there was no way that Lena Cooper could be here.

Chapter 32

THE ZEUS SUITE, which Tommy had designated for us, not only had two bedrooms, but it was a lavishly furnished duplex. Oddly, for a Greek-themed wonderland, the décor in Zeus was all pseudo Louis XIV: gilt-framed chairs and settees upholstered in gold silk, and tables trimmed in ormolu—that decorative brass made to imitate gold.

"I put my things in the upstairs bedroom yesterday," Tommy said, "but if you'd rather have that room I'll switch."

"No, don't. I like being down here because I'll probably get up earlier than you, and this floor is where the kitchenette and the coffeemaker are."

"So everything's perfect!"

Gesturing at the upper floor, I regarded him quizzically. "I'm surprised you picked that room. You don't usually like stairs."

A sudden rush of color flooded his cheeks. "You inspired

me," he said. "I mean, the weight-loss plan you worked out for Francie—and wrote into the show—*boy*, does she look great! Not weighing yourself, giving up just one fattening thing you love, not reading while you eat . . . It sounded weird to me at first, but then all that mail started coming in from fans who are losing weight with Francie. So I decided to give up bread, and start walking some. That's why I wanted the room where I *have* to go up and down the stairs."

"That's wonderful," I said. "When did you start?"

"Yesterday." He ran an index finger along the front of his tight waistband and frowned. "I guess it's too early to see any results."

I gave him an encouraging smile. "Just be patient."

"I think I'll go to the spa and take a steam," Tommy said. I was about to caution him, but he beat me to it. "Don't worry, I won't stay in there too long."

I gave Tommy a thumbs-up, and he sailed off with a happy smile on his face.

It took only a few minutes to empty my duffle, hang up my clothes, and put away my lingerie. I'd brought a cream silk dress and beige high-heeled sandals to wear to the press dinner tonight, and for the show tomorrow, I'd packed navy slacks and a pale blue silk shirt. A down-to-the-knees Bruce Lee tee shirt for sleeping, the dark blue silk robe (a gift from Tommy a few months ago), and fuzzy, black cat-face bedroom slippers completed my wardrobe for the weekend. Penny had given me those slippers. When Magic saw them for the first time, from across the bedroom floor, he dropped down into a crouch and crept toward them with jungle stealth. Watching him, I had no idea what he intended to do, but I was pretty sure he wasn't thinking "welcome to the family." When he got close enough to see that the slippers weren't real cats, he lost interest, stood up, and strolled away.

My initial plan was to shower and fix myself up before the media dinner, but instead I splashed cold water on my face, gave my hair a few swipes with the brush, and left the suite to find someone on the hotel staff who could help me solve the problem of how to get Sean O'Neil on and off stage without the audience noticing how short he is.

Two hours later the showroom's property master came up with a great solution. I could hardly wait to see Sean's face when I showed him what we'd devised for him.

THE MOUNT OLYMPUS is laid out so that one must go through the casino in order to get to any of the restaurants or showrooms. Because the gaming tables are as dangerously alluring as the calls of the Sirens in Greek mythology, few people make it all the way to their original destinations without stopping to gamble. Maybe as a kind of private joke, the casino owners have a large mural on one wall that depicts Odysseus, strapped to the mast of his ship, as he tries to resist those Sirens' calls.

On my way to the media dinner, I passed our two makeup artists, the twin sisters in their midfifties, Molly and Mary Murray. Thirty years earlier they'd been models, and they'd kept their slender figures. Now they were happy grandmothers; instead of toting modeling portfolios, they carried booklets full of family pictures. I watched them chattering with excitement as they gave the quarter slot machines a heavy workout and wished them good luck.

Farther into the casino's kaleidoscope of colors and noise, I spotted Joel Davies and Hugh Jefferson, *Love's* popular "Mr. Hairpiece." They were playing blackjack and concentrating so intently they didn't see me wave at them.

Continuing on, I made it to my destination without trying any of the games, so in that respect, I "beat the house."

The Mount Olympus boasted a dozen inviting places to eat: cafés, bistros, Chinese, Japanese, a steak house, a neon-lighted 1950s-style diner, a sushi bar, a coffee shop, and The Lord Elgin Room. The last was an elegant continental restaurant touted prominently in the hotel's brochures; the private dining room where we were entertaining the press was reached by passing through it.

Named for Thomas Bruce, seventh Earl of Elgin, the restaurant featured replicas of the famous Elgin Marbles, that magnificent collection of sculptures Bruce (a British diplomat in Greece in the early 1800s) had ordered removed from the Parthenon and taken to London. Lord Elgin claimed that the marbles were being defaced by vandals, that pieces were being stolen and used as building material. He justified taking them by saying he was preserving priceless works of art so that the whole world could appreciate them. The British Museum built their Duveen Gallery especially to hold them, but the Greek government has been fighting for decades to get the sculptures back.

The private dining room behind the Elgin—decorated like a mossy grotto, with a waterfall along one side—was filling up with members of the entertainment press when I arrived. All seven of our actors were in their places on the slightly raised dais. Acting partners were sitting together: Rod and Francie at one end, then Link and Julie, and Parker and Clarice. Appropriately, Sean O'Neil was on the other side of Clarice; in the story his character was trying to destroy her relationship with Parker's character, because he wanted Clarice's character for himself.

I noticed Link and Julie had inched their chairs as close together as possible. There was a new sparkle in Julie's eyes; her face was glowing without the aid of makeup.

Tommy joined me. Indicating Clarice, Parker, and Sean, Tommy nicknamed them Cinderella, Prince Charming, and the evil Rumplestiltskin. Eyeing Link and Julie, he whispered, "I think those two spent the afternoon in bed together. If something *is* going on with them, it could be good for the show."

"Unless they break up," I said.

Tommy's smile vanished. "You're right! Oh, God! What if Cody and Amber really catch on with the fans, but off camera they start to *hate* each other?"

"Let's not worry about it now," I said.

I didn't want to upset Tommy, but knowing Link, I doubted

that a romance with Julie would last very long. Yet, human nature was unpredictable. I wasn't sure enough either way to place a bet. In our story, I was good at picking who belonged with whom, but I wasn't so astute in real life. Not even for myself.

Our media guests had found their tables and settled down as waiters began serving. As soon as dinner was over, the interviewing would begin. Our plan was that Tommy would officiate tonight, and tomorrow I'd MC the Daytime Stars on Broadway show. We'd both be on duty at the autographing session after the show.

I asked Tommy, "Do you mind if I don't stay for this dinner?"

"No, it's okay. Go have some fun."

"Thanks," I said. "See you later."

Tommy ambled toward the dais as I slipped out the door.

It was only a few minutes after eleven in New York. Not too late to make a couple of calls. Rather than go all the way back to our suite, I decided to find a ladies' room and use my cell phone.

Restrooms for men and for women were opposite each other just off the main lobby, down a short corridor past the Concierge desk. One was marked Aphrodite and the other Hercules. In case anyone searching for relief didn't know their mythology, there were male and female silhouettes beneath the names.

Opening the door to Aphrodite, I saw that it was a large, comfortably furnished lounge with a sofa and club chairs, and it seemed to be empty for the moment. Stepping inside, I realized that Joel hadn't exaggerated: even in here there were slot machines.

My first call was to Nancy, to find out how things were going with Arnold. Arnold was there, which I took as a good sign, but it meant she couldn't talk freely. She did say that Didi was returning from Boston the middle of next week. I heard Arnold's voice in the background. "Arnold wants to talk to you," Nancy said. She passed the phone to him and he greeted me warmly.

"I wasn't very gracious at the hospital," he said. "I've expressed my regret to Nancy. Now I'm apologizing to you. I appreciate what the two of you did in getting Didi so quickly to Manhattan Orthopedic."

"I'm glad everything worked out."

"One more thing, before I give you back to Nancy. I gather you met Mitchell Cooper."

"Yes." My tone was carefully bland.

"He can be somewhat acerbic, but he's under a great deal of strain, very worried about his daughter. I hope you'll take that into consideration in your assessment of him."

"Does he know where Lena is?"

"He says he doesn't." Arnold paused. "It's a primal instinct to protect one's child. I'm sure you understand that, Morgan."

"Yes," I said. What I didn't say was that while I understood the concept intellectually, it wasn't part of my personal experience. When I was a child and needed it the most, there hadn't been anyone to protect me.

Nancy came on the line again. I told her that I'd be home Sunday evening, and we said good night.

Because I still had the Aphrodite lounge to myself, I dialed Bobby Novello's number and asked him if he had any news about Lena Cooper's whereabouts.

"She's 'in the wind,' as they say on the TV cop shows. Just half an hour ago I talked to the company in Vegas that's watching for her on incoming transportation. So far: nada."

I thanked him for everything he was doing, said good night, and put my cell phone back in my evening bag.

I should have been comforted by Bobby's positive report, but I couldn't shake the uneasy feeling that somehow Lena was going to outsmart his hired gladiators. Maybe it was the curse of having loved my history classes, but I remembered that the Maginot Line, with all of its concrete bunkers, bombproof artillery casements, and antitank traps was thought to be impenetrable. It was supposed to prevent Hitler from invading France. But in 1940, Hitler's army didn't try to breach the line—they went around it, through a mountainous forest, and conquered France.

THE MAKEUP SISTERS declined my offer to treat them to dinner. Even though I promised them the cuisine of their choice, it was no sale. They preferred to stay with the slot machines.

Strolling through the casino, I amused myself by people watching. My old boss, *Love's* previous head storyteller, had called that "the writer's disease."

I was standing just outside a ring of players surrounding the noisiest of the crap tables, watching the action. A gaunt man with a pale, pinched face and sweat-soaked, thinning dark hair was making point after point. Before every toss he would blow on the dice, shake them, rub them between his hands, and then throw to the end of the green felt-covered table as though his life depended on each roll. Maybe it did.

Suddenly I heard a voice close behind me speak my name. Turning, I saw a man who was a couple of inches under six feet tall, with a deep tan, a muscular torso, and powerful hands with tapered fingers. How well I remembered the touch of those fingers.

I was face-to-face with Philippe Abacasas.

Chapter 33

MY PULSE QUICKENED and my mind flashed on a secluded pool in Los Angeles: my naked body pressed against his, our lips and our hands exploring. The memory sent a sudden blast of heat to my cheeks. I wasn't sure if it was a rush of pleasure at the sight of him, or if it was anger because Philippe Abacasas complicated my already complicated life.

I decided to think it was anger.

Philippe took my hand but I pulled it back. "What are you doing here?" I asked. "Did you buy shares in the Mount Olympus, the way you did in Global Broadcasting?"

In spite of the sarcasm in my tone, he smiled at me. His own voice was warm. "You are partially correct, my darling. I do have an interest in a gaming establishment, but not in this one. I read about the event you are having here, so I came to Las Vegas to see you. To talk to you. Shall we go to your suite?"

"No!" The word came out so emphatically that he chuckled knowingly. I was embarrassed again. "What I *mean*—"

"I know your meaning, but I did not come here to make love to you."

I wasn't altogether pleased to hear that; *I* wanted to be the one to say no to *him*.

"There is a place on the hotel grounds where it will be quiet enough to speak," he said. "Will you come with me?"

I hesitated—and felt like a fool. I've lived easily among lions in Kenya—why should I act as though being alone with this man is more dangerous?

Maybe because it is.

I studied him, to see if he'd changed in the months since we'd seen each other. His thick hair, the color of India ink, was cut a little shorter. I thought I saw a few new strands of silver, but it might have been a trick of the lights. His heavy brows arched above gray eyes that darkened to charcoal or lightened to the gray blue color of slate, depending on the time of day or what he was wearing.

"All right," I said. "Let's go talk."

Philippe guided me through the boisterous mob of gamblers crowding around the tables, until we finally reached an exit door. Outside, I took a few breaths of cool night air and felt in complete control of my emotions again.

As we passed the glittering turquoise rectangle of the hotel's deserted pool, I saw that the surrounding wrought-iron gates were locked. Probably to prevent unattended night swimming. Again memories came rushing at me. I slammed the door on the images, careful not to look directly at Philippe.

Beyond the pool, we headed toward what looked like a solid, six-foot wall of hedges, but as we got closer, I saw there was an opening. I followed Philippe into a small garden that was closed off from any view but aerial.

The scent of night-blooming jasmine was heady, but not overwhelming. In the middle of this secluded garden was a smooth marble bench, illuminated by the full moon above and by dozens of tiny fairy-lights that had been woven through the foliage.

Philippe took a handkerchief from his pocket and dusted

the part of the bench nearest me. We sat. When he reached for my hand again, I didn't pull away.

"Philippe, why did you come here?"

He tilted his head slightly, a glint of amusement in his eyes.

"One of my American associates has been recording your daily dramas for me."

Ooops. I felt my cheeks get hot again. So he'd watched the love scene in the pool! "Oh? How do you like the show?"

He raised the palm of my right hand and lightly kissed my fingertips. The touch of his lips sent a wave of electricity through me and I forced myself not to squirm. "You are dressing Gareth like me."

All I could think of to say was, "How long have you been watching?"

"Long enough to note the change. Seeing your work, it was as though you were speaking to me. But tell me, where does this man come from? I cannot quite identify his accent."

"He calls it 'Hollywood European.' "

"You are in a most peculiar business," he said.

"And just what business are *you* in?" I said. "You appear and disappear like a magician's trick."

"I know this is difficult for you, my darling—"

"Don't call me your darling."

He drew back as though I'd slapped him. I saw sadness in his eyes, but I wasn't going to let myself fall under whatever spell he'd managed to cast in Los Angeles. He had asked his questions. It was my turn. "Philippe, are you having me watched?"

Confusion flashed across his face. "I watched for you in the casino—"

"I mean in New York. Are you having me followed?"

Confusion was replaced by shock. "Someone is having you followed? Tell me everything!"

If Philippe hadn't hired the detective, then *who had*?

"One of our actors is being stalked by a disturbed fan," I explained. "I hired a private detective to try to find this fan, and in the course of his investigation he discovered that another detective, someone he recognized, was following *me*. He learned that this other detective's agency had been hired by a man in Europe. No name. I thought—"

"You thought it was I. No. I wish that it were, because then I could guarantee that no harm would come to you. I will find out—"

"No! You won't do anything. I don't need your protection. Now that I know you aren't the client, I'll handle this." *Somehow.*

"But I have resources—"

"I have resources, too! Promise me you won't interfere, Philippe. I mean it."

He saw that I was serious. It took him a few moments, but he agreed. With reluctance.

"If that is your wish."

"It is."

He reached up to my face, and with a smooth index finger he traced the line of my jaw, and then touched my lips lightly. Without thinking, I closed my eyes, and all at once his mouth was on mine. His kiss was gentle until my arms went around him in response. From somewhere deep inside, I finally found the strength to pull away. "No."

He let me go. Reaching for my right hand, he pressed it against his chest. I felt the beating of his heart.

"You say I come and go like a magic trick. For now, that is necessary. I cannot remain for too long in one place. If I really were a magician, I would whisk you away to Taormina, in Sicily, to a place up high that for hundreds of years was a monastery. It is a hotel now. Below the balconies is the Ionian Sea. Taormina is beautiful in the sunlight, but at night it is enchanting. Your D. H. Lawrence wrote *Lady Chatterley's Lover* there. From a hill overlooking the Greco-Roman amphitheater, one has a marvelous view of Mount Etna. When lava flows from the volcano down through the snow on its slopes, it uncoils a ribbon of vapor. Such a magnificent sight! It is my dream to show you."

"It's a fantasy," I said. "I'll never regret the time we . . . spent together, but you and I live on different planets."

He turned his gaze from me and stared into the distance. While he was thinking his thoughts, I studied his profile. Strong chin, prominent, finely shaped nose, full lips. Striking features I might never see again. At last, he inhaled deeply and let the breath out. "The night we met, you asked if Philippe Abacasas was my name, and I replied 'one of them.' There is very little about myself that I can tell you at this moment, but I would like you to know the name at my birth. It was Nico Andreades."

Before I could respond, he asked, "Tell me your name— before you married the late Mr. Tyler."

A limited truth was the best I could do. "It was Morgan . . . Maysfield."

"Now we know each other a little better." He stood up. "May I escort you to your door?"

He offered his hand and I took it.

On the walk back to the hotel, fingers entwined, we were silent. When we reached the entrance to the Zeus Suite and I inserted the key card into the lock, the man I now knew as Nico Andreades leaned down and just barely touched his lips to my right eyelid.

Straightening up, he smiled at me, and melted into the shadows. Gone again.

The *rational* part of me hoped that this time he was gone for good.

The shock of seeing Nico hadn't destroyed my appetite. I hadn't eaten since breakfast and I was hungry, so I put on my robe and ordered a hamburger from room service. When it arrived, I ate everything on the plate, including the decorative carrot that was carved to look like a rose.

I moved the service cart outside the door, so I wouldn't be disturbed, and changed into my Bruce Lee nightshirt. Just as I began to fall asleep in the suite's comfortable king-sized bed, I suddenly had a thought that made my eyes snap open.

When Bobby said that the detective following me had been

hired by "a man in Europe" I was annoyed, but I wasn't really worried because I thought the man was Philippe. Now I knew it wasn't. So some unknown person was tracking my movements. I felt a shiver of fear.

It was long after I heard Tommy come into the suite and go upstairs to his room that I was finally able to sleep.

Chapter 34

NEXT MORNING, TOMMY left the suite early, to have breakfast with the hotel's management. He went armed with a checklist, to make sure we'd have everything we needed for the show this afternoon and for the autographing session later.

I had a quick breakfast by myself in the coffee shop, relieved that I hadn't seen either Nico Andreades or Lena Cooper on the way. Both were a threat to my equilibrium, and I'd had enough surprises for one weekend. Soon as I'd finished a third cup of coffee, I made the rounds of the suites to check on our actors. It was good to see that the performing pairs were awake, in good spirits, and diligently rehearsing their songs and the movements they would make onstage during their numbers.

The show's accompanist had come in early to work with Sean, who would be performing his two numbers alone. Parker, Clarice, Francie, and Rod were all trained singers, but Sean, Link, and Julie were not. They'd been assigned material that was vocally undemanding. Julie had the natural ability to carry a tune, and I'd urged her to take some singing lessons, which she had. The more skills an actor developed, the more they were likely to work, I'd told her.

The songs that the three couples would sing had been chosen to catch particular qualities in their characters, and be appropriate for their storylines. Francie's and Rod's characters were in the early stages of falling in love. First they would sing the wistfully romantic ballad "They Say It's Wonderful," from *Annie Get Your Gun*, and then use their comedy talents in "You're Not Sick, You're Just in Love," from *Call Me Madam*. To celebrate eager Julie's pursuit of reluctant Link, those two would start with "You'll Never Get Away from Me," from *Gypsy*. Later, they'd come back with "People Will Say We're in Love," from *Oklahoma*.

Parker and Clarice played *Love*'s least comedic and most deeply committed couple. The songs I'd selected for them reflected that. First, "I'll Know When My Love Comes Along," from *Guys and Dolls*, and then *Camelot*'s "If Ever I Would Leave You," newly arranged as a duet.

Sean, as befitting his character's villainy, would open the show with a very different kind of song from *Camelot*, that hymn to evil: "The Seven Deadly Virtues."

Near the end of the show, Sean would have his second solo, the dramatic "This Nearly Was Mine," from *South Pacific*. It perfectly captured the bitter truth that Sean's character had lost the women he had pursued.

The big finish would pair Link and Rod as comic gangsters singing and dancing to "Brush Up Your Shakespeare" from *Kiss Me Kate*. Checking and rechecking, I determined that they all knew what they were supposed to do, and when they were supposed to do it.

I left the actors to their rehearsing and tracked down Deke Parsons, the property master I'd met yesterday. With his slightly bowed, jeans-clad legs, his narrow hips, and skin so deeply tanned it almost looked like leather, Deke resembled a cowboy much more than he did a man who'd spent twenty years in charge of props for Broadway shows.

"I repainted it just like you wanted. It's all ready to go," he said.

"Where is it?"

"Most of your actors will go onstage from the artist's entrance on the left side, but I'll take your guy behind the set over to the other side. That's where it's hidden, under a tarp behind the stage right flat." He held up a small black box with levers, about half the size of a TV remote. "I'll be operating the controls for him."

OUR DAYTIME STARS on Broadway show was going to be held in the outdoor concert arena on the grounds of the Mount Olympus. It had a raised stage with state-of-the-art sound and lighting systems, and seating for three thousand fans. By thirty minutes before showtime, every seat had been taken. The tickets were free, but the fans had been required to write in to Global Broadcasting for them. Two weeks earlier, Betty had told me the network had had to hire extra clerical help to answer all the requests.

Approaching the stadium, I saw that several hundred more fans had congregated outside the walls, apparently in the wild hope that seats would become available. I felt bad that so many people had to be disappointed, but as I drew closer to the entrance, I saw Tommy supervising the setting up of a Jumbo Tron screen and speakers.

"What a great idea," I said.

Tommy blushed with pride, but pretended to ignore my praise. "This way, the fans out here can at least see and hear the performers," he said, "even though they won't be part of the audience that can ask questions."

I hurried inside the arena to make sure everything had been set up as we'd planned. It was. The elevated stage was arranged with a line of six high, canvas-back chairs. They'd

been marked with the first names of each of the actors—*not*
their character names. Tommy and I thought it was important
during meet-the-fans events that a clear line be drawn between the performers and their roles. The chairs—really
stools with backs and armrests—were a foot higher than a
normal chair would be. This was so that everyone in the raked
stadium seats would have a good view of the people onstage.

Behind the high stools, masking the backstage area, were
billboard-size canvas flats depicting three familiar sights from
our fictional city of Greendale: the old stone wall of Gareth's
restored castle, where Gareth and Jillian first saw each other;
Link's bedroom (a set we'd used a lot during the past three
years); and the rain-slicked alley where Francie's and Rod's
characters met the night in the story when she saved his life,
and where they'd later played some of their funny but tender
getting-to-know-you scenes.

I found Sean standing in front of the long mirror in the
communal makeup room backstage. Closest to the door, he
was the first person I saw when I came in. Looking past him, I
waved a genial "hello" to the other actors who were getting
the finishing touches from the makeup ladies and the hairdresser. Everyone looked excited, full of nervous energy, like
racehorses at the starting line, just before the gates spring
open.

Sean ignored the others as he stared critically at the dark
blue shirt he was wearing and fussed with the collar. First he
turned it up, spy-in-a-trench coat style so that it nearly
reached his ears. Then he patted it down flat.

Looking into the mirror instead of at me, he whined, "This
shirt is so dull. Why can't I wear my gold chains?"

We'd had this costuming discussion before, but I kept im-
patience out of my voice. Instead I said admiringly, "Sean, the
color is a perfect complement to your eyes and hair, and Nicky
doesn't wear gold chains anymore—not since you turned bad.
With the chains you looked like the cute puppy, harmless
Nicky. Now, without them, you have a *dangerous* air about
you."

"Dangerous, huh?" He liked that. His attitude changed in a flash. "Okay." He leaned in close to me and whispered, "What did you do about what I asked?"

I gave him a conspiratorial wink. "Come with me."

Chapter 35

SEAN FOLLOWED SO close behind that he was almost walking on my heels as we worked our way across the back of the stage toward a large object covered by a tarp. Deke Parsons was standing next to it, grinning like a proud new father.

I introduced Sean to Deke, and then said to the property master, "Let's see it."

Deke grabbed the corner of the tarp, and with a matador's dramatic flourish whipped it off to reveal a gorgeous swan boat! The structure, shaped like a swan and painted a fresh, glossy black—black to represent Sean's evil behavior—was six feet long from bill to tail, and five feet tall from the hidden wheels in its base to the crown of the swan's majestic head.

Sean was dazzled. His "Wow" was barely above a whisper.

"I'm going to introduce you last," I said. "You'll ride the swan boat onto the stage standing up. That will add five inches to your height. You'll do your two numbers from the swan—moving up and down its length. When the others are performing and, later, during the Q & A, you'll perch up on this ledge seat next to the swan's head, which will put your sitting height at roughly the same as Link's and Parker's while they're seated. You'll stay in the swan, and ride it offstage at the end of the show."

"Wow."

"I'll be here behind the backdrop with the controls. The folks out front won't see me," Deke told him.

Squinting into the aperture Deke would look through, I saw that the whole stage was visible. So, too, was the arena. I took my first good look at the audience.

I'd expected the crowd to be made up mostly of women of all ages, and it was, but there were quite a few men out there, too. A quick scan gave me the impression that there were at least a couple of hundred males in the audience. Many seemed to be college age, but I could see gray heads, too. Perhaps they were retirees who'd gotten hooked on the show while watching it with their wives.

Although I peered as hard as I could, I didn't see anyone who looked like Lena Cooper, not that it was realistic I would, in all those people. Still, I had the reassuring thought that every one of the hotel's security staff had the woman's photo. It was unlikely that she could be here. Even more comforting than the fact of tight security was the *sense* I had that she wasn't here. For the first time in days, I didn't feel uneasy.

It was time to start the show. I left to make sure the actors were in place as Deke was explaining to Sean how the remote control device operated the swan.

Because the stage was curved in front and in back, it was impossible for the actors standing at the artists' entrance on the far left side of the stage to see Sean and the swan boat on the far right end.

Link, Julie, Rod, Francie, Parker, and Clarice were assembled in a line, ready to go on when their names were announced. Like Sean, they were rigged with microphones so that whatever they sang or said would be heard by the audience. The tiny speakers were artfully concealed in clothing or by long hair. Only if they were seen from the back would the little electronic boxes—each the size of a cigarette pack—affixed to their belts or waistbands be visible.

Right on schedule, the show's accompanist played a fanfare. I took one deep breath, let it out, and walked onto the stage to face three thousand eager fans. The moment I appeared, the crowd broke into applause, but this only lasted for the three or four seconds it took them to realize I wasn't one of the actors. As their warm greeting quickly died, I picked up the cordless microphone that had been placed for me on one of the stools and, moving down to the edge of the stage, addressed the audience.

"That's okay," I said, acknowledging with a smile the last few perfunctory claps. "I know you didn't come to see *me*—whoever the heck *I* am." That line got a few giggles. "I'm Morgan Tyler, one of the producers of *Love of My Life*. I'm going to introduce the members of our cast who are here today—and then I promise to stay out of their way!" The statement was greeted with such unflattering enthusiasm it made me laugh.

I didn't mind not being who they wanted to see. I preferred to avoid the spotlight, but I'd had to learn to speak to an audience in order to give the quarterly presentations of our upcoming story lines to the network's executives, in the hope of winning approval to go ahead. It was a tough room in which to perform, because *that* audience had the power of life and death over stories I really wanted to tell—and the power of professional life and death over Tommy and me.

In happy contrast, the three thousand people I faced today represented the hundreds of thousands of viewers whose loyalty kept our show on the air and kept Tommy and me employed.

I moved a few steps back and to one side, turned toward stage left, and announced the name of the first actor to emerge. One by one Link, Julie, Rod, Francie, Parker, and Clarice came on stage to wild clapping, stomping, whistling, and squealing. I was afraid the audience would be too tired to applaud for Sean, but when he emerged from behind the stage right flat, standing up and waving to the fans from his stunning black swan boat, the people pounded their palms with a fresh burst of energy. None of the six actors who were already sitting on their stools knew about the swan boat. To their credit, when they saw Sean make his unusual entrance, they stood up and applauded him, too.

This was a great reception for all seven of the actors, and I was happy to have it captured on tape, both by our own network crew and by the Mount Olympus camera team. They were shooting from all angles, with the hotel's female camera operator up onstage.

Looking out into the audience, I saw that small cameras and picture phones were going off all over the stadium, as fans recorded the scene on stage. I signaled Jimmy One, who was in the audience in the third row on the far left aisle, and he swung his video rig around to catch the sea of picture-snapping fans.

The swan came to a smooth stop at the end of the line of actors, deliberately next to Clarice. Just as we'd planned for the media dinner the night before, grouping the trio of Parker, Clarice, and Sean at one end was a subtle reference to their interwoven stories.

As the applause began to wane, the first six actors resumed their seats on the high stools. The fans quieted down, and the accompanist began his musical introduction to Sean's first song, "The Seven Deadly Virtues."

As the black swan glided further downstage on hidden wheels, Sean rested an elbow on the swan's head. With a properly wicked expression on his face, he began to sing, "The seven deadly virtues, those ghastly little traps . . ." By the time he reached the line "Let others take the high road, I will take the low . . ." he sounded positively gleeful in his disdain for everything decent and brave in human behavior.

I knew we'd made the right decision in turning Sean's character into a bad boy who brought a shiver of danger into every relationship. Playing evil brought out unexpected charisma in him.

Judging from the hand clapping and the snapping of pictures, the fans loved Sean's number. It was the perfect warm-up for the next song: Link and Julie doing the teasing "You'll Never Get Away from Me." I saw that their performance had more sexual subtext than when they'd rehearsed the routine in New York.

Through one song after another, mixing comedy and drama, the actors—even untrained singers Link, Julie, and Sean—performed as though they'd spent their whole lives in musicals. From the far right side of the stage, I felt myself beaming.

For the big finish, Link and Rod donned fedoras and flashy jackets, teaming up for the comic gangster number from *Kiss Me Kate*, "Brush Up Your Shakespeare."

They were hilarious.

Glancing at my watch, I realized there'd been so much applause after each performance that the entertainment had run considerably longer than the hour we'd allotted for it.

By the time Link and Rod took their bows, we were thirty minutes over. That meant the time fans would have to ask questions of the actors had to be cut down from ninety minutes to an hour. It couldn't be helped. We had to keep to our schedule because Tommy promised the Mount Olympus management that we'd be out of the stadium in time for the stagehands to strike our backdrops and make the complex sound, lighting, and set preparations necessary for the "Tribute to Motown" show that would play the arena tonight.

With the help of the accompanist pounding out what he called "wrap up" music, the fans settled down enough for me to announce that they would now be able to ask the actors questions. "Anything you want to know," I said.

From behind me, Link called out, "But keep it clean, folks!" That got a big laugh.

As we'd planned, at this point the actors moved their stools downstage to the curved apron, placing themselves much closer to the audience. From behind the flats, property master

Deke Parsons maneuvered Sean's swan boat downstage, too, and stopped it next to the repositioned line.

"Okay," I said, "who'd like to ask the first question?"

Hundreds of hands started waving at me, but the first to catch my eye was a girl ten rows back from the stage.

"The girl in the red top," I said, pointing to her. She stood up and Joel hustled over to thrust his cordless mike toward her.

"I want to ask Link: of the women you've had, who's the best kisser?"

Link leaned forward and gave her one of his sexiest grins. "Do you mean *on the show*?" The fans laughed.

Julie's hand shot up. "He told me *I* was."

Playing along with the gag, Francie's hand shot up. Pretending outrage she said, "He told me *I* was!" Lots of laughter.

"Seriously, folks," Link said, squeezing Julie's hand, "I can't answer that. My character's slept with every woman in the show except Clarice."

Clarice feigned horror as she responded, "What a *terrible* thing to say about me!"

That got the biggest laugh of all.

During this exchange, Joel pulled down a set of steps concealed beneath the stage's apron. It was time for me to take my cordless and start roaming through the audience as Joel was doing.

"Over here," Joel yelled, pointing to a teenage girl who was dressed like a pop diva. He aimed the microphone at her. She stood up and said, "Clarice—I'm fifteen and I want to be on a soap like you. My mother's trying to make me stay in school, but didn't you start acting when you were fifteen?"

"Actually, I was twelve when I got my first part—and fifteen when I was cast on *Love of My Life*—but I had to go to school at the same time," Clarice said. "I'll tell you that was *hard*. It's better to get your education first. Susan Lucci graduated from *college* before she got the part of Erica Kane."

Link added, "Stay in school, honey. But take acting lessons

at the same time, and get some experience in school shows and community theater productions."

A very heavy young man in the fifth row stood up awkwardly and asked Francie, "What diet pills did you take to lose so much weight?"

"Absolutely no pills!" Francie said. "I'm losing weight in real life just the way I'm doing it in the story. The details of the plan are posted on the show's Web site for anybody who's interested, but *please don't take pills.* There's too much risk involved. What's your name?"

"George," he said.

Francie smiled and leaned forward, talking to the young man as though he was the only person in the stadium. "George—please don't start *any* nutrition plan without getting your doctor's approval first. Promise me?"

"I promise," he said.

Francie aimed her hands toward the young man and applauded him. "Good for you, George! We don't want to lose you—or any of you out there."

George gazed at her worshipfully and sat back down.

In the second row on my side, an older woman with a pretty face and silver curls was waving at me wildly. She wore a bright pink cotton shirt and matching pink slacks and carried a large straw purse with a pink flamingo on it.

"In the second row," I said, "the woman in pink." She was one seat in from the near end of the row. Leaning carefully past the person on the aisle, I aimed the microphone toward her.

"This is for Rod," she said. "Back home in South Carolina, I have a twenty-six-year-old daughter who's just crazy about you! Are you married in real life? And if you're single, would you be interested in meeting my daughter?"

Up on stage, Rod blushed as fans in the audience laughed at the brazen question and at Rod's embarrassment.

Rod stammered something, but I didn't hear his answer because a man in the first row, directly in front of me, suddenly stood up. He held a cell phone flat on the palm of his left hand, and it was aimed at the stage. I thought it was an odd way to take a photo and then I realized that it *wasn't* a cell phone. I screamed "Gun!"

Loud shots fired and the laughter in the stadium abruptly died. Someone screamed, and people near the shooter scrambled to get out of the way.

Without pausing to think, I leapt at him, striking at the back of his head with my cordless mike. My momentum sent us both crashing to the ground and I felt my slacks rip up the side. I seized the hand that held the gun and clung to it with all my strength. He was bigger than I, and much more powerful, but I wouldn't let go his wrist.

Swearing, he beat at me with his free hand. I knew I couldn't hold onto him for more than another few seconds. I had a confused glimpse of Rod and Link vaulting down from the stage, and then I was pulled away from the shooter's wild thrashing. It was Joel. He pushed me out of the way, then joined the fray.

I stood up and clutched at the rip in my slacks, holding the two sides together, hoping I'd been quick enough so no one saw I was wearing red panties. The shooter was spread-eagled on the ground. Rod and Link each knelt on one of his outstretched arms, and Joel sat down on his back with a thud.

I looked up onstage and silently thanked God that the actors seemed all right.

"Are you all okay?" I called.

Julie gave a shaky laugh. "We're fine."

"Can't say the same for the swan," said Clarice.

I saw what she meant: bullets had blasted a big chunk out of the head of the swan, exactly where Sean had been sitting. Fear shot through me as I realized I didn't see Sean.

Chapter 36

A FEW ROWS away, a woman screamed, "Nicky's been shot!" Reality clashed with unreality—she'd used the name of the character Sean played on the show.

Fans in the back were rushing forward to see what had happened, filling the aisles and colliding with those who were fleeing from the shooter.

A dozen big, uniformed security guards were trying to push their way through the crowd but were having a tough time, caught as they were between the opposing forces of curiosity and panic.

As I reached the steps to the stage, Sean's head slowly rose up from inside the damaged swan.

Parker called down, "He's okay, Morgan!" He leaned into the swan and helped Sean get to his feet.

I saw Sean's mouth working but no words were coming out. He was clearly in shock.

Francie left Julie and hurried over to Sean.

"Take deep breaths," Francie told him.

Sean looked at her dumbly.

Francie grasped Sean by his upper arms and gave him a gentle shake, trying to jog him out of his stunned condition.

"Breathe in!" she commanded. "One . . . two . . . three. Exhale . . . That's good, Sean. You're going to be all right. Again—breathe . . ." Inhaling and exhaling with Francie, Sean caught her rhythm and his dazed expression began to fade.

I turned back to Sean's attacker. Link, Rod, and Joel had him secured.

The gun had skidded under a seat near my foot. I leaned over Link, grabbed the green silk handkerchief from the pocket of his gangster jacket and carefully picked it up.

Holding it so as not to smudge the shooter's fingerprints, I examined the bizarre weapon. It looked just like millions of other cell phones, but it was heavier. Something else was different, but it was very hard to see unless one examined it closely: a tiny line ran around the middle of the phone, indicating that the case was not all of one piece. Needing to use both hands, I forgot about the rip in my slacks as I carefully twisted it at the line. It opened. I saw a chamber that had held four .22 caliber bullets. The phone's antenna was the barrel, and the gun was fired by pressing numbers on what looked like a perfectly normal keypad. No wonder the man was able to bring it in undetected!

Hearing deep, strangled gasps behind me, I swung around to see that they were coming from the now completely helpless shooter. With two fingers holding the cell phone gun by the antenna, I used my other hand to pull at Joel's shoulder. "Let him raise his head—he's going to suffocate!"

"Tough," Joel muttered, but he shifted enough of his weight so that the shooter was able to lift his mouth and chin and gulp in some air.

With his upper torso off the ground far enough so that he could breathe again, the shooter turned his face toward me. Fat tears began to spill from his eyes, cutting through the dirt caking his face.

The man who had almost killed Sean was in his forties, with puffy cheeks and not much chin. Wisps of graying brown hair barely covered the dome of his bulbous head.

I knelt beside him. Keeping my voice gentle, I asked, "Who are you?"

"Bill Kulik," he said between sobs.

I'd never heard of him. I glanced up at Link and at Rod, but they both shook their heads, indicating he was a total stranger to them, too.

The security guards, shouting, "Stand back!" and "Keep calm, folks!" and "Everything's all right!" had finally waded through the mass of fans and were getting the crowd under control.

Any moment the police would be here, but I needed an answer while I still had the chance to talk to Kulik. "Why did you try to kill Sean O'Neil?"

"To save Dinah," he said. Dinah was the name of the character Francie played.

"What do you mean?"

"You people are going to fire somebody . . . budget cuts . . . I got fired in a budget cut. I didn't want it to happen to her—I love Dinah."

"But what made you think—"

"It was in the papers," he said. "You were going to fire somebody! If I killed him—there's your budget cut. I had to save Dinah! Don't you understand?"

Suddenly, I *did* understand. This man had fallen for the network's cruel publicity stunt—the lie that one of our actors would be fired to cut the show's costs. That cynical ploy to hike the ratings had almost got somebody killed, and now would send this poor, unstable man to jail.

The Law of Unintended Consequences, I thought bitterly.

"Dinah was never going to be fired," I told Kulik. "Don't believe everything you read in the papers."

Before I could talk to Kulik any further, officers from the Las Vegas Metropolitan Police Department arrived. (I learned later that when the shooting started, so many people in the audience had dialed 911 on their cell phones that the emergency system had jammed briefly.) I turned the cell phone gun over to the first uniform on the scene. He dropped it into a plastic evidence bag. With both hands free again, I used one of them to hold my ripped slacks together.

Another officer was collecting the videotapes from our Jimmy One and Jimmy Two, and from two of the Mount Olympus cameramen.

Two? Where was the casino's third camera operator—the woman?

Before I could give that any thought, two plainclothes LVPD detectives arrived, ID badges clipped to their jackets. They'd come in through the artists' entrance and were surveying the arena from the stage. I waved them down to our little group.

As the two detectives started descending the steps, the uniformed officer to whom I'd given the cell phone gun hurried over and met the detectives halfway down. The uniform handed the evidence bag with the disguised gun in it to the older of the two detectives, and said something that made all three men look at me. Correction, the older detective, who was now holding the evidence bag, didn't so much "look" at me as *glare*. He muttered something to the uniformed officer, gave him back the evidence bag, and stalked over to where I was standing, next to where Link, Rod, and Joel were holding Kulik down.

The older detective asked, "What happened here?" and pulled a small notebook out of his jacket pocket. Matt and G. G. carried similar little notebooks.

I explained briefly about our show and the shooting that had brought it to a halt.

His next question was an accusation. "You picked up the weapon?"

"With this," I said, holding up the green silk pocket handkerchief. "I was afraid someone in the crowd might take it."

The younger detective, not to be left out of the accusation business, snarled, "You probably damaged the prints."

"It's not exactly a mystery as to who fired the weapon," I said, indicating Kulik.

They looked down. The younger detective asked, "This the shooter?"

"Yes." Who *else* did he think would be prone in the dirt, with three men holding him? But I held my tongue.

The older detective grunted. Matt and G. G. grunted, too. That made me wonder whether police academies gave classes in "grunting," or whether I just brought that out in members of law enforcement.

I didn't wither under his glare, nor flinch at his grunt. Our standoff was broken when this representative of the LVPD said, "I'm Detective Reed." Indicating his young partner, he added, "This is Detective Doyle. Give me your names." I did, including the names of the actors on stage. He wrote them all down, put the notebook away, and barked to Link, Rod, and Joel, "Off!"

They stood up and backed away as Detective Doyle hauled Kulik to his feet and snapped handcuffs on him. Kulik's beefy shoulders drooped as he heard his Miranda rights recited to him.

"We'll want your statements," Detective Reed said. He glanced up at the stage. "All of your statements." He handed me his card.

"Of course, but may we finish our event first?"

"Yeah, okay. What time are you done?"

"At six. Where do you want us to go?"

"If you're staying at the hotel," he said, "we can do it here."

We settled on 6:30. Joel, Link, Rod, the other actors, and I agreed to meet the detectives in the living room of the suite I shared with Tommy.

I watched with a combination of relief and sadness as Detectives Reed and Doyle took away the man who had come to our fan weekend with the sole intention of killing Sean. No longer a mortal threat, Kulik's feet moved in a spiritless shuffle.

Trying to shake that image from my mind, I glanced

around the arena. While some fans had fled the stadium, the vast majority had remained to watch the real-life drama.

Spotting the cordless microphone I'd used to hit Kulik, I puffed into it and was surprised to find it was still live. I gestured to Rod and Link and they followed me back up onstage.

Facing the audience, I said, "Sorry that our Q & A had to be cut short, but I have two pieces of good news. First—and most important—nobody was hurt."

The fans started clapping. I raised my other hand to quiet them. "Second, we're still going to have our 4:30 autographing session, as scheduled, in the Athena Ballroom. There's a sign in the lobby directing you to the Athena's location. Link and Julie, Rod and Francie, Parker, Clarice, and Sean will all be there, so we hope to see as many of you as can make it."

Huge applause at that. When they quieted again, I said, "However, there's going to be one new rule: you won't be allowed to bring your cell phones into the autographing room." That announcement was greeted with a loud chorus of disappointed *Ahhhhhhs*. I couldn't blame them for that; the action had been confined to such a small area I was sure few if any of them had seen the nature of Kulik's weapon, and I had confiscated it pretty fast. I hoped the police would manage to keep that detail out of the press. The last thing I wanted—and probably the last thing law enforcement wanted—was for the public to hear about a cell phone gun. From what I'd seen when I examined it, it didn't look as though it would be too hard to make. There were too many weapons in the hands of the wrong people already.

Chapter 37

I FOUND TOMMY outside the stadium. When he spotted me exiting through the artists' tunnel, he rushed over and threw his arms around me in a fierce bear-hug.

"Oh, Morgan! You're alive!"

"We're all fine." I managed to extract myself from his grip, pulled back, and was surprised to see tears running down his face. I used the only thing I had—the green silk handkerchief from Link's gangster costume—to dab at his cheeks. "Tommy, please don't be upset. Nobody was hurt."

He grabbed my hand in both of his and held on. "I was so worried! We heard shots and then people started screaming, and on the big screen I saw the actors throw themselves onto the floor of the stage. I saw you, too, from the back—I recognized your hair and that blue shirt. You jumped on somebody, and then you fell out of sight! By the time I pushed my way through the crowd, security guards had locked the stadium doors. When the police got here, they started letting some people out, but they wouldn't let me in! What happened?"

Before I could answer, Tommy suddenly blushed. "I saw your . . . uhhh . . . red under thingy on the TV." Suddenly remembering the rip in my slacks, I grabbed the two sides of the fabric and held them together. Tommy said reassuringly, "Probably nobody else saw anything."

With Tommy clutching one of my hands, and me using the other to hold my pants together, I filled him in as I led him back toward the hotel. When I told him the reason Kulik had tried to kill Sean, Tommy jerked to such an abrupt halt I almost got whiplash.

"The publicity stunt. Those *fffing bastards*!"

I was stunned—that was as close as I'd ever heard Tommy come to swearing. He had expressed my feelings exactly. "I've got to change my pants and make a call," I said. "Will you go handle the autograph session?"

Tommy nodded. "Sure."

"Thanks. I'll join you as soon as I can."

"Please be careful!"

"I will," I assured him. "Don't worry."

His face was mournful, and fresh tears glistened in his eyes. "Oh, Morgan." His voice was so low I had to lean forward to hear his next words. "I love this business, but I really hate some of the people in it."

There was nothing I could add to that.

BACK IN OUR Zeus Suite, I changed into black panties and black slacks, put on a fresh blouse, and called Winston Yarborough, the founder and chairman of the board of the Global Broadcasting Network. It was a little past 6:30 in New York, but I guessed that the boss of bosses would still be in his office. Using my cell phone, I dialed his private number.

Winston Yarborough himself picked up.

"Win, it's Morgan." Months ago, when we were working

together to solve a difficult problem facing the network, the chairman had insisted I call him "Win." It had taken me a while to get comfortable with that familiarity. "First, I want you to know that everybody is all right—our people and the fans in the audience—but we just had a close call here in Las Vegas. A disturbed man tried to shoot Sean O'Neil."

"O'Neil? Oh, yes—he's one of your actors." Yarborough prided himself on knowing the names of most of Global's employees, and what they did in the company. It was an astonishing feat of memory. "Tell me."

I did, ending with Bill Kulik explaining why he tried to shoot Sean. "It was that stupid publicity stunt—planting the lie that Global was going to cut one of the actors from each of the shows. Kulik believed it. He said he lost his job in a budget cut, and I think the rumor we'd be dropping cast members sent him over the edge."

"That is unfortunate," Yarborough said.

Sensing he was about to dismiss the matter, I jumped in before he could. "I believe we're at least partly responsible for Kulik's condition," I said. "It would be a marvelous humanitarian gesture if you would arrange that the network pay the cost of getting Kulik the mental and legal help he needs." I fought to keep any hint of sarcasm out of my voice as I added, "The PR people could make a great story out of that."

Silence on the other end of the line. I knew he hadn't hung up on me because I could hear him breathing.

At last he said, "You have made an excellent point, my dear. Where is Mr. Kulik now?"

"The Las Vegas police arrested him. Detectives Reed and Doyle. Do you want me to find out—"

"No, don't do anything else. I'll handle the matter from here." There was a new, hard edge in his voice. "This is not to be repeated, but I am going to find out which of my executives approved that publicity stunt and make sure that he or she contributes to Mr. Kulik's expenses."

"That's fair," I said. "Thank you."

"When will you be back in New York?"

"Tomorrow night. We're booked on the noon plane and we'll get in—"

"Just a minute," he said abruptly. A second later I heard a man's authoritative voice—not Yarborough's—in the background, but I couldn't hear what the voice was saying.

The chairman of the board spoke to me again. "Our real-life drama is on television—both CNN and FOX News."

Yarborough had a wall full of television monitors in his office. The feed from the major networks played all the time, but he only turned up the sound when he saw something that interested him.

"This story can be a publicity bonanza for us. Have the actors give as many media interviews as possible."

"They'll be happy to."

"And I will make those arrangements we discussed," he said. "Call me when you get back to New York."

I told him I would and we said quick good-byes.

No sooner had I pushed "end" than my cell phone rang. I saw a familiar number on the screen.

I pushed the answer button and said, "Hi, Penny."

"Morgan, are you all right? I just saw you on the news—"

On the other end of the line I heard her muffled protest, and then another voice came on—male and angry. It bellowed, "Are you crazy!"

"Is that a rhetorical question, Matt, or do you want to know what happened?"

"I *saw* what happened—you jumped a big guy!"

"Well, you said *you* don't want to see me anymore, so I figured he looked pretty interesting—"

"Don't make jokes! What were you *thinking*?!"

"I wasn't thinking. It was instinct."

"You could have been killed!" He was yelling so loudly I had to hold the phone away from my ear.

"I wasn't killed, Matt. I just ripped my slacks."

"So I saw!"

I heard a welcome little click in my ear. "Sorry to cut this pleasant chat short, but I've got another call coming in."

Right in the middle of his hollering, "Don't hang up on me!" I hung up on him, and greeted the new caller with a relieved, "Hello."

It was Nancy. "Morgan, are you all right!"

I had to go through it all again. At least Nancy didn't yell.

Just as I managed to convince Nancy that her best friend was still in one piece, the phone in the suite began ringing. I tried to ignore it, but instead of it cutting over to the voice mail message system, it just kept on ringing. And ringing. Whoever was calling must be insisting the switchboard keep trying.

"That phone is driving me crazy, I'd better get it," I told Nancy. "I'll call you when I get home tomorrow."

As I disconnected the cell, I crossed the dozen feet to the bedside phone and picked it up. I barely had time to say "Hello."

"Morgan. Thank God." It was Chet. His calm tone didn't disguise the relief in his voice. "I saw you on TV. Do you want me to come to Vegas? I can get a private plane in an hour—"

"No, Chet, don't. I'll be back tomorrow. But thank you for offering, and for not yelling."

His tone remained composed, but there was a note of concern in it. "Why don't I come out there and keep you company?"

"I'm hardly alone. I'm with Tommy, Joel, seven actors, two makeup ladies, a hairdresser, and two cameramen." All at once a realization struck me. "I just remembered something."

"What?"

"Four men and a woman were filming our event—two men from the network and the other three who were shooting a promotional piece for the hotel. When I saw the Las Vegas police confiscating their tapes, one of the hotel camera people—the woman—was missing. She was shooting from the stage, and must have slipped out with her tape."

Chet finished my thought. "And sold it to the media. For footage like that, she probably made a bundle. You looked great, by the way."

I didn't like the sound of that. "Tommy said he only saw me from the back."

"You were full frontal—so to speak—on CNN. Smacking the guy on his head and throwing yourself onto his back. I have to tell you, it made me jealous as hell." Then I could almost see him smiling as he added, "By the way—red panties under navy blue slacks . . . There are *two* Morgan Tylers."

"And both of us are saying good-bye!"

BY THE TIME the actors, Joel, and I had given our statements to the satisfaction of Detectives Reed and Doyle, and they had packed up their tape recorders and notebooks and departed, it was after nine P.M.

Tommy announced he was taking everybody to dinner. "A champagne and caviar celebration."

I begged off, claiming that I wanted to work on a script. The truth was I was exhausted. All I wanted was to sink up to my earlobes in a warm, foamy bath.

An hour later—clean, relaxed, and blissfully alone—I put on my Bruce Lee T-shirt and went into the suite's living room to pluck some fruit from the management's complimentary basket. I found something better: a note from Tommy propped up on a tray from room service. In his neat, precise handwriting, it said, "Enjoy!"

While I was soaking, Tommy, in one of his thoughtful gestures, had ordered my favorite snack: a plate of deviled eggs. With it, a bottle of merlot (opened, so it could "breathe") and a platter of smoked salmon. I was too tired for smoked salmon, but I poured a glass of the red wine and ate the entire order of deviled eggs.

Chapter 38

I WAS SOUND asleep when the phone rang. Opening one eye, I peered at the digital beside clock. Big green numbers said four A.M.

That snapped me fully awake. *Now what's happened?* I tried not to sound as afraid as I felt. "Hello?"

"Tommmmeeeee. Oh, Tommmmmmeeeee?" It was a female voice, and she didn't sound entirely sober. She demanded, "What are you doing in Tommy's bedroom?"

"This *isn't* his room."

She was insistent. "Of course it is, because the hotel person put me through." In a childlike voice she said, "Can Tommy come out to play?"

"Look, this really isn't his room, but if you'll give me your name and number I'll go upstairs and have him call you back." For Tommy's sake, I was determined to be polite.

"Oh, pooh!" She expelled a deep sigh. "All right. Tell Tommylamb to call Fuchsia."

"Fuchsia?"

"That's my name—Fuchsia, like the color."

I turned on the bedside lamp and sat up. "Where can he reach you?"

"I'm at the Kitty Kat Lounge up on Tropicana Avenue." She giggled a little wildly. "Tell him to hurry, or my cute little *window of opportunity* will be closed."

I wanted to gag.

"Now you be sure to tell him that?" A lot more giggling. It sounded as though another girl was with her.

I assured Fuchsia-like-the-color that I would repeat every word. (And then some, I added silently.) Hanging up, I wiggled my feet into the black cat bedroom slippers, put the robe on over my T-shirt and went upstairs to give Tommy his message.

He didn't answer my knock on his door. I called his name and knocked again. Still no answer. Leaning against the door to listen, I didn't hear any sound from inside his room.

"Tommy?" I turned the knob and carefully opened the door. "Tommy?"

Silence. I ran my hand over the wall next to the door, found the light switch, flipped it on, and got a shock. The room was empty—and the bed hadn't been slept in.

I felt my heart begin to pound. *What's happened to Tommy?*

It was now 4:15 in Las Vegas, which meant 7:15 in New York City. Matt would be awake, and probably still at home.

I ran downstairs and snatched up my cell phone. Not wanting to worry Penny if she answered their home phone, I dialed Matt on his cell. He picked up on the second ring.

"Matt, I'm sorry about our fight yesterday—"

He must have calculated the time in Las Vegas because he didn't waste words on small talk. "What's the matter? Are you all right?"

"It's Tommy—he's missing."

"Be more specific."

"We have a two-bedroom suite. It's after four in the morning and he isn't in his room."

"Hmmm. How old is Tommy, forty?"

"Thirty-five."

"And he's a bachelor?"

"Matt, what's that got to do—"

"You're upset because a thirty-five-year-old unmarried man is staying out all night in *Las Vegas*?"

Matt was making fun of me, but he had a point. "Do I sound like a total idiot?"

There was amusement in his voice. "Maybe not *total*. But your worrying about him seems a little weird."

That was too much. "A man I had lunch with was murdered, a girl who should be in a mental hospital has been stalking Link, and a deluded victim of cost-cutting just tried to shoot Sean to save an actress's job. Welcome to my world!"

The sharp sound of a buzzer interrupted us. Matt heard it too. "What's that?" he asked.

Profound relief washed over me. Hurrying to the front door, I said, "Tommy probably lost his card key."

As I reached for the knob Matt said, "Don't hang up—I want to hear you explain why you're calling the police on him."

I opened the door, but it wasn't Tommy on the other side. It was a maid with an armload of towels and a laundry cart. Then she stepped closer and I saw her face. "Lena?"

Dropping the towels, her hand came up and she sprayed me in the eyes with something sharp and blinding. Before I could run, or scream, I felt a needle's jab in my arm. From far, far away, I heard Matt's voice calling, "Morgan? Morgan!"

A heavy, suffocating blackness closed over me, and I was falling.

Chapter 39

IT WAS THE jolting that woke me.

My skull felt as though it was full of tiny jackhammers attacking tiny blocks of cement. I didn't mind the pain in my head; it meant I was alive.

Little by little, as my mind began to clear, I took inventory of my situation.

It wasn't good.

I was lying on my right side, bound at the wrists and ankles, blindfolded, and inside something that was moving. A car.

I pressed my chin down to touch my shoulder and the skin of my jaw felt the texture of silk. I must still be wearing the T-shirt and robe I was in when I opened the door to the suite. Wiggling my toes, I felt the soft cat slippers on my feet.

Okay. This is encouraging. While I'm not ready to meet and greet distinguished visitors, at least I'm not naked.

Rubbing my cheek against the floor of the car, I managed

to loosen the blindfold enough to slip it off my eyes. Unfortunately, it was too dark to see anything.

Because my hands had been tied in front of me instead of behind my back, I was able to stretch my arms out enough to explore a little. A few inches above my head, I touched metal. Okay, I was in the trunk of this moving vehicle. Judging by the guttural whine of the motor and the clattering of metal parts, it was an old clunker, being driven over a road that was paved but hadn't been well maintained. Every time we hit a pothole, my teeth rattled and the pain in my head shot up into the red zone: Agony.

The biting cold of a steel slab beneath my bare right leg meant there was no carpet, not even a rubber mat on the floor of the trunk. Another sign the car was old. Twisting as much as possible in close quarters, and using my hands and feet, I searched for anything I could utilize to free myself or to wield as a defensive weapon.

Nothing. There wasn't even a spare tire. *I* was the only object in the trunk.

A little bit of air was coming in from someplace. So were exhaust fumes and the odor of gasoline, a combination that was slightly nauseating. Instead of breathing through my nose, I tried to take in just enough air through my mouth to stay conscious.

There was some traffic noise outside, but not much. Since I'd been awake, only three or four vehicles had passed us. Way off in the distance, I heard the toot of a horn and the squeal of a truck's air brakes, but it didn't sound as though that vehicle was on the same route we were. Apparently, we had taken "the road less traveled."

The car I was in was moving at a steady pace, as though the driver knew exactly where she was going.

She . . . Lena.

A car! That was how Lena got to Las Vegas without being spotted and stopped by Bobby Novello's army of hired help. She drove.

Bobby had been sure he had everything covered. His East

Coast troops were watching the departing planes, trains, and buses in New York and New Jersey. His Nevada operatives had staked out the arriving planes, trains, and buses. It hadn't occurred to any of us that Lena Cooper might *drive* to Las Vegas. I hadn't thought of it because Bobby told me the DMV had revoked her driver's license. Because she couldn't have rented a car without one, she probably bought this junker for cash, from somebody who didn't bother about formalities.

Mentally, I kicked myself. What an idiot I was, blithely assuming that the woman who had broken into Link's apartment and behaved like a rampaging tornado, and who might already have committed a murder, would balk at driving without a license!

My eyes still burned. Lena must have blasted me with pepper spray before she jabbed me in the arm with the drug that knocked me out. I hoped she'd at least used a clean needle.

A new thought: why didn't she kill me? She had the perfect opportunity when we were alone in the suite. I presumed she'd bundled me into the laundry cart she had when she came to the door disguised as a maid. But she must have taken a big risk unloading my unconscious body into the car.

I felt a wild surge of hope; maybe Lena wasn't planning to kill me after all.

The wave of euphoria didn't last very long because the practical side of my brain kicked in, forcing me to admit that being kidnapped and driven heaven knows where could not be regarded as a *good* sign. Even by a perpetual optimist like me.

The previous head writer on *Love of My Life* once told me, "After talent, which should be a given, the single most important quality a writer must have is the absolute refusal to face facts." That had sounded good at the time, but I don't think he'd ever been trussed up like a Thanksgiving turkey and dumped into the trunk of a car. There are just some facts that *have* to be faced.

How much time had passed since I'd opened the door to the suite? How long had I been unconscious? No light was coming in with the air, so it must still be dark outside.

Jeopardy wasn't exactly a stranger in my life, but this was the worst spot I'd ever been in. I had no idea how much time I had before the car stopped and the next chapter in this horror story would begin.

Exploring again, I traced my fingers along the trunk's lid and down one side, then moved inward until I touched a patch of metal so rusted-out it formed a lattice of holes. The casing around one of the lights was corroded, too. I poked the tip of my finger into one of the rust holes, but the metal was sharp and cut my skin. Carefully, I withdrew the finger. I didn't dare injure myself. If I was going to survive, I would need every part of my body in good working order.

I squirmed around so that my feet were near the rusted metal. If I could kick it out, I might be able to attract the attention of a car coming up behind us. How could a trailing driver miss the sight of human feet waving at him from the closed trunk of the car ahead? While I was getting into position, the car slowed a bit, and then it swerved into a sharp right turn and speeded up again.

Suddenly we were bumping along a road so rough it made the previous surface we'd been on feel like a super highway. I was bouncing around like a ping-pong ball in a lottery drawing. Using my arms to shield my head from bashing against the top of the trunk, I tried to think. We'd left the main road. Sooner or later this car was going to stop. When it did, I had to be ready with a plan of action.

AS NEARLY AS I could track the time, it had been at least an hour since we'd left the main road. I maneuvered myself around so that I was again facing the rear of the car.

The rusted-out patches were letting in little shafts of weak light now. It was the pewter gray intimation of dawn.

Had Tommy come back to the hotel? And if he had, would he think to look in my room? Probably not. Why would he? Nothing was planned for this morning. Tommy or Joel might not realize I had disappeared until it was time to leave for the airport.

I strained to remember my conversation with Matt. I didn't think we'd said good-bye before I answered the door. Even though we were being pleasant to each other, would Matt assume I'd hung up on him again?

I realized the car was slowing down. In another few seconds it stopped, and the driver killed the engine.

Killed the engine. I shuddered. Under the circumstances, that was a really unfortunate choice of verbs. I vowed never again to use the word *kill* carelessly.

Hardly daring to breathe, I tensed, listening.

Silence. No traffic sounds. No indications at all of human life. Not even the barking of a dog. It was a good guess that we were far away from anyone who could help me.

With nothing to use as a weapon, I clenched my fists into tight balls. I would pretend to be unconscious, and when Lena pulled me out of the trunk, I'd surprise her by shooting my fists up and ramming her under the chin as hard as I could.

I heard the driver's door open and close.

I was ready.

Then I heard another sound that sent a spasm of fear through me.

The passenger door opened and closed.

Lena was not alone.

Chapter 40

FOOTSTEPS CRUNCHED ON the surface of the road as two people approached the rear of the car. I had hoped to overpower Lena by surprising her with the double-fist upper cut, but with my hands and feet tied how could I escape from two kidnappers?

I had to come up with an idea fast.

Voices outside the car: a man's and a woman's.

I strained to hear what they were saying, but I couldn't make out the words.

The woman was speaking in Lena's drab monotone. There was something familiar about the man's voice, too. In its timbre, its resonance. It reminded me of . . . Link?

No, it couldn't be Link. He'd never be a party to kidnapping me!

Or would he?

When the problem with Lena began, Chet had asked if I was sure that Link and Lena hadn't had some prior relationship. I told him Link denied it, and I was positive he was telling the truth.

The voices became more intense. They seemed to be arguing, but I couldn't distinguish enough to make sense of it.

If the man were Link, he might be here to help me . . .

No, Link would have stopped her before we'd come way out to—wherever we were.

It couldn't be Link . . .

Or could it? We'd worked together for three years, but I didn't know much about him. I knew he was keeping a secret—but, then, to be fair, so was I.

Had he discovered that I'd had Bobby Novello investigate him a few months ago, to find out what he was hiding? I'd told Bobby if Link's secret wasn't something that would make me fire him or turn him in to the police—such as if he'd murdered someone, or if he abused women or children or animals—then I didn't want to know what it was. Let Link have his privacy.

Bobby cleared Link of suspicion in that previous case, assuring me Link wasn't concealing anything that would force me to take action.

The conversation outside the car ceased. Metal scraped against metal as a key was inserted in the trunk's lock.

Out of time and options, I drew my legs back, prepared to kick with all of my strength at whoever opened the trunk. It could be my last act on earth, but I was not going to die without putting up the fight of my life.

The lid of the trunk rose. I saw Lena's torso; she was wearing the same blue coat that I'd been watching for around every corner. The moment the lid was far enough open, I thrust my legs out and smashed her in the midsection with my heels. She let out a piercing cry and reeled backward. Off balance, she fell to the ground with a thud.

Struggling to her feet, Lena shrieked, "She's awake!"

Suddenly I was screaming louder than Lena, cursing at her, demanding to be let go—praying for the miracle that there was someone in this desolate place who would hear me. Fueled by righteous anger, a surge of adrenaline, and a furious will to live, I hooked the back of my knees over the edge of the trunk. I was almost out of the car when the man—concealing his face with a wool blanket he held up in front of him—lunged. Throwing the abrasive fabric over me, he shoved me backward with such force it caused my head to bang against the metal roof of the trunk. I saw shooting fragments of colored lights and heard a cacophonous ringing of bells in my ears.

I lashed out again with my legs and caught the man on the side of his chest. I heard a satisfying *crack* as he yowled in pain. Raging, I kicked him again. Then someone stabbed a needle deep into my arm. I felt myself sinking back into the cold black ocean of unconsciousness.

Chapter 41

SCORCHING RAYS BAKE my flesh . . . My mouth and nose are full of sand . . . I'm in the middle of a simoom . . .

Nancy whispered: "What's a simoom?"

"A hot, dry wind in the African desert."

Matt: "There isn't any wind."

Chet: "You aren't in Africa."

"Then where am I?"

Nancy: "In trouble."

Matt, echoing: "Trouble"

Chet, urging: "Wake up . . . wake up . . ."

Penny, pleading: "Don't die . . . don't die . . ."

Their words became chants accompanied by the music of a thousand discordant bells. Then their voices began to fade. My friends were disappearing.

"Don't leave me!"

My cry was too late. They'd vanished.

Struggling against the monster that was trying to smother me, I fought my way up a long, spiraling, lightless cone, all the way to the funnel's mouth. All the way to consciousness. The little jackhammers were back. My eyelids felt weighted down with grit. Slowly, I managed to force my eyes open.

I was lying facedown. Outdoors. On a hot, hard-baked dirt surface. Gradually, I became aware of stones digging into my flesh. I could feel the heavy weight of the sun on my exposed skin. Moving carefully, experimentally, I discovered that the bonds on my wrists and ankles were gone. Using my hands for leverage, I eased my chest off the ground. Too light-headed to stand up yet, I maneuvered into a sitting position. Thick, searing air settled around me like a shroud, making it uncomfortable to breathe deeply.

It seemed as though every muscle in my body ached, but a quick check showed no bones were broken. Now that I was sitting up, the throbbing in my head began to subside a little. So did the ringing in my ears.

Doing a slow 360, I scanned my surroundings, hoping to see some landmark I recognized. Nothing was familiar. All I could see was a limitless vista of scrubby, wilted plants that had been bleached of any trace of color by the blistering sun. The land was mostly flat, with a few outcroppings of rocks, and mountains many miles in the distance. The sun blazed almost directly overhead, which meant it must be close to noon. The hottest time of the day, and no shelter that I could see from where I sat.

Hoping for a better view, one that would suggest a direction to go, I got unsteadily to my feet. I realized that there was something in the robe's pocket that was causing the material to sag. I plunged my hand down and pulled out a miracle—a half-filled liter bottle of water.

Water!

It was such a thrilling discovery it took a few seconds before I realized someone—Lena?—had put it in my pocket.

But *why*? Did she, or he, or some unknown player want to save me? Or to have me die in this desert more slowly?

Holding the bottle, staring at it, I realized I was desperately thirsty. It took every ounce of self-control I had, but I limited myself to three small sips. I couldn't guess how long this half bottle would have to last.

The little amount of water seemed to help me think. Screwing the top on tight, I clutched the bottle and forced myself to think logically, to come up with a plan.

Sharp rocks gouged painfully through the thin soles of my slippers. In this harsh, stony terrain, they weren't much better than being barefooted.

It was clear I had a horribly long trek ahead of me in this pitiless sun. Suppose I chose the wrong direction, away from civilization, and ended up deeper in the desert? That would mean almost certain death.

I decided to head *away* from the mountains. Civilization, a road, a hunting trail, tire tracks that led to *something* were more likely to be found on flat land.

I took inventory of my assets; it was a short list. Besides the nearly useless slippers, I was wearing my knee-length Bruce Lee T-shirt and the dark blue silk robe. To reach anywhere, I had to traverse harsh, rocky terrain. In my current wardrobe, my tender city feet would be so badly lacerated within a hundred yards I wouldn't be able to walk. If I couldn't walk, I'd very likely die of starvation and dehydration. Unless impatient vultures got me first.

None of those images was appealing.

Okay—I'll use what I've got.

Carefully, I put down the water bottle, untied the robe, and shrugged out of it. I needed the sleeves to protect my arms, but with the T-shirt on, I could cut the material off at the waist.

The fabric resisted my efforts to tear it apart. Not wanting to risk breaking a tooth, I peered at the ground until I spotted a jagged rock nearby. Attacking the silk with the sharpest edge, I made a hole and started ripping.

I put the top part of the robe back on and tied the two ends together under my bust. Then I ripped the rest of the fabric in two.

Using the sharp rock again, I hacked at the robe's long silk belt until I was able to tear it in two parts.

Folding the bulk of the silk over and over until I had two thick pads, I took my slippers off, stuffed the pads inside, and put the slippers back on. My emergency innersoles wouldn't last forever in this rough desert. I had to find help before I wore them through.

As a last act of creativity, I took the two long, narrow strips of belt fabric and used them to secure the slippers on my feet by winding the bands over and under, over and under, and finally tying them around my ankles.

The sun was blazing down on me, threatening to cook my brain, and I didn't have anything to protect my head. I knew I wouldn't last long if I didn't find shelter.

I picked up my precious—priceless—bottle of water and set off, walking carefully in my improvised desert boots, my back to the mountains. I wasn't worried about encountering snakes. During this brutal time of day, every self-respecting reptile was dozing under a rock or down a hole. But at night it would be a different matter.

No use worrying about that yet.

THERE ARE TIMES when it's better to be lucky than to be smart.

Just when I thought I was too beaten down by the heat and too weakened by hunger and thirst to go on more than another few yards, I rounded a pile of boulders and found myself facing a frame of weathered timbers as thick as railroad ties.

Oh, thank you, God!

The sturdy timbers marked the entrance to what looked like an old mine that had been hacked into the rocks, probably by men who had risked their lives to find their fortunes. With a last surge of energy, I rushed headlong toward that dark mouth in the rocks.

Chapter 42

STEPPING THROUGH THE opening, I saw that I'd guessed right; what I'd found was a long-forsaken mine. The excavation's ceiling was barely higher than the top of my head. Men taller than my five feet, six inches would have had to stoop.

Outside, the air was so searing hot it was painful to take a deep breath. It wasn't much cooler inside the mouth of the mine, but at least here I was safe from the fierce sun.

It took a few moments for my eyes to adjust to the contrast from blinding bright to sudden dimness. As my vision gradually sharpened, I saw that the mine's entrance led into a tunnel of such utter blackness I couldn't distinguish anything farther than a few feet down its length. The place reeked of dust and decay and of things long dead. Sound was dead in here, too. The scrape of my slippers on the dirt was harsh in my ears.

Broken segments of metal tracks were partially embedded in the tunnel's floor. Against the rock wall, lying on its side, was a battered old cart, caked with dirt, the metal corroded.

Decades ago, maybe a hundred years ago, it must have rolled on those tracks, transporting whatever had been hewed out from the rocks. Picturing the scene, I imagined how awful it must have been laboring in this hellish landscape, surrounded by desolation. I hoped the miners who'd done the hacking and the hauling had found enough gold or silver to make their labor worthwhile.

Taking a few more sips of water, I looked at the cart again and imagined myself riding in it—the way Sean rode in the swan boat—rolling across the desert flats, propelled by something I could use as an oar . . .

Why not? If I could find an oar substitute to use. Setting the water bottle down, I went to the cart and grabbed the high side of it, intending to tip it upright.

The moment my hands touched the rim, I realized the thing was made of iron, and probably weighed a ton. Refusing to face reality, I pulled at that cart with all of my strength. I groaned and tugged and strained until my head felt light and there was a high-pitched whistle blowing in my ears. Finally admitting defeat, I let go. My palms were sticky with blood. A wave of nausea swept over me. Fearing I was about to faint, I sat down on the ground. Energy spent, I leaned my head against the side of the gritty cart and closed my eyes. Just for a minute.

I awoke with a start to discover I was lying on the ground. At first I didn't know where I was, but as I took in my bleak surroundings, I began to remember. Outside, the scorching sun had gone down. Cool darkness must be approaching, but it wasn't yet night. A few inches from my nose, a foot-long lizard with scaly, lead gray skin stared at me as its pale pinkish tongue flicked in and out of its mouth.

I wondered if that lizard was as hungry as I was and if I could catch it.

It must have read my intent because it turned rapidly and darted into the safety of the dark tunnel. I thought, ruefully, that when it comes to self-preservation, animals are much smarter than human beings. In Africa, the animals sensed when we were on their turf with only the benign intention of photographing them. They would be surprisingly cooperative, letting us get close enough to capture amazing moments. Even female lions with their cubs seemed to know we posed no danger to them. But if we were after food—for example, stalking an old male Tommy, then suddenly all of the many thousands of Thompson's gazelles vanished into the bush, becoming as invisible as the extinct Greater Kudu. Back at camp on those nights we made do with biscuits and hard cheese.

Here I'd been lusting to eat a lizard! Without any way to cook it, what was I thinking? What I wouldn't give for some of those stale biscuits and the awful cheese I used to hate. I took another swallow from the bottle. There wasn't much left. It was so hot; I must have been drinking more than I'd thought I was.

How long had it been since I'd eaten anything? About twenty-four hours. Medically insignificant; I'd be able to live for quite a while without food.

In the desert, without water . . . different story.

I simply had to get to civilization before I died from dehydration.

Grasping the rim of the cart—careful not to stand too fast—I pulled myself up. It was time to start walking.

AS NEARLY AS I could calculate, I'd been trudging through this barren landscape for about three hours. The moon was bright; at least I could see the ground well enough to avoid stumbling into prairie dog holes and snapping an ankle. Light was the good news. The bad was that the temperature had plunged from ferociously hot during the day to so cold now that I was shivering in my flimsy T-shirt and the little bolero top that was left of my robe. At least I was still able to walk in my padded slippers. Silk was a tough fabric. I vowed to thank Tommy again for the robe and to write a note of appreciation to the manufacturer. "Highly recommended for kidnap victims forced to wander in the desert." Maybe they'd ask me to give an endorsement.

No water left. That's okay. It's night. I won't be so thirsty at night.

When I get out of this mess I'm going to buy some pepper spray.

When I get out of this mess . . .

Optimistic, making plans for later. I wondered what odds the gamblers in Las Vegas would give that I'd even have a *later*?

I COULDN'T KEEP track of how much time had passed since I left the old mine, but I'd discovered that it didn't feel so cold if I just kept *thinking*. About anything.

The cynic's rebuttal to my favorite poem, Kipling's "If," went "If you can keep your head when all about you are losing theirs—it's just possible you don't understand the situation." Not bad . . .

My favorite part of the original poem goes, "If you can hang on when there's nothing in you, except the will that says to you, hang on . . ."

Something like that.

Might have mangled the words a little, but that's the idea. Hang on . . . Hang on . . .

I can't remember the name *he* called me, the terrible man I hated—the name he gave me before I was found . . . I can't remember . . . That's good, forgetting some things . . . but we really don't forget . . . memories come sneaking back in at night, when you think you're safe . . . I'm not that little girl any more. I'm Morgan now . . . Morgan . . . My feet are hurting . . . sharp rocks getting through the pads . . .

Trying to think of a new story for the show . . . A young story line . . .

Two high school girls, seniors, rivals in love with the same man . . . maybe an older man . . . One girl's rich and the other's poor. The poor girl thinks the rich girl has everything . . . wants to hurt her. She's seen something that she knows will devastate the rich girl . . . she's seen the rich girl's mother kissing a man who's not her husband . . . it wasn't just a friendly kiss, either. It's obvious rich girl's mother is cheating on rich girl's father. Poor girl can't wait to drop that little bombshell . . . sometime when it's going to hurt rich girl the most . . .

Poor girl doesn't know it, but rich girl envies what the poor girl has: the poor girl's loving mother . . . A loving mother . . . hard for me to write . . . never had one . . . Ask Tommy to find a Madonna type actress—Christ's Madonna, not the singer . . . someone who looks like . . . Penny. Penny Cavanaugh . . . Matt's Aunt Penny . . .

Head aches . . . too tired to think of story . . . feet hurt too much . . .

Have to think about something . . . have to keep going . . . "when there is nothing left in you except the will that says to me . . ."

Can't remember the rest . . .

Matt's face in my head . . . and Nancy's . . . Chet's face . . . Penny's face . . .

Nico's face . . . no, don't want to think about Nico . . . put him away in the story I'm writing . . . keep him locked in a script where he can't confuse me . . .

I don't want a fantasy lover. I'm not afraid of real life any more . . .

I can't swallow . . . throat feels dry as sand . . . I'm so thirsty . . . I want to cry, but I can't . . .

Up ahead . . . a glow . . . ?

Getting closer . . . it's fire . . . camp fire . . . Indians . . . I mean Native Americans . . . sitting around a campfire. Wrapped in blankets . . . looking up at me . . . faces bright in the dancing light of the flames . . . I hear a scratchy voice that sounds strangely like mine, "I'm sorry to bother you," my distant voice is saying to the Native Americans, "but does anybody have a cell phone?"

The last thing I hear is a man's cultured voice: "She's fainting!"

Chapter 43

MY EYES BLINKED open to see an unfamiliar room. I was lying in a narrow bed. The right side of my face rested against a man's chest.

My first word was, "Oh!"

"It's okay, honey. You're all right now."

I turned my face up to the voice. "Chet?"

He was next to me, lying on the bed. His long legs were stretched out on top of the white sheet and blanket that covered me; his arms cradled me gently. I was in a private room—there was only the one bed. The room was large and clean and smelled of disinfectant. The walls were painted a fresh white and dotted with a series of framed seascapes. Daylight filtered in through sheer pale green curtains drawn across the window.

"She's awake!" Bobby Novello got up from an armchair in the corner.

I licked my lips; they felt dry and cracked. "I hate to sound like a cliché, but where am I?"

"You're in North Las Vegas Memorial Hospital," Chet said. "It's a fine facility—you've been getting great care."

With his free hand, Chet reached toward the nightstand and picked up a glass of water with a straw, holding it so that I could take some welcome sips. I wanted to throw away the straw and gulp it all down, but I restrained myself. There was an IV attached to a needle inserted into my left arm. I guessed it was hydrating me.

"How long have I . . ." My voice was hoarse; I cleared my throat. "What day is this?"

"You disappeared thirty-six hours ago," Chet said. "It's 4:30 Monday afternoon now."

Bobby pulled a wooden straight back chair that was beside the bed even closer and leaned toward me. He tried to comb his thick head of rosy gold curls with his hands. I saw that his handsome face was tight with worry, and his eyes looked puffy from lack of sleep.

"You were found in Death Valley late last night, near the Nevada–California border," Bobby said. "From the condition you were in—blistered, bleeding, pretty much out of your head—it's a miracle you survived."

"You stumbled into the camp of a family of Paiute Indians," said Chet, "and succeeded in becoming a local legend."

I was afraid to ask. "What did I do?"

Bobby grinned. "You very politely asked if anybody around the camp fire had a cell phone. Then you keeled over."

"Lucky for you, one of them did," Chet said. "They're a family of modern Paiutes who live in Reno. They were out in the desert for a yearly celebration of their ancestors. The man who had the cell phone is a doctor. He gave you first aid until they could get you to the nearest emergency room."

"On the way he called the police, to find out if they had any idea who you were," Bobby said. "Boy, did they!"

I was concentrating hard to follow this tag team form of storytelling, but what Bobby just said was confusing. "What do you mean?"

"Since six o'clock Sunday morning, every cop and highway

patrol officer in Nevada—and along the borders of California, Utah, and Arizona—has had your description. The head of your network pounded on the governors to make your disappearance their priority."

"Winston Yarborough? How did he find out?"

Chet and Bobby exchanged a brief glance before Chet said, "You were talking to Phoenix when you were grabbed. He heard it. When he couldn't get you back on the phone he called the Mount Olympus's manager and made him check your room. The door was slightly ajar, your cell phone was on the floor, a chair had been knocked over."

Bobby picked up the story. "Phoenix called the Las Vegas cops, told them you were 'family' and to use every effort to find you. He put it a little more crudely, but that's the gist. Then . . ." Bobby tossed the conversational ball back to Chet.

"Then Phoenix called me."

"*You*?"

"Yep. Even though he can't stand me." Chet's tone was sardonic. "His jaw clenches whenever we're in the same room, but I've got to give the man credit. He wanted to come out here and lead the search for you, but he's stuck in New York on a case he can't leave. So he called me."

"And Chet called me," Bobby said. "While we were on our way to the airport to get the plane Chet hired, I called my Nevada guys and started them looking for you."

"Penny heard what happened because she was there at the house with Phoenix. While he was calling the Las Vegas PD, she called Nancy." Chet's voice warmed with admiration as he added, "Your friend Nancy doesn't waste any time—she went right to the head of your network. That Yarborough is a man who can move mountains—or at least galvanize politicians."

I was fighting back tears. For one of the rare times in my life, I didn't know what to say.

Bobby said, "There's one funny bit. It was a wild scene when we got here. Your photos going out over the wires, 'Breaking News' TV stories every half hour, cops pulled off regular tours. One of the uniforms asked me, 'What does this woman *do* that makes her so important?' "

"What did you say?"

"I told him you write a soap opera."

I heard Chet correct Bobby, saying, "She calls it daytime drama," when I noticed I was clenching something in my left hand. Carefully uncurling my fingers I saw an object that shocked me. I must have made a sound, because suddenly Chet and Bobby were asking me what was the matter.

"Nothing," I said. "Nothing, really."

"What's that in your hand?" Chet leaned over for closer look. "It's a rose?"

A white rose. Just the blossom. Wilted now, it must have been closed in my hand for hours. Doing my best to make the question sound casual, I asked, "Who's been in my room?"

"Nobody—not since Bobby and I arrived a little before six this morning. Except nurses, to check your vital signs."

"There was a doctor here," Bobby reminded him.

"A doctor?"

"Oh, yes. That's right," Chet said. "He was sitting with you when we came in. Then he left."

"What did he look like?" I asked.

Chet shrugged. "Frankly, I was so happy to see you alive I didn't notice."

"Early forties, five-ten, 175 pounds, black hair, gray eyes, ID badge in the name of 'R. Michaels, M.D.,' wearing light blue hospital scrubs and expensive shoes," Bobby said. "It was too dim in here to see the brand of the shoes."

Chet and I stared at Bobby, awestruck. His cheeks colored slightly in embarrassment. "Well, I do this for a living," he said.

Bobby looked at me, an unspoken question in his eyes. Before he, or Chet, could put the question into words, I asked them, "When can I go home?"

Chet stood up and slipped his shoes on. "I'll find out."

As soon as Chet was out of the room, Bobby said quietly, "You know who the guy in the doctor drag was, don't you?"

My fingers tightened around the wilted white rose. I didn't want to lie to Bobby, so I replied, "There's nothing to worry about."

"You and I might have a difference of opinion on that subject," he said.

Chapter 44

CHET RETURNED TO the room, beaming. "A doctor's going to come by in the next half hour to look you over. If he doesn't find anything alarming, you'll be discharged."

"Wonderful!" I was so eager to be part of the action again, I started to get up.

Bobby leaned forward to stop me. "Don't. You'll rip out your IV."

"Try to be a *patient* patient, okay?" Chet said.

I wasn't happy about it, but I settled back against the pillows.

Chet took a second straight-back visitor's chair from against the wall and placed it beside Bobby's. "How much do you remember of what happened?"

I told them about Lena surprising me at the door of the suite with pepper spray and the needle with a knockout drug, of waking up in the trunk of an old car, and discovering when the car finally stopped that a man was with Lena.

"Did you recognize him, or had you seen him before?" Bobby asked.

"I couldn't see his face, but I heard his voice. There was something familiar about it, but I couldn't place it at the time. He sounded like an actor, his voice had that kind of trained resonance. At first I was afraid it was Link—"

Chet shook his head. "When Tommy got back to the suite about six o'clock Sunday morning and found it swarming with cops, he raced around to all the other rooms to see if you were there. Link was with a woman—Julie something."

"Julie Lawson," Bobby said.

Chet nodded, "That's her name."

"I finally figured out it wasn't Link," I said, "but I *had* heard that voice before. It nagged at me for hours while I was wandering around. It was so elusive, always just out of reach. Finally hit me, incredible as the idea was. The voice I'd heard was Mitchell Cooper's—Lena's father."

"The creepy-crazies don't run it that family, they *gallop*," Bobby said. "But Cooper's rich enough to hire somebody to do his dirty work."

"Rich enough," Chet said, "but involving somebody else in a murder would leave him vulnerable to blackmail."

"I've been thinking about that," I said. "I don't believe they really wanted to kill me. Or maybe one of them didn't want to."

Chet looked at me quizzically. "What do you mean?"

"Somebody put half a bottle of water in the pocket of my robe."

"It couldn't have lasted very long," Chet said.

"That little bit of water made the difference between my staying alive or suffering a terrible death because I was too weak to find help."

Bobby held up a hand. "Let's stay focused on the case. Morgan, we need something to substantiate what you've said. Can you remember anything about the place where the car stopped? Anything you saw that might help us find it again. We might be able get tire tracks or footprints. We need concrete evidence to nail them."

"Lena opened the trunk." I closed my eyes to concentrate, trying to recall what I might have glimpsed behind or around Lena, any object or landmark. Slowly, a picture began to come into focus in my mind.

"Behind Lena to one side, there was a kind of big plant, tall. It had spiky, armlike branches. But there was something wrong—it was sheared off on one side . . ." I opened my eyes. "Yes! I guess that's why it made an impression. It should have had those spiky things sticking out in both directions, but they were only on one side. How do you find something like that in hundreds and hundreds of miles?"

Bobby stood up and took a handful of colorful pages out of the pocket of his windbreaker. "Soon as we got here I started grabbing brochures and maps." He chose a few and fanned them out in front of me. They had pictures of desert scenes and hiking trails. In the third folder I saw something similar. "There, that's the kind of plant it was," I said. "Do you have a pencil or a pen?"

Chet pulled a ballpoint pen from his pocket, clicked the tip into place, and handed it to me.

I started striking off half of the branches on the picture. "It looked like this," I said. "But how can you hope to find it?"

Bobby tapped one of the other brochures with an index finger. "This is a list of desert tour guides. One of them might be able to tell us where this spot is. They know Death Valley even better than one of my other clients knows the porno channels."

Chet turned to me. "Do you remember anything about the highway you were on? For example, did you hear any sounds?"

"When I woke up in the trunk, I had the impression we were on a back road—paved, but full of potholes. Only a few cars passed us. I heard a big truck—one of those eighteen-wheelers. But it sounded as though it was on another highway some distance away. I was going to kick out the taillight to attract another driver's attention, but before I could do it, Lena's car turned right onto an unpaved surface. From then on I didn't hear any other cars. After about an hour on that road, we stopped."

"What about the car?" Bobby asked. "You said it was old."

"Old, and big. Pieces in the back were rusted out, and so was the casing around one of the taillights."

"Good. That should narrow the search a little."

"When I was trying to climb out of the trunk, I noticed the car was dark green. It was an old paint job—pretty faded, but still green."

"What about the make?" Chet asked.

"I'm sorry—I've never been able to tell one brand of car from another."

Suddenly the door was flung open. Tommy rushed into the room, skidded to a stop beside the bed, gaped at me—and promptly burst into tears.

Before he managed to get control of his emotions, the door opened again and in came Detectives Reed and Doyle. Their jackets were rumpled and they were both in need of a shave.

"You held out on us," Reed said accusingly.

Chapter 45

CHET SNAPPED AT the detective, "Don't talk to her like that. She's been through hell!"

To defuse what threatened to become an unpleasant situation, I tugged at Chet's sleeve and said lightly, "It was just a very small corner of hell. I'm all right."

As soon as the detectives entered, Tommy had retreated to stand against the wall near the door. I didn't know whether he was posing as wallpaper, or planning to make a run for it.

Because it was clear from their sour expressions that Detectives Reed and Doyle were annoyed in the extreme, I thought it best to give them my complete attention. I asked, "Holding out on you? I don't know what you mean."

Reed said, "You made us think the guy who took a shot during your show was just some random nut."

"Then you get snatched, and suddenly we got TV sharks and politicos, and our own brass comin' down on us," Doyle jumped in. "We're ordered to drop everything and find *you*, Princess Hot-Shit."

I said, "Wait a minute!" but they didn't wait. So much for my power.

"You should of told us there was more goin' on than just a potshot at some unknown actor," Reed said.

"Sean O'Neil is not unknown—he has millions of fans!" *Well, at least tens of thousands.*

Chet said, "How could Morgan possibly have any idea she was going to be violently attacked and then kidnapped?"

Doyle snorted derisively. Ignoring Chet, he said to me, "You want us to believe you were involved in both a shooting and then a kidnapping—"

"Reed: "In less than twenty-four hours—"

Doyle: "In less than twenty-four hours. That's just a coincidence?"

"I know it looks strange, but it's the truth."

"Like the saying goes, 'Truth is stranger than fiction,'" Bobby remarked.

Reed fixed Bobby with a look. "And just who are you?"

"Robert Novello, a friend of Morgan's."

Doyle shook his head and said to his partner, "Lou—he's that"—he stopped himself, apparently searching for the right word—"he's that . . . *short guy* we heard about—the one who's been running all the local PIs."

Reed planted his fists on his hips, thrust his jaw out pugnaciously, and snarled, "Keep your hired muscle out of our way, or they'll get their licenses yanked."

Bobby was more affable than I would have been. Instead of a clever retort, he smiled pleasantly and said, "Absolutely. As an indication of our willingness to be helpful, we can give you information about the kidnapping and the car used to transport Morgan."

"And just where did you get this information?"

I said, "I told Mr. Novello and Mr. Thompson what I know."

Doyle looked at Chet. "You Thompson?"

"Yes."

Doyle's tone was scornful. "What do *you* do?"

"A little of this, a little of that."

"Chet is here as my friend." I scrunched my eyebrows at Chet in a for-heaven's-sake-behave-yourself look.

If, in flattening himself against the wall, Tommy was trying to make himself invisible, it hadn't worked, because he was the next target of Reed's scrutiny. "Who are you?" Reed demanded.

"Ta-Ta-Thomas Alexander Zenos."

"What's your part in this?"

Fresh tears filled Tommy's eyes. He clasped his hands and raised them to his chin as he wailed, "I should have been there! If I hadn't gone out Saturday night—"

"Mr. Zenos and I work together," I said quickly. Protectively. "He hasn't slept, and he's very upset about what happened this weekend."

Obviously sensitive to his distress, Chet said, "Tommy, can you go back to the hotel and get some clothes for Morgan? She's going to be discharged in a little while."

Tommy looked from Reed to Doyle and back to Reed. "Is it all right? For me to go?"

"All of you—out! We want to interview Ms. Tyler."

"Bobby and I will be in the hallway," Chet said.

When my three friends had left the room, I made the effort to smile up at Detectives Reed and Doyle. "Alone at last," I said. "Why don't you sit down and get comfortable?"

Reed and Doyle claimed the two straight back chairs and pulled out their little notebooks. Even though I was feeling weak and battered, I wanted to get through this as quickly as possible so I could leave the hospital. Adjusting the pillows behind my back, I took a few sips of water and began to tell my story.

I repeated everything I could remember, everything except my belief that the man with Lena Cooper was her father. I left that out because I didn't have any proof. At least, not yet. Mitchell Cooper's home turf was New York. If I was right, and

Cooper had been involved in my kidnapping, then Matt and G. G. wouldn't want him spooked before they had evidence for an arrest. There were too many places in the world where a rich man could hide, beyond the reach of the law.

Reed and Doyle listened carefully, and only interrupted with questions a few times. When I finished my tale, the two detectives were markedly less hostile.

Noticing that the glass on my bedside table was empty, Reed offered to pour more water for me. I accepted.

As I drank, Doyle stared at me, an unexpectedly sympathetic expression on his face. "You looked a lot better on Saturday."

I laughed. "Well, being pumped full of drugs and left as a banquet for the buzzards isn't exactly like spending the day at a spa," I said.

THE STAFF DOCTOR who came around examined me, unhooked the IV, and pronounced me well enough to leave North Las Vegas Memorial.

"Take it easy for a few days," he said. "And go see your personal physician for an examination as soon as you return to New York."

"I will," I said. It was a lie. Nancy and Penny would have seven kinds of fits if they found out, but it would take more than sunburn, a headache, and sore feet to get me to a doctor. I don't like going to doctors—except Magic's veterinarian. Now if Dr. Marks treated people . . .

As soon as the doctor left, Chet, Bobby, and Tommy came in. Tommy carried my duffle and tote bags. "This is everything from the hotel. I had the maid pack you up." He added shyly, "I didn't think I should be handling your lingerie."

"You could have asked me to do it," Bobby said with a mischievous wink.

Tommy ignored him.

I got out of bed carefully, mindful of how little a hospital gown covered. Chet, Tommy, and Bobby gallantly turned their backs.

"It'll just take a couple of minutes to get dressed," I said. Pulling clothes out of the duffle, I picked up my tote bag and headed for the bathroom. "I'll leave the door open a little so we can keep talking."

When I saw my reflection in the bathroom mirror, I winced. My face was red, and my skin was beginning to peel. My lips were as rough and cracked as a dry riverbed. My hair had the texture of cactus, and was matted with dirt. In short, I looked even worse than I felt.

I heard Tommy say, "I gave the hospital our company's insurance information, took care of the paperwork, and tipped the hotel staff. We're all set to go home."

"What about the others?" I asked. "Joel and the actors and staff?"

"Joel took everybody back to New York this morning, after we learned you were safe in the hospital," Tommy said. "On Sunday they mutinied—refused to leave Las Vegas until you were found."

I felt a sudden sting in my eyes. What Tommy had just said touched me more than I was able to admit without breaking down. "We've got a good group," I managed to get out. Then I seized a brush and battled with my hair, trying to force the bristles through the tangles. After a futile minute, I gave up and put on my clothes. "What time does the next plane to New York leave?" I called through the partially open door as I zipped up my slacks.

"Whenever we get there," Chet said. "I kept the executive jet on for our return trip."

"That was optimistic of you," I joked.

Bobby said, "Chet swore you were too stubborn to die. I'm glad he was right."

"That's sweet of you, Bobby."

"Not really. You haven't got my bill yet. Speaking of which—I'm not going back to New York with you guys."

"Why not?" I came out of the bathroom dressed in slacks, shirt, and my red blazer, but carrying my ankle boots. I'd tried to put them on, but it was too painful because of the cuts on my feet, so I settled for wearing two pairs of socks.

"While the doctor was checking you out, I made some calls," Bobby said. "I'm meeting three of my Las Vegas PIs and some tour guides tonight. Soon as it's light tomorrow we're going to try to locate the place where the car stopped. We'll search for tracks—vehicle or shoes—or anything else that can help us nail Poppa Cooper and his Little Girl Blue."

IN THE TAXI on the way to the private airfield where the jet waited, three questions nagged at me. One: Why would Lena Cooper risk being locked up for years in order to kidnap me? Two: That water bottle made no sense—was she trying to kill me, or to save me? Three: What in the world did Mitchell Cooper have against me that would lead him to be party to my kidnapping and possible murder?

Chapter 46

CHET HAD ARRANGED with the pilot to stock the plane with sandwiches and thermoses of coffee for himself and Tommy and hot soup and apple juice for me.

While the pilot was doing his final preflight check, I peered at the digital face of Tommy's watch. "Eight o'clock—eleven in New York. Did you pack my cell phone?"

"Yes, but it's broken." Tommy added sheepishly, "I lost mine, or left it somewhere."

"Take mine," Chet said, pulling it out of his jacket pocket. "I programmed Phoenix and Nancy on speed dial for you."

"Thank you."

"Are you going to tell Nancy about Mitchell Cooper?" Chet asked.

I nodded. "The question is *when*. I don't want to tell her over the phone. Nancy's not just my friend, she's my attorney. But Mitchell Cooper employs the firm, too. Specifically, he's Arnold Rose's client."

Tommy's eyebrows shot up in surprise. "*Nancy's* Arnold Rose? Oh, that's sticky."

I pressed the button Chet indicated and heard the phone ring in the town house on East Sixty-Eighth Street. Almost immediately, Penny answered. "Morgan?"

"How did you know?"

"Chet called a couple of hours ago to say you'd be flying home tonight. I'm all packed and ready to go."

Was I back in the desert, wandering around with only half my brain functioning? "Ready to go where?"

"To your place. Call your building and tell them to let me in."

"Penny, we won't land until about four A.M. your time. Why don't you come over tomorrow?"

"After what you've been through, I am absolutely *not* going to let you be alone—at least not for the first twenty-four hours after you get back." There was a stubborn, don't-argue-with-me note in Penny's voice.

"You've been spending time with Nancy," I said with affection. "You're getting just as bossy."

"Never mind that. Call your building." I heard Matt's voice saying, "Let me talk to her." When he had the phone, I said, "Matt, thank you for everything you did."

"Not much, as it turned out. From what I heard, you rescued yourself."

"Lena Cooper kidnapped me," I said. "A man helped her."

"Tell me."

"I think the man was her father. I didn't see his face, but I heard his voice. That—my suspicion—was the one thing I left out when I told the Las Vegas police what happened."

Matt was silent for a moment before he said, "I'll come over with G. G. tomorrow about noon. Don't leave the apartment."

I promised. "Tell Penny I'll call the Dakota and have them let her in. And thank her for staying with me."

"No need. I wouldn't have been able to stop her if I'd tried." The tension left Matt's voice. I could almost hear him smiling as he added, "That cat of yours is a pest—he's been sleeping with me."

"No accounting for taste," I joked and hung up before he could reply.

IT WAS 4:30 in the morning in New York when the taxi carrying Chet and me pulled up in front of the Dakota. Tommy, who lived on the East Side, had taken a separate cab. There is always traffic in Manhattan, but at this time of day it was perhaps the lightest. Still, I couldn't help wondering where those other cars were going at this hour.

"Wait here while I take the lady inside," Chet told the driver. "Then we're heading downtown to Waverly Place."

"The soles of my feet are still tender," I told Chet. "Let's take the elevator."

"Thank God," Chet said with mock relief. "Even if you haven't eaten for a couple of days, I wasn't looking forward to carrying you up two flights of stairs."

Outside my front door, I looked up at Chet and said, "I don't know how to thank you for rushing all the way to Las Vegas, and for Bobby, and the plane . . ."

"We can talk about that when you're all healed up," he said softly. He rang the bell and smiled as he smoothed back a lock of hair that was falling over my eyes. "I'd like to kiss you, but you're a mess."

"That's what Detective Doyle said."

He dropped his hand. "What!"

"Oh, not the kissing part—just that I look awful."

Penny opened the door, and Nancy was right behind her. With a little cry, Penny threw her arms around me in a fierce hug. "Oh, Morgan!"

"Thank you for bringing her home, Chet," Nancy said.

"My pleasure."

Penny released her grip on me, and then hugged Chet, while Nancy grabbed my hand. I could see the profound relief in the eyes of my dear friend.

"I'm taking a couple of personal days away from the office," Nancy said, "so I can be sure you don't do anything foolish."

Suddenly, coming toward us from the direction of the kitchen, I heard the sweet sound of thundering paws.

Chet asked, "How can a seven-pound cat make so much noise when he runs? I thought cats were supposed to be light-footed."

My heart lurched with happiness at the sight of Magic. I scooped him up in my arms and pressed him lovingly against my chest. He rubbed the top of his silky head beneath my jaw and purred loudly.

As Nancy and Penny and I exchanged good nights with Chet, he put my duffle and tote bags down inside the door. "I'll come over this afternoon, so we can make plans."

As soon as the door closed behind him, Penny asked, "Plans? What plans?" There was a note of alarm in her voice. "You're not going to marry Chet, are you?!"

I thought I was too tired to laugh, but that produced a chuckle. "We've only had two dates. I've seen a lot more of Matt."

"Matt is the one I'm rooting for," Penny said.

But Matt is refusing to see me any longer. I wondered if he'd told that to Penny.

Penny and Nancy each took one of my bags and preceded me toward the bedroom. Magic was still in my arms.

"Penny brought you food and I brought moisturizer and creams for your burns," Nancy said.

"Are you hungry?" Penny asked. "As soon as Chet called yesterday morning to say you'd been found, I started making you soups."

"Soups? Plural?"

"The best ones after a fast and for building back your strength: chicken with rice, chicken with dumplings, beef and barley, and split pea with onions, carrots, and a smoked ham bone. I made a few other things for you, too. The meals are labeled and dated and in your freezer."

"In all the years I've known you," Nancy said with an amused smile, "I've never seen your kitchen as well-stocked as it is now. You provide everything for Magic and forget about yourself."

"I'll gorge later, Penny. Right now I just want to take a bath, put on a clean T-shirt, and go to sleep."

I CAME OUT of the bathroom feeling almost normal: soaked clean, shampooed, teeth brushed, gums flossed, creamed, moisturized, and dressed in an oversized New York Knicks shirt.

My emergency air mattress had been taken from its storage bag, inflated, and dressed with sheets and blankets. Nancy and Penny were in their nightclothes. They'd partially unpacked their overnight bags, and the outfits they planned to wear when we got up were hanging on the closet doors. Nancy noticed the smile on my face and guessed what I was thinking. "Girl clutter. Like being back in the dorm."

"Better," I said. "We don't have to study for exams."

"In a way, *life* is one long exam," Penny said. "But it's too early in the morning to be philosophical."

I wholeheartedly agreed.

Penny had claimed the air mattress, and I climbed into the king-size bed. Nancy was already on what I called "the guest side," even though in the three years I'd lived at the Dakota, Nancy and Penny had been the only overnight guests I'd had.

Magic strolled in from the bathroom, where he'd been pushing the bath mat around. He looked at the air mattress. Apparently deciding it wasn't important in his life, he walked right across Penny and jumped up onto the bed, settling himself in the space between Nancy and me.

"Now that he's home, I'm going to miss him," Penny said.

I asked her, "When he was staying with you, did he really sleep with Matt?"

"Every night. I took him in with me, but each morning I woke up and found him on Matt's bed."

I was just about to turn out the lamp on the night table when I saw a thick package wrapped in brown paper and tied with cord. The paper looked liked a recycled grocery bag. It was addressed to me, in unfamiliar handwriting. "Where did this come from?"

"It was downstairs when I arrived. The person at your desk asked me to bring it up." Penny said.

I tilted it so I could see the return label. The package was from a Mrs. Gordon Stoddard, with a Syracuse, New York, address. It took a moment before memory kicked in. "Oh, this is from Nora Stoddard, Wade Maitland's sister. It's his book manuscript. I promised her I'd read it."

Nancy yawned. "As though you don't already have enough to do. You shouldn't be so accommodating to strangers."

"I couldn't refuse. Her brother was murdered right after he and I had lunch together."

We got comfortable, and I turned off the bedside light.

Soon, I heard Nancy and Penny breathing deeply and evenly. I'd shut my eyes, but sleep wouldn't come. Maybe it was because I'd spent so much time knocked out from the drugs Lena injected into me. Whatever the reason, I realized that right now I was completely awake.

Careful not to disturb my houseguests, I picked up the package from Maitland's sister and crept out of the bedroom.

At the kitchen table, I opened the package. *Next to Greatness: Wives of Famous Men*. The first three chapters were well written and moderately interesting, but most of the historical vignettes were familiar ones. I was beginning to feel sorry that I'd agreed to read it. Then I turned another page—and suddenly Wade Maitland's manuscript became an entirely different book.

Chapter 47

CERTAIN INCIDENTS MAITLAND described were so startling I reread them. By the time I reached the last page in the box, I felt emotionally drained. If Maitland had lived to finish it, this book would have sold for a lot of money, put Maitland on the best-seller lists, and made him a media celebrity. Readers have an insatiable appetite for nonfiction works exposing the rich and flourishing.

During some of the most shocking passages describing Mitchell Cooper's actions, Maitland had referred to substantiating documents. The burglar who'd invaded Maitland's house in Connecticut might have taken them, but I didn't think so. At the time the killer stole Maitland's hard drive, he wouldn't have read the manuscript, so he wouldn't have known the documents existed. I wished I'd known Maitland well enough to guess where he might have hidden them.

Magic was now curled up atop the open box of manuscript pages. A shaft of bright morning sunlight coming in through the kitchen window fell across the lower half of his body, making his black fur shine like polished ebony. The strong light illuminated the even blacker stripes beneath his dark topcoat. "A little tabby action going on there," Nancy had remarked when she noticed the phenomenon a couple of weeks ago. I thought of Magic as my miniature jaguar. When I reached out to stroke him, I was rewarded by the sound of his contented purring.

While I was mulling what I'd read, Penny and Nancy rushed into the kitchen.

"Quick, turn on the TV!" Penny said.

Not waiting for me to get up from the table, Nancy grabbed the remote from the counter and activated the kitchen set. "Mitchell Cooper is holding a press conference!"

Penny said, "We had the TV news on while we were dressing."

As the picture came on, I saw that Arnold Rose was standing close beside Cooper.

"I'm begging you," Cooper was saying, "and I address this especially to anyone in law enforcement—please do not harm Lena when you apprehend her! Yes, it's true that Lena is a suspect in the murder of Wade Maitland, the man with whom she was obsessed and whom she stalked relentlessly. And it's true that when she was emotionally fragile, she poisoned his dog."

Nancy's voice dripped with sarcasm. "Some people are going to think she's worse for poisoning his dog than for murdering the *man*."

"The dog survived," I said. "Let's listen."

"Sadly, Lena has been troubled for a long time," Cooper went on. "And I'm afraid the situation has gotten worse. Saturday night in Las Vegas my daughter kidnapped a television writer, Morgan Tyler, and tried to murder the woman. Fortunately, Ms. Tyler was rescued. I'm thankful for that, but it's very important to remember that when Lena tried to kill Ms. Tyler, she did *not* use the gun."

I head Penny's sharp intake of breath. "Gun?

"You didn't tell me she had a gun!" Nancy said accusingly.

"I never saw one." I shushed them as Arnold Rose leaned close to Cooper, covered his mouth with his hand to foil lip-readers, and whispered something into his client's ear.

Cooper shook his head vehemently. "No, Arnold! I *want* people to know about the gun." He took a step away from the lawyer, whose expression changed from worried to positively flinty.

"Look at Arnold's face," Nancy said. "He's *furious.*"

Cooper spoke directly into the nearest video camera. "The gun my daughter is carrying belongs to me. I feel guilty about that because I was careless. I failed to lock the firearm away, and so I fully intend to pay whatever penalty the law requires. Even though Lena took the gun from my apartment, where I have a valid Premises Permit for it, I take issue with those who have described my poor girl as armed and dangerous! Lena is not a murderer at heart—she's sick! Very sick!"

Nancy was shaking her head in disbelief. "That man just painted a target on his daughter's back."

Penny stared at the set, incredulous. "It's as though he's inviting a police officer, or someone, to shoot her on sight. He can't know what he's doing!"

Cooper knows exactly what he's doing.

"What's a Premises Permit?" Penny asked.

"It's what I have," I said. "I can keep my Glock here in the apartment, but I can't carry it outside. If I want to take it up to the shooting range outside Manhattan to practice, I have to lock the Glock in the glove compartment of the car, and keep the ammunition for it in the trunk. If I don't do that, and I'm stopped by the police for any reason, they'll revoke my permit."

"And those are very hard to get," Nancy said.

A reporter for the ABC affiliate called out: "Mr. Cooper, do you have any idea where Lena is now?"

"No. I'm praying she'll come home to me, so I can get her the help she so desperately needs."

One of our GBN reporters asked: "Where was she seen last?"

Cooper replied, "The car she used in the kidnapping was found abandoned in Philadelphia."

From WCBS: "That's pretty close to New York."

Again, Cooper spoke directly into the camera. "Lena, if you can see me, or hear my voice, *please call*—you have all my private numbers." He nodded toward Arnold. "This is my attorney, Arnold Rose. He and I will meet you wherever you are, Lena—*anywhere*—and we'll bring you safely to the authorities so you can tell your side of the story. Don't be afraid, Lena. And please *don't do anything foolish!*"

I shook my head in disgust. Mitchell Cooper was in front of a bank of cameras, endangering his daughter's life, when he should have been in jail for his part in my kidnapping and attempted murder.

And for the far worse things I'd read about in Wade Maitland's manuscript.

MATT CALLED TO say that he and G. G. were delayed on an investigation and might not get to the Dakota until late afternoon.

By three o'clock Nancy, Penny, and I had seen six replays of Mitchell Cooper's press conference. The story of the missing heiress, the murdered professor, and the kidnapped TV writer was all over TV. Much to my surprise, it was even a subject on talk radio: "Crazy stalkers—should we send them to hospitals or to prison?" I switched it off before impassioned callers started flooding the airwaves with their wacky proposals.

At noon, Penny went out to get newspapers and came back with an armload. All of the New York dailies, and *USA Today*, carried the story and pictures of the fugitive Lena Cooper. The *New York Post*, the *Daily News*, and Long Island's *Newsday* printed my picture, too; it was a photo taken last May when I won the Daytime Emmy Award for writing *Love of My Life*. The *Post* included the picture of Wade Maitland that was on the back of his book jackets. Almost every piece quoted the phrase "armed and dangerous" in reference to Lena.

"How can these papers have so much detail?" Penny asked. "Mitchell Cooper was only on TV this morning."

"For this story to make it into print," I said, "Cooper had to have given it out last night." I asked Nancy, "Have you talked to Arnold since the press conference?"

"Half an hour ago. I don't know if it counts as talking, but we had words."

That distressed Penny, "Oh, Nancy, are you and Arnold fighting?"

"Call it a conflict of interest," she said. "Arnold's being loyal to Cooper and I'm standing by Morgan."

UNTIL NANCY, PENNY, and I could get together with Matt and G. G., I had deliberately kept what I'd read in Wade Maitland's manuscript to myself.

It was close to six o'clock when our favorite homicide detectives finally arrived. They were hungry, thirsty, and tired from a day that had stretched almost two hours beyond the usual end of their tour.

Penny had dinner ready, and Nancy had uncorked two bottles of good red wine. After we'd finished Penny's Sicilian lasagna (a recipe adapted with her own embellishments from a cookbook written by actor Alan Alda's parents), fresh asparagus vinaigrette, a red cake shaped like a rose, the wine, and were having coffee, it was time to share what I'd read in the manuscript.

With the first words out of my mouth, I had everybody's attention. "Mitchell Cooper's very rich wife didn't commit suicide—he murdered her."

Chapter 48

"THERE'S A LOT more to the story Maitland tells," I told my dining companions.

"You mean, to his *allegations*," Matt said.

"Don't get technical, just listen."

"I want to see that manuscript."

"Later, Matt. Let me finish."

"Cooper's a client of our firm," Nancy reminded Matt. "If you take possession of the book, I'll need a copy of it."

"Anybody want that last little piece of the red cake?" G. G. asked.

Penny urged me, "Go on," as she put the final petal on his plate.

"Just because I'm eating, don't mean I'm not listening," G. G. said.

I resumed the story Maitland had laid out. "Cooper's wife's maiden name was Amelia Newton. She was from the oil-rich Oklahoma Newtons. When she was twenty, Amelia's father and brother were killed in a fire at one of their wells, leaving her the sole heir, the last of the Newton line. Cooper met Amelia a few weeks after the fire, and he married her a couple of months later. Apparently, she was still in a state of shock and grief when Cooper swept into her life. Their only child, Lena, was born just eight months after they got married. According to Maitland, who tracked down retired family servants, they weren't a very happy couple. Cooper wasn't an affectionate father, but Amelia adored her child."

Matt was drumming the fingers of one hand on the table. "It's been a long day. Can't we skip forward to the alleged murder?"

"Murder-zzzz," I said. "More than one. Okay, but you're going to want to go back and ask questions."

"We're used to that," G. G. said dryly.

"Amelia supposedly committed suicide when Lena was six years old," I told them. "A man named Jud Larsen—he'd been Amelia's boyfriend before Cooper came along—refused to believe she committed suicide. A few weeks after Amelia died, Larsen confronted Cooper, claiming he had proof that Cooper murdered Amelia, and he said he was going to take it to the police. Lena overheard the argument. She was just a little girl, but Maitland said she remembered it vividly. Before Larsen could show his proof to the police, he died in a single-car crash. When police and paramedics got to him, Larsen was dead. Because he reeked of liquor, and his blood alcohol level was over the legal limit, the police wrote it off as accidental death, alcohol-related. They didn't have any reason to do a deeper investigation. Nothing was found in the wreck that connected Jud Larsen to Mitchell Cooper."

"This is all very interesting," Matt said, "and I mean that. I'm not being sarcastic. I'd like to nail Cooper—at the very least for what he tried to do to you—but we've got a jurisdictional problem."

"Jurisdictional?" I said innocently.

"He means Maitland was killed in Westport, Connecticut— that's Westport's case," G. G. said. "Maitland lived in

Hartford—the burglary is Hartford's case. You were snatched in Las Vegas, so that's *their* case. Cooper's wife was from Oklahoma—"

I was waiting for one of them to say that.

"Amelia Cooper was *from* Oklahoma, but she died *here*, in Manhattan," I said. "The Cooper Building on Fifth Avenue was just completed, and the Coopers were living in the penthouse. That's still his legal residence. Larsen's car crashed into the side of a condemned building on Tenth Avenue. That puts Amelia Cooper's and Jud Larsen's cases in the NYPD's jurisdiction."

Matt did a quick calculation in his head. "If Lena Cooper was six, and those two events really were murders, that means they happened eighteen or nineteen years ago. There's no statute of limitation on murder, but . . ."

"It's a long shot there'd be any useful evidence left," G. G. finished the thought for him.

"I watch those *Cold Case* stories on TV," Penny said. "Don't your precinct houses have basements full of old boxes with clues?"

"It's not that easy," Matt said.

"I'm sorry about Amelia Cooper and Jud Larsen," Nancy said, "but the person I'm worried about is Morgan. Lena Cooper kidnapped her, Mitchell Cooper helped, and my best friend nearly died. What can we do about that?"

"I have an idea," I said.

G. G.'s snort was almost a laugh. "This I wanna hear."

Penny gave G. G. a tap on one bulging forearm. "Stop being so negative," she said reprovingly. "Let Morgan talk." After her rare display of annoyance, which surprised everyone at the table, Penny stood up and began refilling coffee cups.

When she got to me, I put my hand over the top of my cup, signaling I'd had enough. "Before I tell you my idea, there's more of Maitland's story you should hear."

"Go on," Matt said. No longer did he sound impatient.

"There's a lot of dialogue in the book, and much of it is conversations between Lena and her father. Maitland made starred footnotes, indicating which conversations were direct quotes that came from Lena, and which were recreations based on the investigating he did. Maitland was a skilled researcher. His three published books were all biographies. They didn't sell many copies, but according to the reviews I looked up, they were highly regarded for the accuracy of their scholarship, and they gave him academic prestige. He spent quite a lot of time with Lena, before he became alarmed about her mental state. When we had lunch together, Maitland told me he had been encouraging her in her studies, but I'm beginning to think that soon after she started confiding in him, he got the very commercial idea of writing a book exposing Mitchell Cooper. For years, Cooper's been on media lists of the richest people in America, so a tell-all about him would be much more likely to find a publisher than the history of women married to famous men Maitland had been trying to write. When Lena told him things she'd kept secret for years, Maitland must have realized a potential gold mine had fallen into his lap because she was in love with him."

Nancy corrected me. "Obsessed with him."

"Sometimes you don't know the difference until a relationship is over," Matt said.

My eyebrows lifted. "You sound like the voice of experience."

"Not really," he said.

Not really—that was man-speak meaning "yes."

Matt sat up straighter and focused on his fresh cup of coffee.

I said to Matt and G. G., "Did you see Cooper's press conference this morning?"

Matt replied with distaste, "Yes. The man's a fool."

"Somebody should've told him he could get his daughter killed," G. G. growled.

"I think that's exactly what he wants," I said.

"That would be insane," Nancy said.

I shook my head. "No, it would be the perfect crime. Cooper's motive is spelled out in Maitland's book. Remember,

I said the Cooper marriage wasn't happy. Mitchell Cooper didn't know it at the time, but a few months after Lena was born, Amelia Cooper made a new will, specifying that Lena was to inherit all of Amelia's money and holdings. According to the will, which Maitland found in public records, Lena will gain control of the fortune when she's twenty-five. Her twenty-fifth birthday comes in four months. Her father is her only living relative."

I let that sink in.

Penny was the first to speak. Her voice was full of sadness. "What terrible things people will do for money."

Suddenly Nancy and Matt looked at each other and then at me. I could see the same thought had occurred to them both.

Matt put it into words. "Assuming this story is true, Cooper could have found out about the book, killed Maitland, and then torn his house apart trying to find the disk or the manuscript. He probably found the disk, and he took the hard drive out of the computer, but he couldn't be sure Maitland hadn't printed out the pages."

"Which, as it turned out, he did."

"Maitland was murdered just after you two were together," Nancy said. "Cooper could think that Maitland gave you a disk or the manuscript—which would motivate him to try to kill you, or get his daughter to kill you."

"This is pretty convoluted," I said, "but I believe Cooper convinced Lena to kidnap me, and helped her, so that he could frame her for my death and for Maitland's. If Lena is locked up in a mental hospital for the rest of her life, or in prison, or killed by somebody who heard she's armed and dangerous, Cooper gains control of the Newton fortune."

"Nice story," G.G. said. "But without any proof, we're just talking gas."

"Footnotes or no," Matt said, "a manuscript doesn't constitute evidence."

The four faces around me assumed glum expressions. But I was smiling. "In his book, Maitland claims that he has the documents to substantiate his murder claims."

Four faces lighted simultaneously. "Great," Matt said. "Where are they?"

"Well," I admitted, "his book doesn't say. But that's what inspired my idea. The idea I don't think any of you are going to like."

Chapter 49

MATT'S EYES, AND G. G.'s, Nancy's, and Penny's were riveted on me. "Before I tell you the idea, there's something you should know. Shortly before I went to Las Vegas, I found out I was being followed."

"Followed? Who was following you—"

"A private detective was watching me, Matt. All I could find out was that his employer was a man in Europe. I didn't tell you about it because I was afraid you'd think it was connected to Maitland's murder and that you'd do everything you could to stop me from going to Las Vegas."

"Bingo!" he said. "And if I'd kept you in New York you wouldn't have almost died in the desert."

"Okay, so in retrospect it seems as though I should have told you."

"Damn right!"

Surprising me, G .G. was the voice of reason. "Don't get

so hot, Matt. If she didn't know who was tailing her or why, there's nothing we could have done."

I wanted to shout, "See, Matt!" but for once my better judgment prevailed. From their expressions, I could tell Nancy and Penny weren't happy to hear about the detective either, so I quickly moved the subject forward. "I tried to figure out who the man in Europe was and couldn't—but now I think it was Mitchell Cooper. It was about the same time you mentioned he was in Switzerland."

"Then Matt must be right about Mitchell Cooper thinking you have the manuscript," Penny said. "What are we going to do?"

"I'll let him know that I have it."

"How?" G. G. asked sarcastically. "You gonna to call him up?"

"No. I'll have our network's publicity man plant an item in the papers. 'TV writer plans to find publisher for murdered man's manuscript.' Something like that. If we're right about Cooper, he'll come after me, and when he tries something you can arrest him."

Nancy was horrified. "You're going to use yourself as bait!"

"Absolutely not!" Matt yelled.

"I like the idea," G. G. said, blandly disagreeing.

"No," Matt said in a more moderate tone. He'd forced himself to calm down, but the subtext in that little two-letter word was "Over my dead body."

G. G. heard it, too. "All right, if you feel so strong about it."

"What's *your* idea, then?" I asked Matt. I was sure he wouldn't have one, but I was wrong.

"While G. G. and I do some serious digging in those two old cases, *you're* going to stay here in this apartment, without leaving it for any reason. You can work at home for a few days, can't you?"

Nancy answered for me. "Yes, she can. So can I. I'll stay here with her."

"So will I," Penny said firmly. She met Matt's hard-eyed glare without flinching. Penny was tougher than she looked; it was Matt who backed down. Having won, she said to Nancy, "We can take turns going home to pack some clothes."

"I have the perfect compromise," I told Matt. "You want me to stay right here, so I will. That makes it safe to get word out in the papers about my having the manuscript. Now, isn't that reasonable?"

It took some muttering under his breath, but finally Matt agreed.

Indicating Nancy and Penny, he said, "After you get your clothes, I don't want any of you three to leave this apartment. Whatever you need, order in, or G. G. or I will bring it."

"I'm sure Chet will be happy to help us out," Penny said mischievously.

THE HEAD OF Global's PR department released the story I asked him to. That started the clock ticking. The NYPD didn't have the manpower to station anyone at the Dakota, but Matt persuaded his superiors to order a patrol car to cruise past the building at least once an hour. He said he and G. G. would check on us when they were off duty.

Beginning the following morning, there was an almost constant stream of messengers in and out of my third-floor apartment. Betty Kraft sent new scripts from the writing staff for me to review and to edit and to rewrite when necessary. She e-mailed breakdowns for the episodes I intended to write myself. Tommy sent actors' reels for me to look at and asked me to call to let him know which ones I thought we should invite in to audition.

Most of the messengers came from Nancy's law firm. Some of the envelopes and boxes of tapes concerned the preparations for Penny's cable TV show, scheduled to go on the air May twenty-second, which was six weeks away.

Nancy turned the den into her temporary office. Penny planned segments for her show at the kitchen table. For

Penny's convenience, I had the building's engineer set up a DVD player next to the kitchen TV set where she could view material sent over by the Better Living Channel's production team.

I worked at the computer in the bedroom. Every spare moment I had was used to research the people I'd read about in Wade Maitland's manuscript. What I learned from newspaper archives and accessible public records confirmed the personal details he'd written about Mitchell Cooper, Amelia Newton, Jud Larsen, and their backgrounds. I found pictures from Amelia's wedding to Cooper, which was a big social event, even though it was organized hastily. That point was made by several columnists: how quickly invitations had been printed and a dress designer and caterer had been chosen. One opined that it was "highly unusual" for such a big wedding to have no bridesmaids, no groomsmen, no maid of honor, no best man, but I'd already read Maitland's explanation. Mitchell Cooper had lived in Oklahoma for less than six months prior to the wedding and had no close friends. According to the Newton housekeeper, Amelia had decreed that the wedding party consist only of the bride and groom.

Nancy and Matt now each had copies of the book. Ever the careful attorney, Nancy had gone with Matt and G. G. to a print shop, to be sure only two copies were produced. Because the manuscript was not yet "evidence," I kept the original.

Time and again I returned to Maitland's assertion that he had proof of his charges against Cooper. But where was it?

True to Penny's prediction, and to Matt's intense irritation, Chet brought lunch to us every day, and enjoyed it with us.

When Chet arrived with provisions the first day, he also brought three identical gift-wrapped boxes. One was for Nancy, one for Penny, and one for me. They were about two inches high, six inches long, and four inches wide.

I tested the weight of the box on the palm of my hand. Pretending to be disappointed I said, "Not heavy enough for chocolate butter creams."

Nancy and Penny were opening their gifts carefully so as

not to damage the paper. Shamelessly, I ripped the wrapping off of mine. When I lifted the top of the box and saw what was inside, I threw my arms around Chet and gave him a big hug. Stepping back, smiling with delight, I held up his gift. "Mace Triple Action Spray!"

"When you were delirious in the hospital, you were mumbling about pepper spray. This is better. It's tear gas and UV dye. If you're attacked you can blind him long enough to get away, and the dye will make it easy for the police to identify him."

Pleased, Nancy said, "I wanted this, but in New York they make you jump through hoops. You can only buy it from licensed pharmacists or licensed firearms dealers. I never had time to go through that rigmarole."

"I tried to get something like this on the Internet," Penny said, "but none of the companies I found would ship to New York."

"I didn't get these in New York," Chet said. "Don't ask questions." He extended his palm toward the little canister. "May I?"

I handed it to him and he pointed out its features. "A flip-top safety cap. And the finger grip dispenser means you can aim it in the right direction even in the dark, just by feel. You'll get five bursts out of it, one second each. Don't keep it in a purse—you might not have time to find it there, or your purse could be snatched. Carry it in the pocket of whatever you're wearing, or you can Velcro it to your belt, or put it on a key ring. The attachments are in the box."

While he was explaining, he'd looked at each of us in turn, but his gaze came back to me as he added, "You three have brought a lot of fun into my life. I don't want to lose you."

ON THE SECOND day of what Nancy called "our house arrest," Bobby Novello telephoned from Las Vegas. His tone was triumphant.

"It took a while, but we finally found that half-sliced-off

tree-like thing where the car stopped. There was only one set of tire tracks, and they're distinctive: three bad tires, one new, all different brands. It was lucky the car didn't crash. With tires like that it was just asking for a blowout."

"Your desert guides are amazing," I said. "I want to thank them."

I heard him chuckle. "Great minds think alike. I said you'd send each of them your autograph—*on a check.*"

"I will, as soon as you give me their names and addresses. Did you hear the car was abandoned in Philadelphia?"

"Yeah. I e-mailed photos of the Nevada tire tracks to the Philly PD. It was an easy match to the tires on the vehicle they found. The inside was wiped clean, including the trunk, so they didn't get any fingerprints. But I got two clear sets of shoeprints near the tire tracks. I took photos of the area and the landmarks to identify the location. And I got shots of the prints—tire and shoe and signed affidavits from the desert guides about how we found them. I brought plaster with me and made casts of all the prints. Two sets. I had to give a set to the Nevada cops, but they don't know I kept one for us. If the New York blues ever come up with probable cause for a search warrant, we might get lucky and find that the nuts-o Coopers kept the shoes they were wearing."

"You did a great job, Bobby. What now?"

"I come home, pay my bird-sitter, and then we figure out our next move."

"Fly safely," I told him, and we said good-bye.

ON THE AFTERNOON of the third day, I asked Nancy if she'd talked to Arnold.

"He says that they haven't heard from Lena." Her voice was strained.

"I wasn't asking about that. You haven't mentioned Arnold for a while. Is everything all right with you two?"

"It would be, when this Cooper business is resolved, but something else has happened."

The unhappiness in Nancy's eyes stabbed at me. "What?"

"You remember Didi?"

"She's unforgettable," I said wryly.

"Well, she's going to be a lot harder to forget from now on because she and her mother are moving back to New York City next month."

"Yikes."

"Don't get me wrong," Nancy said, "I really want Arnold and his daughter to be close and see each other. Actually, if he were a widower, or if he had full-time custody of Didi, I'd really like to have her as part of my life, too."

Catching my skeptical expression, she said, "No, truly. I think in time Didi would realize that I don't want to come between her and Arnold. I know how much growing up with my own father meant to me."

"I hate to suggest this, but does Veronica want Arnold back?"

It was obvious Nancy had already thought of that and was troubled by the idea. "I came right out and asked Arnold. He says he's sure she doesn't—but he's also told me how competitive she is. Lord, men can be so *dense*!"

AT A FEW minutes after eleven o'clock that night, Nancy and Penny had made themselves comfortable, leaning back against the headboard of the king-size bed as they watched the local news on television. Magic was lying on the desk, next to the pile of Maitland's pages as I typed. I was trying to work out the Mitchell Cooper/Lena Cooper puzzle as though I were creating it as a plotline for the show.

I listed the charges Maitland leveled at Cooper; they worked as motivation for Cooper getting rid of his wife and for covering up that crime by killing Jud Larsen. If Maitland found proof that Cooper was a murderer, then that clearly supplied Cooper's motivation for killing Maitland. Cooper's emotionally needy daughter had turned to Maitland, seeking love. She'd confided in him about her father and mother and about Jud Larsen's fight with Cooper. Although at the time she had been only six, instinctively Lena had believed Larsen's charges because deep down she didn't think her mother had committed suicide.

I wondered about Cooper's obvious dislike of his daughter, and remembered that Lena had been born eight months after her parents married. Was it possible—as it was traditional in daytime drama—that Cooper was *not* Lena's biological father? No, that was too easy. Besides, unfortunately for Lena, she resembled Cooper. More likely that Cooper seduced the vulnerable Amelia and quickly got her pregnant. That was a smart way to stampede a recently orphaned rich young girl into marriage.

I filled up several pages with characters and their most likely motivations. The story that evolved from the exercise paralleled Maitland's book. That brought me back to Cooper's reason for going after me: it had to be my possession of the manuscript.

Magic got up, stretched, and started to resettle himself.

"Magic, you are a wicked cat. I need to study these pages." I leaned over to lift him, but Magic didn't want to move. His front paws hooked onto the edge of the pile, and as I picked him up, the papers went flying onto the floor. "It's all right, you didn't mean to do it," I told him as I gently put him down on the other side of the computer.

I got down on my hands and knees and began to collect the strewn pages from the floor and under the desk.

"Want some help?" Penny asked.

"No, thanks, it's okay." I gathered the sheets quickly and sat back down at the desk to put them in order. As I was reorganizing them, I noticed something scribbled on the back of one of the pages: 1940.

At first I thought it was a date, but by now I was so familiar with the story Maitland told that I knew 1940 didn't fit any of the events. *Maybe it's not a year.* All at once it came to me. Giving him a light kiss on the top of his silky head, I declared, "Magic, you're wonderful!"

Nancy and Penny looked at me. "What's happened?" Nancy asked.

"Maitland wrote 1940 on the back of one of the pages. I'm sure it's not a date. I think it's the number of a safety deposit box!" I felt like jumping up and down and yelling "Eureka," but I remembered I had neighbors. "If I'm right, then I'll bet this is where Maitland put the documents that prove Cooper's guilt!"

Before Nancy or Penny could respond, the house phone connected to the Dakota's reception desk rang. Excited by my theory, I picked it up and said a very cheerful hello.

"Mrs. Tyler?" I recognized the voice of Frank, the former wrestler and my favorite night security man. "There's a delivery guy down here with something for you."

"It's after 11:30. I'll pick it up in the morning."

"It's pretty big," Frank said. "The guy here has it on a dolly, and he said he's supposed to leave it only with *you*."

That stumped me. "What in the world is it? And who sent it?"

"According to the delivery slip, it's from a museum in Cairo—the one in Egypt, not the Cairo in Illinois. It's a gen-u-ine mummy case."

Chapter 50

A MUMMY CASE? Who would send me a . . .

One person.

But with my life in danger, I had to be sure this wasn't some trick of Cooper's—the Egyptian version of the Trojan Horse, perhaps with a bomb inside, or poison gas rigged to be released when the lid was opened, or twenty thousand black widow spiders. The image of all those spiders sent a shudder through me.

I needed information. "Frank, what's the delivery man's name?"

I heard Frank repeat my question, and in a moment he came back on the line. "He showed me ID. Name is Shakespeare. Bill Shakespeare."

A reference to Shakespeare was the code Nico Andreades used to identify himself when he contacted me. My pulse quickened with anticipation, but I tried to keep my voice steady and calm. "Let him bring it up, Frank."

"Okey-dokey."

As I replaced the receiver, Nancy asked, "What's going on?"

"Nothing to worry about, but I want you and Penny to stay here in the bedroom for a few minutes."

Hurrying to the front door, I opened it just as the man who called himself "Bill Shakespeare" emerged from the elevator, steering a six-foot Egyptian mummy case on a dolly. He was wearing a plain dark blue uniform with short sleeves. A cloth cap in the same blue material covered the top of his large head. A fringe of straight brown hair was visible beneath the cap. Of medium height, with a muscular build, and clean-shaven, at a cursory glance he looked like a million other men who made deliveries. I didn't know his real name, but I recognized his face. This was one of the brawny *assistants* I'd spotted close to Nico Andreades.

"Good evening, Mrs. Tyler." His tone was casual; he might have been conveying something ordinary—a bouquet of flowers, or a bag of groceries. "Where would you like your package?"

Choosing a place for a mummy case in my apartment was a problem I hadn't faced before. "I suppose . . . in the dining room." That was the part of my home I used least. Situated between the kitchen, which overlooked the Dakota's courtyard, and the front rooms, which faced Central Park, it didn't have any windows. What it did have were heavy sliding doors that closed it off from the rest of the apartment.

As soon as we reached the dining room, Nico's assistant carefully worked the case off the dolly. As he maneuvered the mummy case upright against the wall, I saw his muscles straining, and a faint sheen of perspiration popping out on his forehead. "It looks heavy."

"The gentleman who employs me wants you to know that the content of the package is unharmed."

Content?

"If you would like to see him, he will be on the bridge you both know at five A.M."

Staring at the mummy case with growing apprehension, I felt my throat tighten. All I could manage to get out was, "What's in that?"

"A gift, Mrs. Tyler. Compensation for the ordeal you recently suffered."

Oh, my god! What has Nico . . .

He reached into the shirt pocket of his uniform. "There is a lock on the left side. This is the key." I was frozen, until the touch of cold metal on the palm of my hand snapped me out of my trance. "I suggest you open the case soon," he said. Then he was gone.

Before I'd fully recovered my wits, I heard Nancy's voice calling from the direction of the bedroom. "Morgan, what's going on?"

Stepping out of the dining room and into the hall, I saw Nancy and Penny coming toward me. I was clutching the key to the mummy case so hard it bit into my palm, but that was the jab of reality I needed to clear my head.

Gesturing at them to follow me, I stepped back into the dining room. As soon as the three of us were inside, I pulled the sliding doors closed.

Nancy spied the mummy case and her lips curved in an expression of wry humor. "You do go to extremes. I've been urging you to redecorate this apartment, but I didn't expect you to start with something like that."

Penny, ever the diplomat, said, "It's such an unusual piece. Perhaps when you have different wallpaper—"

I shook my head at them. "I didn't buy this." Before they could ask anymore questions, I approached the mummy case. Apprehensively, I inserted the key in the lock and felt the mechanism respond. As I swung the cover open, suddenly I felt as though my heart was doing flip-flops against my rib cage. Nancy gasped, and Penny emitted a strangled cry of shock.

From inside the case—bound at the wrists and ankles, mouth duct-taped shut, eyes bulging with terror—Lena Cooper stared at us.

How in the world was I going to explain this to Matt?

Chapter 51

CALL ME PARANOID, but I gave Lena a thorough pat down to make sure she didn't have any kind of concealed weapon. Satisfied she was harmless, Nancy and I began to unknot the ropes that bound her. As we were doing that, Penny used Vaseline to ease the tape off her mouth.

Lena slumped into a chair at the dining room table and rubbed her wrists and arms to get her circulation going again. For once, she wasn't wearing her blue coat. Tonight, she was dressed in a dull shade of brown: a shapeless wool sweater and baggy slacks.

When she spoke, Lena's voice was a petrified croak. "Where am I?"

"In a much more comfortable place than where you left me," I said.

Hearing that, Lena hid her face in her hands, hunched her shoulders, and began to weep great, wrenching sobs. I couldn't help feeling sorry for her, in spite of what she'd put me through.

Nancy was not so forgiving. With tightly folded arms and fury in her eyes, she positioned herself against the dining room doors, on guard duty.

Lena kept crying. Penny looked at me over Lena's bent head. "Maybe she's hungry," Penny said.

I almost smiled. Food was Penny's prescription for most situations.

While Nancy and Penny stayed with Lena, I phoned Matt from the living room. "We're all safe, but you and G. G. need to come over to my apartment."

Instantly, he went on the alert. "What's happened?" I pictured him jumping out of bed and grabbing a pair of pants.

"We have Lena Cooper in custody." I thought *in custody* was a nice way to put it. "Please don't ask any questions right now." In spite of my request, Matt started yelling questions, so I said a polite "see you soon," and hung up.

BY THE TIME Matt and G. G. arrived about twenty minutes after my call, our little girl-party had moved to the kitchen. When they saw Lena Cooper sitting at the kitchen table, eating a bowl of Penny's beef and barley soup, Matt behaved every bit as badly as I was afraid he would.

"Stop yelling," I told him. "It's almost one in the morning and I have neighbors."

"Don't worry," G. G. said. "The walls in this place are three feet thick. I'd be hollering at you, too, but I let Matt have the first go."

"There's no need for either of you to raise your voices," Penny said. "Everything's under control." She handed both men tall mugs of fresh coffee and plates of muffins.

Nancy moved over to stand next to Lena. While they drank coffee and ate muffins, she addressed the two detectives in her most professional tone. "As a member of the law firm that represents Ms. Cooper, I'm acting as her attorney. Before we begin discussing this situation, I want to make it clear that that Ms. Cooper is not required to answer any questions."

"Where's what's-his-name?"

"Oh, G. G., don't be like that," Penny said in mild exasperation. "You know Arnold Rose's name."

"I've left messages for Arnold, but I haven't heard from him yet," Nancy said, "But I'm here, and I can make sure Ms. Cooper's rights are protected."

Matt, G. G., Penny, and I were standing in a semicircle around Lena. She put down her soupspoon. Lena's expression was forlorn, defeated. Her pale blue eyes began to glisten with fresh tears. As though determined not to start crying again, she swiped at her eyes with the sleeve of her sweater. Sitting up straighter in her chair, she looked directly at me. "I'm so sorry about what I did. I didn't want to hurt you. That's why I left you the water."

"It probably saved my life."

Lena focused on the badges clipped to Matt's and G. G.'s jackets. "I want to tell you—"

Nancy cautioned Lena, reminding her that she didn't have to say anything. Lena waved the advice away. "I understand, but I *want* to explain. Please don't try to stop me."

Nancy nodded acquiescence and sat down beside her. The rest of us sat down, too, pulling our chairs up close to the table.

Matt took a small audiocassette recorder out of his jacket pocket. "May I tape this?" Lena agreed, and so did Nancy. Matt activated it, stated his name, the time of day, the location, listed those of us who were present, and said that this was going to be the voluntary statement of Lena Cooper, whose residence was the Cooper Building in Manhattan, and that she was giving it in the presence of her attorney, Nancy Cummings.

For the next hour, Lena kept us enthralled. She went backward and forward in time, but began with meeting Professor Wade Maitland.

I was enormously impressed by Matt's skill at questioning. He made Lena feel safe, and encouraged her without leading. When she started to digress, Matt gently drew her back to what he wanted to explore. Essentially, Lena told the same story that Matt and Nancy and I had read in Maitland's manuscript, but it soon became clear that we knew things she did not.

Lena described falling in love with Maitland and spending as much time with him as he would allow. Because she thought that he returned her love, she confided in him, sharing the secrets she'd kept all of her life. She was devastated when he told her he wasn't going to see her outside of class any longer. Hoping to change his mind, she began to follow him. She went to his house and sat outside, even when it rained and she was cold and hungry. She tried everything to get him to resume their relationship: she called him several times a day, wrote him letters, sent him flowers. When he still refused to see her, she got so angry she poisoned his dog. She told Matt how truly sorry she was about that—she'd never hurt an animal before, and vowed never to do it again. She went to her father and confessed everything, including the fact that she'd told Maitland the bad things about their family. Mitchell Cooper was so furious he used her out-of-control behavior to justify having her committed to a mental institution. But from Lena's point of view, that wasn't such a bad thing because during the months she was there she fell in love again.

With Link Ramsey.

Link talked to her through the television set; she knew everything he said—every romantic word—was really meant for *her*. When she was discharged, Lena said she thought she and Link had gotten married. She remembered a wedding ceremony, but later she thought maybe she'd seen the wedding on television. That part wasn't very clear to her. Then she saw me with Link, and it broke her heart. She desperately wanted Link to love her—she even got into his apartment and waited for him in bed. Lena blushed as she told Matt that she'd never *been with* a man.

Lena wanted to give herself to Link, but when he saw her in his bed, he said some terrible things. Then he walked out on what Lena imagined would be their honeymoon night. She was so upset she punished Link by pouring water all over his bed and slashing his clothes. With no place else to go, she ran back to her father and told him about Link abandoning her, and about the woman he was seeing, me.

It wasn't long after the terrible Link episode that Lena read about Professor Maitland's death. It was clear from the way Lena told her story that she had no idea why Maitland was killed; she thought a stranger must have robbed him. Her father told her that just before Maitland was killed, he'd been seen with a woman named Morgan Tyler. "Isn't she the woman who took Link Ramsey away from you?" her father asked Lena.

Mitchell Cooper persuaded Lena that she could have Link if she got rid of *me*. Lena could do it when I was in Las Vegas—so many people, such huge crowds. He gave her cash to buy an old car, and told her she wouldn't need a driver's license if she went to a private party and was willing to pay too much for the vehicle.

Cooper hired a private plane and met her in Las Vegas. At the hotel, he gave her a syringe.

"What was the drug?" Matt asked.

"I didn't know. He told me it would just make her sleep. He gave me the pepper spray, but I thought of hiding her in a laundry cart."

Lena believed they were going to scare me, take me out in the desert and make me promise never to see Link again.

But when they got way far out in that desolate area, Cooper told her I had to die because they couldn't trust me to keep my promise.

Lena didn't want to do it, but her father said it was the only way she could get Link's love—and his. Reluctantly, she agreed, but she didn't want my death to be painful, so when her father wasn't looking, she slipped a bottle of water she'd been sipping in the car into the pocket of my robe.

At this point, Lena drooped with weariness and despair. "I don't want to live anymore. Everyone hates me. My father will never forgive me. I just want to die." She let her arms flop down onto the table and burrowed her face in them.

"Hey," G. G. said. He stood up, leaned over and with a gentleness that surprised me, he turned her face to the side. "You gotta breathe, kid."

Matt stopped the questioning. He left G. G. with her while he took Nancy and Penny and me into the den to talk.

"We've got to take her into custody for her own safety," Matt said. "She's acting like she could hurt herself."

"I don't want her put in jail," I said. "She's talking about not want wanting to live—isn't that reason enough to put her in a hospital? She'd be safe and watched while we look for evidence against her father."

"Just where do you suggest we look for this elusive evidence?" Matt's voice dripped with sarcasm.

"I found a notation on the back of one of Maitland's pages: 1940. I think it's the number of his safety deposit box."

In a skeptical tone, Matt asked, "Any idea what bank?"

"He lived in Hartford, Connecticut," I said.

Penny added, "People usually choose banks conveniently located."

"Finding banks, getting into locked boxes, that's where you guardians of the peace excel. We amateurs can't do it all for you," Nancy quipped.

I saw the line of Matt's mouth harden, but I sensed it wasn't because of Nancy's flip remark. He pinned me with what I called his cop stare. "You weren't supposed to leave this apartment. With people in several states looking for her, I want to know how you found Lena Cooper, and why you brought her up here."

It was the question I'd been dreading.

Nancy saved me. "As Morgan's attorney," she said, "I'm advising her not to answer that."

Penny smiled at Matt ingenuously. "Why don't you get your friends in Hartford to start looking for the professor's bank? If the proof of Mitchell Cooper's crimes is there, nothing else really matters, does it?"

Matt called Bellevue and arranged to have Lena admitted on the basis that her behavior indicated she was a danger to herself or others.

Lena was more than docile—she was spiritless—as Matt and G. G. took her away. I couldn't help thinking how good Matt was at his job. Excellence was a very attractive quality.

As soon as they were gone, Nancy turned to me. "Okay, who sent your kidnapper gift-wrapped in a mummy case?"

"Was it that very clever Little Person detective?" Penny asked.

"On the advice of my attorney, I'm not going to answer that," I said.

Chapter 52

I MADE SURE Nancy and Penny were asleep before I crept out of the bedroom at 4:30 the next morning. After Matt and G. G. took Lena Cooper away, and before we'd gone to bed, I'd managed to conceal a toothbrush, toothpaste, fresh clothes, and ankle boots in the hall closet. I brushed my teeth and dressed in the kitchen, put down food and water for when Magic woke up, and quietly let myself out of the apartment. Nancy and Penny had set the alarm clock for seven A.M. I'd be home well before they knew I was gone.

The building was so silent it made me think I was the only one awake. To keep it that way, I slipped down the hall to the stairs in my stocking feet, and didn't put on my ankle boots until I reached the courtyard.

Twelve minutes to five. I hurried past the central fountain, out onto Seventy-Second Street, and turned left onto Central Park West just in time to catch the green crossing signal.

Once inside the park's entrance, I veered slightly north and

headed toward the Ramble. The sky was gray, the light too
weak yet to cast shadows, but it was easy to see the path. It
rained in April, and sometimes there were even flurries of
snow, but this morning there was just a slight vapory haze to
the atmosphere. A pair of squirrels, one chasing the other,
scampered past me. A few yards farther, a raccoon stood up
from behind a small boulder, glanced at me, and then scurried
away. I didn't see any human beings—except one mounted
policeman way off in the distance, patrolling in the opposite
direction from the one I was taking.

Reaching the sprawling wild forest that was the Ramble, I
slowed down to catch my breath. I didn't want Nico to see me
panting. He'd think I was eager to see him instead of a little
out of shape since my kidnapping. The reckless part of me *did*
want to see him, but I was trying to keep it in check. I *needed*
to see Nico this morning to talk about the delivery of that
mummy case.

On branches above my head, birds were waking up, trilling
and cheeping. So many birds this morning, an avian conven-
tion! Then I remembered: April was one of their migratory
months. My bird expert, Bobby Novello, had told me that as
many as two hundred and fifty species of feathered beauties
stopped over at the Ramble, flying in and out during April and
October.

I quickened my pace again as I passed through the lovely
sanctuary called the Shakespeare Garden. It was landscaped
entirely with the flowers, plants, and trees mentioned in the
playwright's works.

At exactly five o'clock I reached Bow Bridge. It was one
of the places I loved most in Central Park. I'd first seen this
ornate nineteenth-century cast-iron bridge twelve years ago,
when Nancy and I were freshmen at Columbia. Gazing at the
graceful curves and curlicues of its sixty-foot length, I told
Nancy it looked as though it had been poured like pancake
batter across the lake it spanned.

The sky had lightened to silver when, out of the predawn
mist, the silhouette of a man materialized, walking toward me

from the other end. I recognized the shape of his head and shoulders, and his stride. Simultaneously, our steps accelerated. We met in the center, at the top of the slight rise—the "bow," that gave the bridge its name.

We were within an arm's length of each other.

I won't let him kiss me.

He didn't try. Instead, he reached for my hands and held them against his chest as he studied my face.

"Thank you for the rose, and for being there," I said.

Nico nodded. "How are you?" It wasn't simply a polite question. I heard the concern in his voice, and a darker tone. I realized Nico's anxiety was freighted with anger.

"I'm all right. Completely healed. I was scraped, dehydrated, sunburned, and stupid with injected drugs, but nothing more." Gently, I withdrew my hands. Turning, facing west, I could see the top floors of the Dakota through the trees. The sight of my home kept me focused. "How did you find Lena?"

Nico moved to stand next to me, but kept a few inches between us. He leaned against the side of the bridge and looked out over the water. "From the moment I learned who had done that to you, I let it be known I wanted Lena Cooper captured— but not harmed. The reward I offered would not be paid if she were injured. The amount was large enough to insure her safety." He smiled, but there was no humor in it. "I wanted her delivered to you, in something resembling the way you were transported."

"I'm glad you didn't hurt her," I said. "It's her father, Mitchell Cooper, who wants me dead. Lena thought they were just going to scare me. When she found out what he really planned to do, she left the water that helped me stay alive."

"Why does he want to harm you?"

"I found out he's a murderer." Nico's full lips thinned into a hard line. I could see fury building in him and wanted to cut off any possibility of his doing something rash. "Don't even think about going after Mitchell Cooper," I said firmly. "He'll be arrested soon. Besides, I don't want you to help me anymore."

Nico's face became a mask meant to hide his emotions. Afraid I'd wounded him, I reached for his hand and held it tightly. "Please don't think I'm not grateful, Nico. I am, truly—but if you tried to do anything you'd risk endangering yourself. I couldn't forgive myself for that. Believe me, I'm safe from Mitchell Cooper."

His eyes softened and he gave me a wistful smile. It touched my heart.

"If my situation were different, I would tell you many things. But know this: there is nothing I would not do for you, my darling. *Nothing.*"

"I don't want—"

"Please, let me finish. I must leave soon, but before I do, I ask a favor of you. The mummy case is from the Ptolemaic dynasty. The airholes I put in and the lock I installed diminish its value only a very little. An expert restorer will correct those imperfections. I want you to keep it."

I started to protest, but he placed an index finger lightly against my lips, silencing me. "You sent back my ancient coins, and you refused to accept the house in Los Angeles that I bought for you, the house in which we made love. Please keep the mummy case. If you ever need to sell it, many museums will give you a handsome price." He kissed the palm of my hand. "Think of it, if you will, as a hedge against inflation."

The assistant who brought the mummy case appeared on the bridge, from the direction I had come. He was no longer wearing a delivery uniform; now he was back in a suit and tie. Nico acknowledged him, then looked back at me, with a smile that was as tender as his last kiss. In a few moments, the two of them had vanished into the park.

WHEN I OPENED the door to the apartment, I smelled coffee brewing. Nancy, wearing pajamas, her hair tied back and no makeup, was alone in the kitchen. Her features were pinched with worry. When she saw me, she cried, "Thank God!" Relief immediately turned to anger. "Where have you been?"

"In the park."

"That's crazy! It's dangerous—"

"It's beautiful at dawn, I only went in as far as the bridge, and it's not dangerous because no one is there this early." *Practically no one.*

Sudden realization filled Nancy's eyes. "You went there to meet that *Greek*, didn't you?"

"He told me his real name is Nico Andreades. Please don't call him 'that Greek.' It sounds bigoted."

"You know it's not his ethnicity that upsets me. First, he gives a phony name, now suddenly he tells you his real name—*maybe*. For your sake, I don't want him to be real! You've been seeing him secretly, haven't you?"

"Not really." *I'd actually said 'not really'! I hate that weasely phrase!* "What I mean is, I haven't been seeing him in the way you mean. I have run into him a couple of times." *Three or four times.*

" 'Run into him'? As in completely by chance? I don't believe it."

"I haven't slept with him again, that's what you're talking about, isn't it? When I've seen Nico, we've talked. We haven't made love. Not since—"

"Not since Los Angeles. Well, I'm grateful for that, at least."

I held up my hand and listened for a moment. The only sound in the apartment was Mr. Coffee doing his brewing thing. "Is Penny still asleep?"

Nancy nodded. "So is Magic. Apparently, he doesn't like to get up as early as you do."

The coffee finished brewing. I took two mugs from the cabinet over the counter and emptied the grounds and filter into the garbage can.

"I woke up twenty minutes ago," Nancy said. "You weren't in the bedroom, or anywhere in the apartment. I was about to call Matt."

"I'm glad you didn't." I poured coffee for us, and we sat down at the table.

"So am I—you make him crazy enough. While I was looking for you, I did some serious thinking. It wasn't Bobby Novello who had Lena delivered to you, was it? It was that . . . Andreades."

"Strictly between the two of us, yes. His messenger told me where he'd be this morning, if I wanted to see him."

"And you did."

"I told him I appreciated his finding Lena, but that he had to stay out of my life."

"Is he going to?"

"I think so."

"I hope so," Nancy said. "Okay, new subject. Just before you got home, I called Arnold and told him that Matt and G. G. took Lena into custody, and put her in Bellevue."

"Did he ask how they got her?"

"Not yet. Arnold is solution-oriented; he wants details after he solves the immediate problem. He said he was going to get busy having Lena transferred from Bellevue to a private psychiatric hospital."

"Did he say why he didn't call you back last night?"

Nancy tried to keep her tone blandly casual, but I knew something had upset her. "He was up in Boston, having dinner with Didi. And her mother, Veronica."

CHET CAME OVER a little before ten o'clock to read Maitland's manuscript. With Chet in the apartment, Nancy decided to go to her office for a couple of hours. She said it was to make sure all of the things that needed her attention were being sent over, but I suspected it really was because she wanted to see Arnold.

Chet was settled in the den with Maitland's box of pages, and Penny was working on plans for her TV show in the kitchen when Matt called a little after 10:30.

"We hit a wall," he said. "The professor didn't have a safety deposit box where he banked, or in any other bank in Hartford. Hartford PD also checked his locker at Trinity College, and searched the room where he taught, and his campus office. Whatever proof he had—if he really had it—isn't in Hartford."

"The day we met he was going to the Westport Playhouse. Maybe he had a bank box in Westport."

"Not exactly a convenient location for a man who lived and taught in Hartford."

"Have the Connecticut police try it anyway."

I heard acquiescence in Matt's responding grunt. "I'll call you later."

"Before you hang up, how was Lena, after you took her away last night?"

"*Crazy*," he said. "She told us she'd been an Egyptian queen in a mummy case. When G. G. asked if she was Cleopatra, she said she wasn't pretty enough, then she started crying."

"Cleopatra wasn't pretty! I saw her portrait on an ancient coin. Lena has a better face."

"Fascinating," Matt said sardonically, "but the city pays me to solve crimes."

After we said good-bye, I sat thinking about the investigation's dead end: Maitland didn't have a safety deposit box. Maitland must have been at least a little bit afraid of going up against a man as powerful and ruthless as Mitchell Cooper. He would have hidden the proof in the safest place he could think of.

I picked up one of the white legal pads I used to sketch out ideas. If one of my *Love* characters needed to have a box in a place where a dangerous enemy wouldn't think to look, where would that be? Naturally, it would depend on who the character was. I reviewed the cast in my head . . . When I came to Sean O'Neil suddenly I snapped to attention. Nicky, Sean's character, has a *sister.* Wade Maitland had a sister! I scrambled through the names in my Rolodex until I came to Nora Stoddard.

A few minutes later it was all I could do to keep from running as I hurried down the hall to the den.

"Chet, Maitland's sister has a safety deposit box and the

number is 1940! Maitland put things in it a few weeks before he died!"

Chet stood up and grabbed my hands in excitement. "Our big break!"

"Can you go up to Syracuse right away? Nora will take you to the bank and open up the box."

Chapter 53

FROM THE MOMENT Chet left, I'd been unable to settle down. I paced restlessly through the apartment, but I avoided the kitchen so as not to disturb Penny while she was creating. More than once I stood at my living room window and looked out at Central Park. The sky was darkening; rain was on the way. I couldn't see Bow Bridge, but I knew where it was. At eleven o'clock, I called Nancy at her office to tell her about Nora Stoddard's safety deposit box, and that Chet was on his way to find out what was in it.

"It's at least three hundred and fifty miles to Syracuse. He won't get there before the bank closes," she said. "We'll have to wait until tomorrow—"

"Chet chartered a plane. He estimates he'll be able to pick Nora up and get to the bank by four. We'll know what's in that box by late this afternoon. Look, something Matt said this morning got me thinking about Lena. Did Arnold have her moved to a private hospital?"

"Yes. He got her to commit herself voluntarily to Webber House. It's a top-rated psychiatric clinic, on the Upper East Side. She signed papers agreeing to stay until the doctors feel she can be released."

"Can she have visitors?"

"If arrangements are made in advance, and if Arnold gives permission."

"I'd like to see her about six o'clock tonight. It can't be earlier because I want to take a couple of people from the show with me. Will you get Arnold to okay it?"

"Sure, but—"

When I gave her the names of the two people, I heard the surprise in her voice. "Morgan, we've been best friends for almost half our lives, but I don't think I'll ever totally understand you."

"Are you coming back to the apartment?"

"In about an hour. Since Chet's off on his mission, shall I bring us lunch?"

"No. Penny's inventing a new dish and we're going to be the taste testers."

ALL AFTERNOON I edited scripts, but I was so keyed up I checked the time every five minutes. Luckily for the show, I didn't have to do any serious writing. All that was needed was some touching up of dialogue.

When the phone rang a few minutes after five P.M., Caller ID identified it as coming from the 315 area code: Syracuse. I snatched up the receiver. "Chet?"

"We struck gold."

"Tell me!"

"Maitland had three sets of private laboratory toxicology reports that prove Amelia Cooper was poisoned, and three sets of forensic reports saying the slashes on her wrists that made her death look like suicide were administered postmortem. Jud Larsen paid off gravediggers to exhume Amelia's body and had the tests made using a phony name. He was smart enough to use separate labs with sterling reputations. They all agreed on the cause of death. He also got copies of a receipt that proves Cooper bought the poison, and proof Cooper was in New York at the time Amelia died—when Cooper was supposed to be on a plane to California."

"How did Larsen find that out?"

"The old-fashioned way: he worked hard until he got lucky," Chet said. "Larsen showed Cooper's photo to airline personnel. One of them, a flight attendant who knew Cooper because he was so unpleasant and demanding, told Larsen that she remembered that particular flight because she recognized immediately that the man who was traveling as Mitchell Cooper *wasn't* Cooper. She played dumb at the time, and didn't say anything to anybody because she suspected Cooper was cheating on his wife. She figured it wasn't any of her business. The woman signed an affidavit swearing what she told Larsen was true. It was easy to fly under a phony name eighteen years ago. You didn't need photo ID, or even *any* ID to board a plane in this country. You paid for your ticket and they took your word about who you were."

"Those days are gone forever."

"That's the truth," he said ruefully. "There are a couple of videotapes in the box, too. The labels say they're on-camera statements from ex-employees who worked for Amelia at the time of her death. We haven't had time to play them."

My big fear had been that Maitland's substantiating documents wouldn't hold up. Now I agreed with Chet; we'd struck gold. "How in the world did Maitland get all of that?" I asked.

"Jud Larsen's mother. He tracked her down in Oklahoma and persuaded her to let him go through Larsen's things. Larsen must have been worried about Cooper possibly paying off cops, because he'd taken the precaution of sending the package of evidence to his mother. He asked her to keep it for a while, but be ready to send it back to him in New York when he asked for it. The next day Larsen was killed in what looked like a drunk driving accident. His mother told me she was so devastated that it never occurred to her to open the package.

She just put it away in her cellar, with the other things she was storing for him. She's kept that part of her basement like a shrine to her son."

When I imagined Mrs. Larsen's years of grief, I felt a twinge of guilt because I was so excited at the discovery of the evidence. As soon as Cooper was arrested for the murder of his wife, I was going to make sure Mrs. Larsen knew her son was the hero who made it possible.

"We've got to tell Matt," I said.

"I called Phoenix just before I called you, so he could start working on getting an arrest warrant for Cooper. I'm going to fax him the lab reports right now."

"That's wonderful. When are you coming back?"

"Bad weather's moving in. We can't fly out of here until tomorrow. I'm putting the pilot up at a hotel for the night, but I'm going to stay over with Nora and Gordon Stoddard."

"It's going to rain here any minute. Chet, please, if the weather's still bad tomorrow, stay in Syracuse until it clears."

"You're worried about me," Chet said in a teasing tone. "That's encouraging." Before I could respond, he went on. "Listen, I've decided I'm going to finish Maitland's book for him, and get it published. Cooper's one of the darlings of the Forbes 500. With proof that he's a murderer, this will be a big book. The royalties will put Maitland's nephews through college and grad school. Even though we haven't proved that Cooper killed Maitland, that's poetic justice."

NANCY WAS SO worried about me leaving the Dakota while Mitchell Cooper was on the loose, she refused to let me travel by cab.

"Don't argue," she said firmly, "I've already hired a limo for you." She smiled with satisfaction as she added, "I specified that the driver had to be big and look mean."

It had just begun to sprinkle when, at 6:30 P.M., Nancy's limousine pulled up outside Webber House on East Eighty-Ninth Street between Second and Third Avenues. The driver was, indeed, *big*—but I wasn't going to tell Nancy that with his silver hair and ruddy round face he looked more avuncular than menacing.

"We'll be an hour or so," I told him. "Do you want to go get yourself some dinner?"

He shook his head. "Nah. I'm used to eating late." He got out of the car and opened an industrial-strength black umbrella to shield us from the raindrops, gave me a hand out, then helped the two older women who alighted behind me. The three of us hurried to the shelter of the awning over the entrance and the driver retreated into the limo.

Webber House didn't look like a psychiatric hospital, which was part of its appeal to those who could afford to be there. The gray sandstone building dated from the 1930s, was four stories high, and had black wrought iron casement windows. The front door was painted a fresh, glossy black, matching the casement windows. There was a mini door styled like the windows set at eye level. Shortly after I rang the bell, the little door opened and a woman peered out at me.

"I'm Morgan Tyler," I told her. "These two ladies and I have permission to see Lena Cooper."

"Yes," she said. The little door closed and after a few seconds and the clicking of locks, the big door swung open, and we were admitted into the kind of attractive lounge that might be found in an old-world men's club. To our right a large, comfortable-looking sofa faced an unlighted fireplace. It was upholstered in rich burgundy velvet and flanked by a pair of dark gold velvet club chairs. A coffee table in front of the sofa boasted a low glass bowl of flowers and several magazines.

In her fifties, the woman was solidly built but not fat. She wore a stylish navy blue dress with a white lace collar. Letting her dark hair go gray, she had it coiled into a figure eight at the back of her neck. She looked like the dean of a girls' school.

"I'm Mrs. Putnam," she said. Retreating behind the polished oak desk facing the door, she consulted a large book, similar to a hotel register. "You are Morgan Tyler, and with you are . . ." She looked up at us with eyes full of question marks.

"Molly and Mary Murray," I said.

The answer matched what was in her book, and satisfied her. She pressed a button on the desk and I heard a far-off buzz. "Someone will be here in a moment to take you up, but I'm afraid I must check your bags first to make sure you're not carrying anything we forbid to our guests."

My small clutch bag quickly passed her inspection. What she saw in the larger totes Molly and Mary carried made her smile. "Ahhh, I see. Well, if you intend to leave anything here, it must be given to the nurse. Lena will be allowed to have it as needed. With supervision."

A young woman, probably no older than thirty and wearing a pale blue nurse's uniform, entered the reception area through a door behind Mrs. Putnam's desk. She stood over six feet tall in her flat, thick-soled shoes, and her arms and legs were thick and strong as tree trunks. In contrast to her intimidating physique, she had a sweet face and a soft voice. Mrs. Putnam introduced her as Doris, and said Doris would be Lena's night nurse during the week.

We took a small elevator up to the second floor, where Doris led us through two sets of locked doors until we reached a door that wasn't locked. She opened it for us, and I saw Lena sitting on a single bed, forlornly staring at the floor.

The room was clean and cheerful. A mural of weeping willows covered one wall. In addition to the bed, there was a table and two visitor's chairs. A television set was suspended from the ceiling, angled for viewing either from bed or from a chair. It was tuned to a channel that reran sitcoms. The picture was excellent. The sound was turned low.

Lena looked up when we came in. She started to smile when she saw me, but she drew back in fear when the two women I'd brought with me entered.

"Lena," I said. "I'd like you to meet Molly and Mary Murray. They're makeup artists on our show."

"Hello, dearie," Molly said. Even though the Murray sisters had lived in America for more than forty years, their voices still had a charming Irish lilt. "We've come to give you a little help."

Confused, Lena glanced from Molly to me. "Help?"

"You have beautiful skin," Mary said. "We're going to do for *you* what we do for the girls on our show."

"Trim your hair a little," Molly said. "Shape it to compliment your bone structure."

"And use a wee bit of color to enhance your features," Mary added.

Gradually, the tightness left Lena's shoulders. She inched forward and began to relax.

While Doris and I watched, Molly and Mary worked on Lena.

First, Molly cut Lena's thin hair into a feathered gamin style that gave an illusion of fullness. The graceful wisps that Molly curved forward onto her cheeks had the effect of slimming Lena's face.

When Molly finished cutting, Mary began to apply makeup to Lena's cheeks and chin line that was a little darker than Lena's natural skin tone. The shading was so artful that Lena's face was transformed from a spherical shape to an oval.

As Molly and Mary used their considerable skills, I realized that Lena had the potential to be attractive.

At eight o'clock, I drew Molly to one side. "This is amazing. Are you just about through?"

"Oh, no," Molly said. "I've got to narrow and shape her eyebrows, and remove those hairs in the middle. Mary has to show her how to work with mascara and lipstick. We have a lot to do yet."

"I really appreciate this," I said.

"We're having fun. It's like looking for buried treasure! But you don't have to stay."

"All right, then. I'll go home and send the car back for you."

I said good night to the Murray sisters and to Doris and Lena. Lena mumbled something, but I don't know what she said because Mary was carefully outlining Lena's mouth with a lip pencil.

Doris stepped out into the hallway and signaled for another nurse to take me through the locked doors to the elevator.

Out on Eighty-Ninth Street it was raining harder, and apparently had driven the pedestrians indoors. It was darker than I'd expected; the rain had dimmed the illumination from the street lamps.

Turning toward the spot where we'd left the limo, I was surprised to see it wasn't there. Staying under the awning to keep dry, I scanned the street in both directions. No limo. A traffic policeman might have ordered it to move, I thought. If so, it was probably circling the block. *To heck with the rain, I'm not going to melt.* I started toward the corner. I hadn't gone more than a few steps when I felt something small and round jabbed hard into my back, just above my left kidney.

"This is a gun," Mitchell Cooper said. He was so close his umbrella sheltered me, too, and would prevent anyone who happened along from seeing the weapon in his hand.

Fighting to keep terror out of my voice, I went on the offensive. "You're crazy! Any second my limo—"

"Gone," Cooper gloated. "I gave him a fifty-dollar tip— from you—and told him you said you wouldn't need the car after all. He appreciated your generosity." Cooper jammed the gun barrel harder into my back. "Over there," he said, "into that car."

Chapter 54

THE VEHICLE COOPER shoved me toward was an SUV, dark blue or black. It was impossible to distinguish exact color in the rain-muted light from the street lamps.

"Turn around," Cooper ordered.

I obeyed, and we were face-to-face. Mitchell Cooper wasn't dressed like the cover of *Fortune*; he wore a dark gray jogging suit with the hood pulled up and running shoes. If I could ease enough space between us, I thought I might be able to use Bruce Lee's famous advice to women who faced attackers: "Kick him in the balls and run like hell!" Most people are notoriously bad shots when aiming at a moving target. But Cooper was too smart for that trick. He stood slightly to one side of me, insuring that if I tried anything he could shoot me before I could do him any harm.

There was enough light for me to recognize the make of the pistol. It was a 1934 Beretta 9 mm Short. All steel construction with a V notch sight. I was familiar with it because

I'd seen many in Africa. During World War II, the Italian army adopted the Beretta and assigned it mainly to officers and selected troops for battlefronts in Africa, Europe, and Russia. It was compact, simple to operate, and—too bad for me—extremely reliable.

Blood pounded in my ears and my fingers felt cold. I was more afraid than I'd been on the trip to the desert, because then at least I'd had time to think of a strategy. It hadn't worked, but the planning kept panic at bay.

Keeping the automatic pointed at my heart, Cooper balanced the umbrella between his cheek and shoulder and used his freed hand to wrench open the SUV's front passenger-side door. As soon as it was gaping wide, he told me to toss my clutch bag in, over the top of the front seat. I did and heard it land with a dull thump somewhere in the back.

"Now climb in and get behind the wheel," he said. "You're going to drive."

I did *not* want to get into the vehicle. Impatient with my slowness, Cooper jabbed me again painfully with the Beretta's barrel. I pulled myself up and scooted sideways to the driver's seat. Cooper threw the umbrella down on the sidewalk, climbed in, slammed the passenger door shut, and pressed the lock button.

This was not happening on a film set. No director was going to shout "cut" and stop the scene. The cavalry wasn't poised at the top of the ridge before sweeping down to the rescue. Survival was up to me.

Trying to think of something, I stalled. "How did you know where I was?"

"I paid an orderly to tell me who would be visiting Lena, and when."

"Where are we going?" I asked. My mouth was dry, and my words sounded hollow in my ears.

"A place where your body won't be found until I've died peacefully of old age."

Suddenly I was angrier than I was afraid. I couldn't let it end like this.

Keeping the gun leveled at my chest, Cooper reached into the pocket of his jogging jacket and pulled out a car key.

I began to tremble deliberately, but I was careful not to overdo it. With a pathetic little gasp, I whispered "Oh, God, no, please . . ."

"Shut up, bitch!"

I nodded at him obediently, hoping he'd think he'd frightened me into abject submission.

He snarled, "Let's go!"

I was irritating him. Good. I juiced up the trembling. He passed me the car key, and the moment the metal touched my shaking palm I fumbled and dropped the key into the darkness on the vehicle's floor. Instantly, I cried, "I'm sorry!" and started to sob.

"For Christ's sake—pick it up!"

I flinched, as though fearful he was going to hit me. I leaned forward, stretched my right hand down toward the fallen key at my feet—and instead plunged my fingers into the top of my ankle boot. I grasped Chet's little canister that I carried there. My hand flew up, I turned my face away and I shot a blast of Mace. Cooper screamed in pain. Lashing out at me blindly, his Beretta caught me on the side of the cheek and sent me reeling against the door. I lurched forward, thrusting his gun hand straight up. The 9 mm went off, exploding rounds through the SUV's metal roof. Holding my breath, keeping my face averted, I shot another burst of Mace. Cooper, his upper torso covered in dye, bent over in coughing spasms.

I unlocked the door, jumped out into the pelting rain, and ran around the front end just as Cooper came stumbling out from the passenger side. I was able to use Bruce Lee's advice; Cooper screamed in agony, tumbled backward, and lay sprawled on the sidewalk. Ignoring the soaking I was getting, I knelt down and felt for a pulse. He was only unconscious, not dead.

I heard the welcome shriek of a police siren racing closer and closer.

Chapter 55

COOPER WAS ARRESTED for my attempted kidnapping, and jailed on that charge. With an ice pack on my bruised cheek, I also swore out a complaint that he had kidnapped and attempted to kill me in Las Vegas. I would let the two jurisdictions fight it out. By the following day I knew enough evidence would arrive from Syracuse to have Cooper charged with the murder of his wife. There was as yet no way to prove he had also killed Jud Larsen or Wade Maitland, but some very skilled homicide detectives were going to work on those cases.

Unfortunately, there was no law against the emotional abuse he'd inflicted on his daughter. I was going to keep in touch with Lena, and ask Chet to confer with her doctors. I wanted us to do everything we could to make sure she had the best possible chance to recover and be able to live a normal life.

* * *

THE BRUISE ON my cheek had barely begun to fade when Matt called with news that shook me to my core. "Cooper's been released on bail."

"What?!"

"Money talks, killers walk," Matt said bitterly. A few minutes later, I dialed Nancy at her office. "Mitchell Cooper's—"

"He's out, I know," she said. "I was just about to call you."

"How did Arnold—"

"It wasn't Arnold. Cooper fired him and got Bernie Jakes." She practically spit out the name of the man who was renowned as the sleaziest criminal lawyer currently practicing in America. Sleazy, but effective. It was said Bernie Jakes had never represented an innocent client, but he succeeded in getting many guilty clients off. Now it looked as though he might do it again.

"Poor Lena," I said.

"Forget Lena," Nancy snapped. "What about *you*? Arnold and I are coming over tonight, to figure out how to keep you safe until . . ." She didn't finish the sentence. We both knew that with Jakes in the picture there was no guarantee Cooper would ever be punished. "We'll make some plans," she finished weakly.

The team rallied around. Chet wanted me to stay with him in Greenwich. Nancy wanted me to stay with her. Bobby Novello wanted to stay with *me*. Matt had a policewoman friend ready to move into the Dakota. I turned them all down. I was not going to live in fear, nor was I going to be driven out of my home.

That night I went to bed with my Glock under my pillow. Not surprisingly, I didn't sleep very well, but I must have dozed off at some point because when the telephone rang at a quarter to six it took me a moment to realize what the sound was.

"Are you awake?" Matt asked.

"I am now. What's happened?"

"Cooper's dead. He committed suicide."

I couldn't have been more astonished if Matt had said

Cooper flew to Pluto on a spaceship. "*Suicide*?" I sat up in bed, now thoroughly alert.

"Cooper slit his wrists in the bathtub," Matt said. "He left the water running. When the tub overflowed and leaked into the apartment below, the building's maintenance man went up to Cooper's penthouse and found him."

The irony of it struck me. "Cooper poisoned his wife and then faked her suicide by slitting her wrists."

"Imagine that." Matt's voice was so full of sarcasm I was jolted.

"You don't believe Cooper killed himself?"

For a moment, Matt didn't answer. Then he said, "It *looks* like suicide. Bottom line: a very bad man is dead. Unless something turns up to tell me he didn't kill himself, case closed. Go back to sleep," he said. "You don't have to worry anymore."

But I didn't go back to sleep. I made coffee, drank one mug down quickly, filled it up again and took it into the den. As I sipped, I gazed out at Central Park and thought about this latest twist in the story of Mitchell Cooper.

Chet had said it was poetic justice that the profits from Maitland's book would put his nephews through school. Was Cooper's death another kind of poetic justice?

Had he really killed himself? Or had one of his many enemies managed . . .

All at once I realized I was staring in the direction of Bow Bridge.

Bow Bridge, where I had last seen Nico. Suddenly I remembered him saying, "Know this: there is nothing I would not do for you, my darling. *Nothing*."

The coffee mug cupped in my hands was hot, but my fingers around it suddenly felt cold. Icy. I shivered. *No!*

I sat down on the window seat, but turned my back on the park.

I'd had too little sleep, and too much coffee. My imagination was spinning a madly improbable scenario—one too wild to write, even for me.

* * *

FOUR DAYS WENT by. With no new revelations, the sensational story of Mitchell Cooper's suicide died down, and the media turned its glare on a new celebrity divorce. Case closed. It was April seventeenth. Against pretty big odds I'd managed to survive the past six months, and now I was eligible to claim my inheritance.

In one more irony, I was about to receive a small fortune from a man I had made no secret of despising, and whom I had once been suspected of murdering. Because he was healthy, and had not expected to die in his forties, I was certain he'd put me in his will in order to hurt the unfortunate woman who was in his life at the time. Nancy and Penny—incurable romantics—disagreed. They believed he was obsessed with me because I was a woman who wouldn't give in to him. We'd never learn the truth.

Nancy had insisted on going with me to the Seagram Building at 375 Park Avenue, to the law office of Leo Seligman where the event would take place. Stretching between Fifty-Second and Fifty-Third Streets, the Seagram Building is a spectacular thirty-eight-story tower with alternating bands of bronze plating and bronze-tinted glass. As we got out of the taxi, I shielded my eyes against the glare of spring sunlight bouncing off acres of bronze.

"Two days ago we were having snow flurries," Nancy said.

"Typical in New York, the world's least typical city."

We'd climbed the three steps to the main plaza when Nancy tugged at my sleeve and said in surprise, "There's Matt. What's *he* doing here?"

I turned in the direction she indicated and saw Matt's tall figure ambling toward us from the Fifty-Second Street side of the building. I had told Nancy about his declaration that he couldn't continue to see me if I accepted the inheritance. I tried to make my tone light. "He's probably come to say good-bye to me forever, now that I'm rich."

Matt greeted me with a slight incline of his head, and said, "Hi, Nancy."

Nancy shot him a glare. "I'll meet you up in Leo's office, on twenty-nine," she told me. At her most imperious, she added to Matt, "You are an *idiot*."

She glided the final few yards across the plaza toward the entrance, causing both male and female heads to swivel in her direction as she passed.

Matt, too, watched Nancy enter the building. "You told her how I feel."

"Yes."

He folded one of my hands into his. "Will you give me a couple of minutes before you go up to that office?"

"Have you changed your mind?"

Without answering, Matt guided me to the comparative privacy of a group of slender trees on the uptown side of the building. Beneath a lacy canopy of branches, he drew me into his arms and kissed me gently on the lips.

"What are you going to do with that money?"

I was going to use most of it to help people. But the thought of saying that out loud made me embarrassed. The other thing I planned to do I couldn't tell him either: I was going to hire Bobby Novello to track down a monster from my past. I'd long fantasized about bringing this man to justice— even if it wasn't conventional justice.

What I said was, "I'm going to pay Nancy back the rest of the money she advanced me for the down payment on my apartment. Then I'll get rid of the mortgage. Nancy's financial person will invest what's left."

"I hope all your stock buys go south," he said softly. His arms tightened around me and he kissed me so hard I could barely breathe.

At last, Matt withdrew his mouth from mine and stepped back. Without another word, he took my hand again and escorted me to the building's entrance.

"You can run, but you can't hide," I joked. "Penny's TV

show goes on the air next month, and I'm going to be there for her. You'll have to see me sometimes."

"I can handle it." Releasing my hand, he said, "Take care of yourself."

With that, Matt turned and started back across the plaza, toward the Fifty-Second Street corner of Park Avenue. A beam of sunlight caught glints of red in his dark brown hair.

"Go to hell," I whispered and wondered, *Will he look back at me?*

No, it was eyes forward all the way.

I watched until he was out of sight. Then I entered the Seagram Building through the brass-framed revolving doors. In a few minutes, I was going to sign papers that would put a certified check for eight million dollars into my hands. The irony of this situation was that I'd never before made any decision in my life by thinking about the money involved. After five years in show business, I'd met enough very wealthy people to know that money can't buy happiness. Happiness is having loyal friends, and the possibility of love. I didn't intend to buy happiness with my unexpected fortune, though.

What I intended to buy was a certain kind of freedom from the past.

LINDA PALMER was a wildlife photographer in Africa before she turned to writing. She teaches novel writing at UCLA Extension and lives with several pets in Studio City, California.

Visit her website at www.lindapalmermysteries.com.